I0647389

POPULAR PUBLICATIONS · FACSIMILE EDITIONS

Terror Tales #10
(June 1935)

Starting in 1934, editor (and publisher) Harry Steeger unveiled *Terror Tales*: perhaps the flagship magazine in Popular Publications' so-called "Weird Menace" lineup of titles. Running for almost 50 issues, *Terror Tales* showcased some of the best suspense, mystery and terror stories to see print in the pulps. This facsimile of the June 1935 issue contains stories by Nat Schachner, Hugh B. Cave, H.M. Appel, Arthur J. Burks, John H. Knox, Wyatt Blassingame, and Robert Newman.

Authors:

*Nat Schachner, Hugh B. Cave, H.M. Appel, Arthur J. Burks,
John H. Knox, Wyatt Blassingame, Robert Newman*

Illustrators:

John Newton Howitt, Amos Sewell

TERROR TALES

Volume Three   June, 1935   Number Two

TWO FEATURE-LENGTH MYSTERY NOVELS

Railroad to Hell............................By Nat Schachner   **4**

Kent Chandler and Jane, his lovely bride, scoffed at the lurid legend. But when the madman pastor rose from his grave to lead his vengeful host, Kent knew a brave man's fear, and Jane explored the abysses of despair!

The Scarlet Widow............................By Hugh B. Cave   **44**

Mark Andrews could not understand the bond which made his wife turn to her mother—the strange widow who wore scarlet. But he learned what it was—from a horrible creature which haunted the night and the dank graveyard, seeking screaming victims for its obscene lust!

TWO GRIPPING MYSTERY-TERROR NOVELETTES

The Ice Maiden............................By John H. Knox   **82**

At first, they thought Colonel Homquist's fantastic tale a gigantic hoax—until the creature from the Arctic began to murder them, one by one!

Blossoms of Doom............................By Arthur J. Burks   **110**

Had Jon Lynn really come back, investing that crawling vegetation with an animation which—for Mary and her lover—meant a ghastly, terror-haunted death . . . ?

BLOOD-CHILLING SHORT TERROR TALES

Attic of Terror............................By H. M. Appel   **34**

Thrashing that lewd half-wit started a hell on earth for Ray Green and his beautiful young bride. . . !

The Child Who Lived With Death   By Wyatt Blassingame   **69**

Paul Reece stared at that innocent three-year-old. . . . Was Death really peering from those guileless eyes?

They Did Not Need a Hell!............................By Robert Newman   **101**

An ancient manuscript and a corpse brought Charles and Tessa Colton to the red brink of hell itself!

—AND—

The Black Chapel............................A Department   **126**

Cover Painting by John Howitt
Story Illustrations by Amos Sewell

Published every month by Popular Publications, Inc., 2256 Grove Street, Chicago, Illinois. Editorial and executive offices, 205 East Forty-second Street, New York City. Harry Steeger, President and Secretary, Harold S. Goldsmith, Vice President and Treasurer. Entry as second-class matter pending at the post office at Chicago, Ill., under the Act of March 3, 1879. Title registration pending at U. S. Patent Office. Copyright, 1935, by Popular Publications, Inc. Single copy price 15c. Yearly subscriptions in U. S. A. $1.50. For advertising rates address Sam J. Perry, 205 E. 42nd St., New York, N. Y. When submitting manuscripts kindly enclose stamped self-addressed envelope for their return if found unavailable. The publishers cannot accept responsibility for return of unsolicited manuscripts, although care will be exercised in handling them.

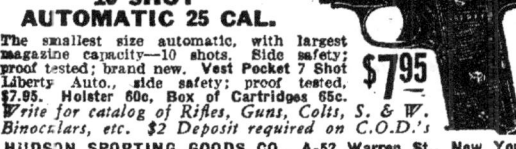

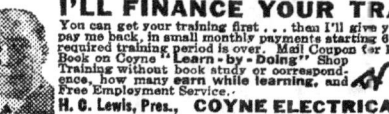

Classified Advertising

3

RAILROAD TO

Kent Chandler and Jane, his lovely young wife, scoffed at the lurid tales of restless spirits haunting the deep ravine called Devil's Gap. They did not believe that the victims of that awful accident which had sent Jane's father to a disgraceful death could come back from the grave to exact a hideous vengeance. But when Everlasting Fayre, the madman pastor, rose from his year-old sepulcher to marshal his vengeful minions, Kent knew a brave man's fear, and Jane explored the most profound abysses of despair!

HELL

By Nat Schachner
(Author of "The Devil's Brewers," etc.)

A Complete Mystery-Terror Novel

JANE CHANDLER hurried up the wooden steps of Abner Tracy's General Store. She had a good deal of shopping to do, and she wanted to get back to Kent before it grew too dark and the threatening storm was raging.

Yet, for a tiny second, her hand trembled hesitantly on the doorknob. Pale, yellow light struggled dimly through the grime-encrusted windows, and voices made a confused murmur within.

It was almost a year since she had last been in this mountain village of dreadful, haunting memories. Her eyes lifted involuntarily to the backdrop of the hills. There, silhouetted blackly against the light-fading sky, thrusting gaunt, skeletal fingers out into the abyss of Devil's Gap, were the broken remnants of the railroad trestle.

On the other side, ascending the steep slope of Thunder Mountain were the unseen rails her father, Henry Stanford, had built. Up near the very top, hidden by misty distance and the thickening shadows, were the huge drums around which the steel cable wound to haul the cars up the terrific grade to the plateau. It was the steel cable which had snapped, precipitating screaming women and children into the devil-haunted depths of the chasm.

Jane straightened her slender shoulders defiantly. It had not been her fault; it had not been her father's. She was not afraid to face the mumbling villagers, even though they knew that Kent, the young engineer she had married a month before, had come to Devil's Gap to rebuild the trestle so that Henry Stanford's railroad could run again along Thunder Mountain and into the upland country.

Her small hand firmed on the knob, twisted. Loud talk eddied around the half-dozen men in the store as she entered.

A booted mountaineer peered slowly at Jane and jerked erect with an explosive gasp: "Old Henry Stanford's gal!"

A sudden hush fell on the men. Their heads craned in her direction, froze. An alien influence ringed her in as she walked to the counter. She pushed a penciled list across the pine boards.

"Mr. Tracy, will you please get these things for me right away?" she ordered steadily. "I'm in a hurry."

The storekeeper's round, normally ruddy countenance was slightly pale now. His jaw dropped at the sight of his cus-

tomer. But he forced his lips into the semblance of a welcoming smile.

"Why certainly, Mrs. Chandler," he greeted her. "Of course! Glad to see you again. Hear you're married now. Don't know as I rightly remember Mr. Chandler."

"No." Jane fought to keep the quiver out of her voice. Why had Abner Tracy winked that violent warning to the men behind her back? Why had they stiffened into strange silence at her approach? What caused the secret terror that lurked in the far corners of Tracy's eyes? "Mr. Chandler's never been to Devil's Gap before."

Tracy fumbled for the supplies. His fingers trembled with queer nervousness. He jittered the parcels down in front of her as if he were striving frantically to get her out of the store before. . . .

A stealthy mutter beat upon her ears. It came from behind. "There's a curse on her! I seen Everlasting Fayre myself last night!"

The blood misted in a frozen vapor around Jane's heart. Then she whirled on the man who had whispered, tiny fists clenched. "Joel Harris," she demanded, "what nonsense are you spreading? Everlasting Fayre's been dead a year. He—he died with the others."

The man glowered at her sullenly. "It's the truth," he insisted. "I seen him plain as day, standin' in the middle of the road. He raised his hands to the sky, like he always done when he were a-preachin', an' he called down the curse of the sp'rits of the Gap on your dad and all his kin forever!"

"You hush up, Joel!" Tracy shrilled angrily. He turned imploringly to Jane. "They're just a bunch of superstitious hill-billies, Mrs. Chandler. Don't you be taking any stock in their wild talk."

"It ain't no wild talk," a tall man spoke up. Jane knew him too. He was Zeke

Lowe, the teamster who trucked supplies from the village along the treacherous old trail road into the back country. "I seen Everlasting too. So did other folk." A growl of assent swung around the silent circle. "His hair and his beard was stiff with blood, and his face were a funny grey. He preached agin your pa and anyone what tried to build that bridge again. Cursed you all with the curse of the Gap, he did!"

"For God's sake, Zeke, keep still!" Tracy expostulated.

But Lowe rumbled on:

"There he was, a-shoutin' 'bout how the devils of the Gap broke the cable 'cause they resented the bridge over their haunts, and how next time they'd take a mightier vengeance. Then my hosses started running hell-bent-for-election, and old Everlasting sorta vanished back into the cemetery."

JANE breathed hard, as if she had been running. She fought to keep her sanity. It was impossible, what they said. Fayre was dead—she had seen his crushed body, had seen him laid in his grave—and the dead stayed dead.

"I—I don't believe it," she forced through tight lips. "You must have had a drink too many when you saw that, Zeke."

"I never touch a drop," he answered shortly, finally.

The silence grew oppressive. A man got up from his box, went shuffling into the dusk. Another arose without a word and followed him, sliding past the girl as if the curse of the fanatic, half-mad preacher were in truth already upon her. Then another, and another, eyes averted, breathing heavily.

Joel Harris said with a grunt. "Old Everlasting never did like the railroad. He prophesied 'twould make the spirits mad. He warned the women not to take

the cars to the Social t'other side of the Hills. But they had their minds sot on't, an' wouldn't listen no how. So Fayre, he went along, figurin' as how a preacher could fight the devils. There he made a big mistake." Harris shook his big, powerful body as if he were a dog, and thumped slowly out of the store.

The light from the reflector-lamps seemed to haze before Jane. The store was suddenly cold. The shadows in the back swirled with the misty faces of those long dead. "It's all buncombe," Tracy said kindly. "Just you go home and forget it, Mrs. Chandler."

But Zeke Lowe, face gaunt and stubbled with beard, shook his head. His little red eyes lingered secretly on the girl. Then he too sidled out the door.

Jane stammered something incoherent, snatched up her bundles, fled into the gathering darkness. She must get back to Kent, her husband. She had left him poring over blueprints in the little cottage they had rented only that afternoon. He was alone, absorbed in the plans for the rebuilding of her father's railroad. He knew nothing of Fayre's ghost, of the demons who lurked in the Gap, of the curse upon her family. If he did, it would have made him laugh. Of course, they were ridiculous, the things she had heard, but. . . .

She hugged the packages tighter to her bosom, hurried on. The single, dusty street was deserted. Shadows crept noiselessly down Thunder Mountain, hemming her in. Lightning played over its bald, precipitous peak, and thunder growled warily in the distance. Jane's French heels tapped loud and eerily on the flagstones.

Why was there no one else in the street? It was not yet very late. When she had entered Tracy's Store, there had been men sitting on their front porches, shambling down the road. But now. . . .

She tried to laugh at her growing fears,

but the laugh was choked off in her throat. Accursed? She and all her kin? She half-smiled. Mere superstitious rot! Yet the silence was unbearably ominous. Not even a dog lifted its voice. The houses along the street seemed blank, untenanted—where warm, cozy lamps had gleamed before!

The road took a sudden turn. There, glimmering ghostly white in the invading night, lay the cemetery. The tiny plot of ground had swelled beyond its bounds in one dreadful day. The pitiful headstones —crowded close together in death—like the bodies whose graves they marked had been that fateful day—seemed to sway in the darkness.

"Accursed! Accursed!" they seemed to moan with soundless fury. "Henry Stanford's girl. Accursed!"

God! That taller tombstone, towering over its companions, seemed to rear itself into the air, as if the bearded, big-thewed Everlasting Fayre were clawing out of his coffin at the very sight of her.

Jane stumbled on. It was madness, of course; nightmare imaginings induced by the silly gossip in the store. How Kent would rumple her hair and hold her in his arms and laugh! If only she were already in the cottage!

The muttering thunder rumbled weirdly among the crags. It sounded to her exactly like the mocking laughter of evil spirits lurking in the boulder-strewn Gap. Good Lord! There she was being silly again. She forced her head up in defiance, and stopped suddenly short. For one dreadful instant, the blood congealed in her veins. A package dropped with a dull thud from her nerveless fingers. What were those strange flickers of flame crawling up the mountainside, along the outer rim of Devil's Gap? It was pitch dark now and the forked lightnings had died away. Yet those thin, quivering fires moved with horrible celerity, higher and

higher. They appeared to be splotches of yellow light seeking an unknown goal; bodiless flames, alive with some hideous life of their own.

A strangled moan forced its way through Jane's gelid lips. She started to run wildly, madly down the black road. The things she had purchased in the general store scattered along the backward trail unheeded. One overwhelming thought hammered in her skull, poured fiery liquid through her veins: she must get back to Kent before it was too late. Only in his arms would she be safe. . . .

THE strange lights converged and vanished suddenly. The night was an ominous, all-embracing blackness again. Silence brooded over mountains and the Gap. Jane slowed to a stumbling walk, groping her way fearfully along the curving road. Her laboring lungs gulped in the warm night air. It had been an illusion—she tried to tell herself—a queer exhalation of phosphorescent vapor such as often lures the unwary traveler into the foul recesses of a swamp. But inside her shapely head, beyond all doubt and argument, she knew what they were. . . .

They were the spirits of the Gap, gathered in a conclave by the avenging ghost of Everlasting Fayre. Once before, they had glutted their hate on those who had dared thunder on rails over their unholy haunts; now they gathered to wreck their wrath on the defiant humans who invaded their fastnesses again.

Jane hastened her pace. Her heart squeezed at the thought of Kent alone in the little cottage, bent over his plans and figures, unwitting of the risen figure of Everlasting Fayre, of the evil Things of the Gap. Why had she ever left him alone? Jerry Shannon, his young, freckled-faced assistant, had gone to the county seat to check a shipment of supplies. He wouldn't be back until late. Tomorrow the laborers would pour in, ready for work. But tonight, now. . . !

She was running again, blindly, a sudden, horrible fear for her husband clamping her throat. Lightning sent a jagged streak across the mountain. Was that thunder which rustled like cracking paper on the heels of the flash? Thunder? Great God! Thunder did not move on stealthy feet through the shadows of the encompassing trees; thunder did not slither into ominous silence a fractional second after she stopped suddenly, ears straining for further sounds! *Thunder did not resume its creeping stride the moment she flung herself forward again!*

Frantic with fear, Jane raced over the pebbly, rutted road. Around the next bend, almost half a mile away, was the cottage. Kent's strong, warm arms would keep her safe from the nightmare horrors of the night. But half a mile! God, would she ever make it?

The Thing behind had abandoned secrecy. It was racing after her, pounding the hard dirt with heavy, thudding pace. She dared not look behind, she dared not falter a moment in her pistoning stride. Her lungs were panting bellows of fire, her heart a clanking weight that tore at her ribs. The breath whistled in her throat, mingled with the fierce exhalations coming from behind.

The Thing was gaining on her. The pounding grew nearer. Hot foulness seemed almost at the nape of her neck; hideous, clawing fingers stretched eagerly for her running, trembling body. The bend in the road! She flogged her failing limbs to renewed spurts. There, not a hundred yards away, was the cottage and. . . .

Merciful Heavens! The house was dark, a mere indistinct blob against the cupping hills. Kent was in bed, asleep, exhausted from his day's work, unknowing of the dreadful Thing that pursued his wife.

She tried to scream, to shriek for help. But the muscles of her throat were constricted with nightmare paralysis; the tortured breath failed in her bursting lungs. The pounding feet behind were hammer-strokes in her ears, almost upon her!

Jane forced her dying strength into a last desperate spurt. A clutching paw fastened the thin stuff of her dress, ripped the cloth. A savage snarl rasped through the darkness. Then she was flinging her icy body against the door that led into the house. For one dreadful instant, it resisted the struggle of her thrusting slenderness. The crunching of feet on cinders was loud in her ears. A gloating chuckle pierced her hammering skull; ice-cold fingers gripped her shoulder.

"Kent! Kent!" she screamed insanely. The desperate wail racketed through the blanketing night, reverberated through the narrow foulness of the Gap, flared up the mountainside in ghastly, mocking echoes.

The fingers on her shoulder tightened, lanced like glacial splinters into her flesh. Jane jerked forward uncontrollably. Terror gave her super-human strength. Pain gashed her shoulder as she smashed into the door again. The she flung herself headlong. The creaking barrier had yielded.

Even in the shattering concussions of her fear, she knew what she must do. She scrambled up from hands and knees, crashed the wide-thrust door shut on the charging, black-solid figure outside, slammed the wooden bolt home just as the pine barrier groaned under the heavy impact of her pursuer.

She shrank back from the quivering door, back almost to the low-glowing embers in the fireplace. There was no other light. The red shadows made wan splotches on the faded wallpaper of the nearer wall, died into grey-black nothingness again.

"Kent!" she screamed. "Help!"

THE Thing outside hesitated. She could hear its lumbering feet scuffing against the wooden sill of the door. Another such blow and the flimsy pine would not hold.

She crouched low, moaning faintly. There had been no answer to her anguished cry; there was no other sound in the thick silence except the stertorous gasping of her own breath, the dreadful scraping noise beyond the door.

Thud—thud—crunch! Thank God! Tears of relief rolled down her cheeks. The Thing was going away, going down the cinder path back to the road. He had heard her call Kent, and had thought. . . .

Panic fear filled her again. What had happened to her husband? He was not in the cabin. He had said he would work late, had sent her off to the village with a tender hug and an admonition to be back before it was dark. Even if he had been tired, and fallen asleep, he should have heard her screams. He was always a very light sleeper. The hearth fire, too, was low; dull ashes overlaid the faint red of the still-live embers. The lamp was out and the peculiar smell of kerosene told Jane that the wick had burnt untended. Dim in the clustering gloom, she could see the table and the spread plans. Kent never left his papers out when he was finished; he had a passion for neatness and orderliness. Swift realization burst like an exploding shell within her brain. *Kent had been taken from the cottage! The Things in the Gap had struck against her husband!*

A great cry crashed through the darkness. Jane did not even know she had screamed. She raced madly across the room, flung aside the heavy curtains that veiled the window, and glared out. Kent, her adored Kent, taken by four demons! She remembered those climbing flares on the mountainside. Nausea churned her stomach. In a searing flash she envisioned the awful truth. The vengeful Things of the Gap were taking him to their secret lair. They. . . .

Lightning gashed the heavens. A blinding, corpse-white flame darted across the black background of the night. Out there, on the road, facing the house, silhouetted for one terrible moment in the flood of streaking light, was a looming figure.

It faced the house with right arm uplifted, as if it were invoking the terrors of the sky, the infinite rage of Hell, on the doomed house and all its occupants. The glow from the storm illuminated tawny, blood-dabbled beard and hair, hideously contorted features, grey with the greyness of death. Mad, measureless hatred showed in the bottomless pits that should have been eyes.

One dreadful instant, and the lightning wiped it out of existence. A crash of thunder split the heavens, drumming a receding tattoo among the crags. The blackness closed over firmament and earth with clamping tightness.

But Jane had seen—and recognized—the apparition. It was Everlasting Fayre, the fanatic madman who had preached of everlasting Hell, of damnation and of the demons of the Gap to the superstitious natives of the hills. Everlasting Fayre—who had dropped to his death with all the women and children when the cable had broken—whose body had lain mouldering in the little cemetery for almost a year. Risen from his grave, an avenging corpse, he had come to doom with dreadful curses the kin of Henry Stanford.

Out of the darkness of the night came a low, sinister chuckle. Then that, too, was gone. The room, the night, the earth itself whirled dizzily around the girl. She tried to hold her slipping senses, to grope blindly for physical support. Her fingers clawed along the wall, flexed even as her body crumpled. A single shooting star blazed across the vault of Jane's consciousness. Then the waters of oblivion flowed over her head. . . .

CHAPTER TWO

The Village of Desolation

HER eyes opened wearily, closed again. Good Lord, she must have fallen asleep while waiting for Kent. What was taking him so long? It wasn't like him to go out and leave her alone in a desolate, old house, buried in the middle of the wilderness. Strange too, how her head ached, and how very hard the bed seemed!

She opened her eyes again, dazedly. Only a little glimmer of red showed pallidly on the hearth—the last dying embers of a forgotten fire. There was a strange odor in the house, too. Her nose crinkled in disgust. It was the acrid smell of burnt-out wick, of raw kerosene. . . . She heaved herself erect, looked wildly around. She remembered now.

"Kent!" she cried hopelessly. The darkness muttered with eerie whispers, but her husband did not answer. Fear seized her abruptly by the throat, choked off further sounds. Kent, the man she loved, was dead or worse! Outside, hidden by the enveloping blackness, were the dreadful Things of the Gap, marshaled by Everlasting Fayre, the corpse who was their leader. They were waiting, waiting tirelessly for her. Soon they would come, crawling and slithering along the walls of the house, seeking entrance. Soon their grave-cold fingers would caress her body, and they would take her—even as they had taken Kent—to the unholy fastnesses of the chasm that was their hideous home.

Her straining ears seemed to hear first faint rustlings, the thud of approaching feet. No, no! That was merely the pounding of the blood through her heart; the mad whispering of her own thoughts.

Then a quick frenzy seized her. She shrieked defiance to the evil beings who waited hungrily for her; she stamped and yelled until the slender whiteness of her throat was a raw ache. The madness left her finally, a cold, whimpering little girl, even as she had been years before when the lights were out, and she conjured shapes in the shadows on the wall of her bedroom.

Shadows! Walls! Ghosts! She raised her heavy head, tried to pierce the dun murk. Not a sound; silence as of the grave, just like that of the untenanted coffin of Everlasting Fayre! She laughed insanely, and the laughter frightened her. If she stayed here, she would surely, certainly, go stark mad. And Kent! Perhaps he was still alive, perhaps the climbing demons had not harmed him yet. . . ?

She jerked forward, stumbled to the door. She would go to the village and get help. There would be men there who could forget the past and the loss of their families long enough to help her find her own dear one, and save him from Fayre and his attendant devils. Men like Abner Tracy, the storekeeper; like Zeke Lowe, the teamster. They were men of business, accustomed to the outer world. They were not afraid of demons and corpses, as the other natives were. Yet Zeke himself had seen lights, had beheld the gory figure of old Fayre. That meant. . . . She stopped with fingers frozen on the bolt. She too had seen!

Then the madness enveloped her again. Fear for her husband, for the mate to whom she had sworn love and fealty through life, made her mind plunge along a single, narrow groove. Those men would help; they *must* help! Jerry Shannon, too, would be back. It was late; the train had no doubt come in while she lay there in a faint.

The bolt creaked rustily back; the door swung open. She ran stumbling and panting down the path, the crunch of the cinders loud in her ears. There was no moon, but the sky had a dull glare that portended a storm. Thunder grumbled ominously in the distance.

The night was thick with shadows and strange noises. The road seemed to open before her, as if to lure her on and on, and to close behind her with stealthy rustlings and gloating, obscene laughter. But a driving, half-insane purpose forced her on the dolorous way. God! How long that mile seemed! Somewhere in the distance, the demons lurked; somewhere Kent was being dragged to a horrible fate. She must get help; men—strong and human—to fight bravely against the loathsome creatures of the night. What could her slender, feminine strength avail against corpses and clawing devils? In her terrible frenzy, she did not stop to think, to understand. . . .

Thank God! The road twisted, led into open fields. Just ahead lay the village, sprawling like a shapeless beast in the dim, reflected glow of the storm-bellied sky. No lights showed from the vaguely outlined houses. There was no light even in the General Store. At the farther end stood the railroad station, the terminus from the county seat, dark with sullen gloom.

No sound, no motion. . . . The village seemed an empty husk from which all life had been sucked by strange forces. Good God! It was impossible. Her quivering body slowed to a creeping, sagging walk. What had happened; where was everybody? Not even a dog barked. Death emanated from the untenanted town, death and the effluvia of approaching madness. Had Devil's Gap also been invaded by other-world visitants; had the inhabitants been dragged shrieking from their beds, even as Kent. . . ?

THE thought of her husband pumped the hot blood through her veins. Far off, so far away it seemed from another planet—came a thin, long-drawn-out sound. *Whoo-oo-ooh!* Joy flooded her then, sent her stumbling on. That was the whistle of the locomotive, pistoning its solid, substantial wheels along the single track. The train was coming, bringing crew and passengers—and Jerry Shannon! Jane's mind clung to that comforting thought. Jerry, with his broad Irish face and merry grin, would know just what to do. Not all the devils in Hell could stop him from finding his Chief.

The whistle died into a thin wail, like the trailing gibber of a wraith, and was gone. The blood that had raced so warmly just a moment before clabbered now to thick jelly. Bands of steel compressed her skull in a crushing vise. *The train was departing from Devil's Gap!* It had already been in, discharging its load and passengers.

Jane swayed crazily. That meant Jerry Shannon had come, had already been engulfed in the eerie menace that overshadowed the village. That meant. . . .

A new sound crashed through the muttering night. Something was banging and clattering down the road—out of the empty, plague-stricken village—coming directly for her with a dreadful, desperate tattoo, smashing and rocking through the murk in a wind of its own creation.

Jane tried to fling herself out of the way of this onrushing juggernaut, this unknown thing that already was almost upon her. But her body was anchored with unyielding lead, and her feet were numb, rooted weights.

Then the darkness split. Two horses,

lathered with foam, eyeballs glaring with equine madness in the flicker of lightning that ran over the heavens, manes flowing stiff behind them in the wind of their flight, galloped straight for the fear-rigid girl. A great wagon bounced and jounced in the hard ruts behind them, and a man stood up in his seat, lashing them with whistling whip.

His face seemed distorted into a mask of terror. A black beard studded the grey, drained parchment of his face. His mouth was slack and loose; his little red eyes were fixed balls of mania.

Again hope flared through the girl. She flung up a slender arm, cried quickly: "Zeke Lowe! It's Mrs. Chandler. Stop! I need help!"

But the teamster seemed neither to hear nor to see. His eyes were fixed on far-off horrors. Again he lashed wildly along the horse's steaming flanks with his heavy bull-whip. The great animals surged forward, trembling under the biting blow, their iron hooves drumming on the hard-packed earth.

Jane leaped just in time. The team hurtled, in a fury of noise and motion, over the spot where she had stood. Already they were a banging, diminishing blur in the distance, yet Zeke Lowe's whip still belabored them. Then the bend in the road snatched them from sight, and all sounds were cut off as if the earth had swallowed them abruptly.

Jane's knees were water-weak. They seemed to ebb away from her, unable to support her body. What dreadful thing had sent the fear-crazed man on such an insane flight; what horrors lurked in the streets of the ominously dark and silent village?

Jane clenched her teeth, forced her unwilling limbs to move. In spite of devils —in spite of corpses who should be moldering quietly in their graves—she must go on. Only in the village was there possibility of help. Someone must still live—someone able to help her seek her husband.

The flagstones made hollow noises under her weary feet. The houses were ominous with unseen menace. No lights showed; no sound rang out to challenge the click of her heels. Yet somehow, the skin along the ridge of her spine prickled from the glare of hidden eyes. She was being watched, she felt sure—every move she made, every little dragging gesture! Those hidden eyes bored tunnels of ice into her beating skull, into the frozen marrow of her bones. As if—as if dead women, dead children, were reaching out for her with grave-cold thoughts, cursing this last living Stanford who had dared return to Devil's Gap. . . .

SHE tasted salt blood on her lips. She had not known she had bitten them through. Ah, there was Abner Tracy's Store, the only one in Devil's Gap! It was a flourishing business, the sole source of supplies going to the back country—supplies that reached the hill-folk with difficulty by means of circuitous mountain roads and Zeke Lowe's trucking service.

The store also was oppressively dark and silent. Queer, too, for Tracy prided himself on his lamps and the shiny reflectors that spread an even glow around the piled-up shelves. He usually kept open until quite late—for at least an hour after the arrival of the last night train. What had happened to Abner Tracy? Despair coursed sluggishly through Jane's veins. Tracy had been her last hope, the last straw at which she could clutch. He was sane and sensible, not superstitious like the others. He had mocked all the shuddering dreads that made the natives avoid the Gap from which the village had taken its name. And now. . . ?

The door yielded slowly to her trembling hand. The darkness within was like a clammy shroud. It assailed her nostrils with prickling odors of hay and flour and cider and dried beans. Dread squeezed her heart. A short, quick scream rasped her throat. Something had stirred, something that loomed as a darker shadow where the counter should have been.

Jane whirled madly and tried to flee. But it was too late. There were quick scuffling steps, a grip of steel on her shoulder. "No, you don't!" A man's voice, strange, harsh, croaked.

The grip tightened, held her immobile. Then there was a sharp, scratching noise, the quick flare of a match. The light dazzled her terror-wide eyes, illuminated briefly her shrinking form.

The man gasped. "Mrs. Chandler! What? Hold on a minute!" His grip relaxed. The sounds his feet made were loud in the dark. There were fumbling murmurs, and the splutter of another match. The yellow glow cupped momentarily; then the store sprang into familiar illumination. The man had lit a reflector-lamp.

Jane swayed on unsteady legs, but the pounding in her heart grew more bearable. She recognized her captor. She had met him the year before, when her father was building the railroad. His shrewd, dark features and faultless clothing had been a familiar sight in the little village. Her father had never liked him, and had told him so in blunt, plain language. He was William Kirkland, representative of the C. R. & R. Railroad that fed into Devil's Gap.

But Jane was not thinking now of former dislikes, of rivalry for business. Kirkland was a human being, flesh and blood—not a lurking demon of the Gap, not a corpse from a long-sealed grave.

"Thank God, it's you, Mr. Kirkland. I—I'm so frightened."

He stared at her with narrowed eyes. The first shock of their meeting was over.

"What's the matter?" he asked gently.

"I—I don't know. But my husband—you know Kent Chandler?—he's gone. They—they've taken him, and—" tears were streaming from her eyes. "You must help me get him back!"

"Take it easy," Kirkland advised. "Who took him, and where?"

"The spirits of Devil's Gap, and Everlasting Fayre. They took him up the mountain, and they're going to kill him."

Surprise showed in his eyes, and a dawning suspicion.

"I know you'll think I'm mad," she went on, "but it's true! You must believe me. I saw Fayre myself—a year-old corpse—and he chased me all the way to my house. Zeke Lowe saw him too; so did—"

Kirkland was upon her with a swift, catlike motion. He gripped her arm so tightly that it hurt. "Where is Zeke now?" he demanded.

She shrank from the fierceness of his gaze. She was suddenly afraid of this man. The stories she had heard of his unscrupulous methods raced through her hammering brain.

"He—he just left the village!" she gasped. "Tearing down the road with his team as if the devils were chasing him too. You—you're hurting me."

"Sorry," Kirkland muttered, releasing his powerful grip on her arm.

She felt a little braver then. "You had an appointment with him?"

"Why—uh, yes. That is, nothing special." He laughed, but there was no true merriment in his laughter. "I came in on the last train, and found the village dead. Even Abner Tracy's gone. Then you come with a story—"

"It's true," she assured him earnestly.

KIRKLAND looked at her a long time, and little lights crawled in his coal-black eyes. Involuntarily Jane moved back, suddenly afraid. He laughed as she did so. "I can see something has frightened the whole village half to death, and you too, Mrs. Chandler. Now I'll tell you what you better do. You stay here in Tracy's store where you'll be safe, and I'll go and see what it's all about."

Jane said very low: "All right." Then a thought struck her like a blow. Kirkland said he came on the last train. In that case. . . !

"Where is Mr. Shannon?" she asked. "Didn't he come with you from the county seat—from Meredith?"

There was a frown on Kirkland's dark face as he moved hastily toward the door. "Shannon?" he echoed hurriedly. "No, I guess I didn't see him." Then the sinister blackness swallowed him up greedily. Not even the sound of retreating footsteps came above the low whisper of the breeze.

Jane darted to the door, bolted it. She was terribly afraid. She knew Kirkland had lied. He had seen Kent's young assistant come off the train. The blood roared in whirlpool rapids in her heart. What had happened to Jerry since then— Jerry, to whom she had clung as the last desperate hope for saving Kent?

The store became suddenly a place of dreadful menace. The familiar sacks of potatoes, of meal, the bales of hay, took on strange, threatening shapes. The lantern swung slowly, rocked by an invisible wind. It cast eerie, moving shadows on the fly-speckled walls. The far-off rear of the store was a pool of ghostly, uninvaded darkness.

Jane shivered, clenched her hands until the sharp nails drew blood from the palms. She was alone—alone in a village of death and desolation, a village from which every human being seemed to have vanished! What dreadful horror had driven Abner Tracy to desert his store? What pursuing Thing with scorpion whips had lashed Zeke Lowe into mad

flight? Where was Shannon? What . . . ?

She moaned, and the sound made her shrink affrighted. Kent, her husband, was being tortured even now, a helpless captive in the hands of a risen corpse and his crew of unholy demons, while she, who loved him more than life itself, remained cowering in the village store. Kirkland had gone to his rescue, but what could he do—a dapper city man, a pusher of pens and a schemer of schemes—with pine wood. A scream formed in the recesses of the chasm?

Great God, what was that? She shrank against the counter on unsteady legs; her hands gripped desperately for the smooth pine wood. A scream formed in the hollow of her throat, died in strangling constrictions.

Something was in the back of the store, where the lantern glow tried in vain to penetrate against piled bales and boxes and barrels. Something was crawling and slithering with terrible slowness out toward the light!

Jane's limbs were gripped in nightmare paralysis. Her skin was a tight casing that made breathing almost impossible. Her bones were grating dust and powder. The corpse that had once been Fayre was coming for her again, coming to claim her for his own!

Merciful God in Heaven! There, in the sharp dividing-line between yellow light and the impenetrable dark, a hand emerged. It was a long, grey hand, inching its way over the white-dusted floor—a hand of corpse-grey veins and sinewy fingers, spattered with blood.

Jane stared, unable to move; unable to breathe. The hand crawled forward, clutching, gripping with bloody fingers at the smooth boards, arching along in dreadful parody of life.

Farther and farther into the light it slithered—a bodiless, gory hand. The store rocked and swayed before Jane. She tried to run, screaming, from that ghastly, crawling thing. But stark horror held her fast.

An arm followed, evil, black-shrouded, slithering along the flour-dusted boards. Then—oh God, why was she tormented so?—a head, face down, groveling with infinite effort; forward, ever forward.

Jane's brain seemed to explode. The frozen torrent of her blood seethed in an overwhelming flood. Roaring fragments filled her skull. Her mouth gaped wide, and her throat twanged like a great harp. She screamed, and the noise went racketing through the store with dreadful concussions of sound. Her limbs jerked forward, toward the door, toward the waiting menaces of the night. Anywhere, except with this Thing that crept, face down, like a blind worm, into the shadow-laden light.

Jane gasped, froze in midflight. At the sound of her shriek, at the pounding noise of her racing heels, the Thing that crawled like a worm lifted its gory head. Eyes filled with agony stared up at her. The head lifted, revealed for a moment a freckled face and fell down again, twitching. "Water!" came in a smothered moan.

It was Jerry Shannon, Kent's assistant!

CHAPTER THREE

Snared by the Dead!

JANE forgot her fears, forgot everything but the sight of that young lad, hurt and broken, inching along toward the safety of human-kind. Little sounds of pity welled from her as she ran to him. She lifted him with pity-strengthened arms into a chair.

His tousled red hair was stiff with dirt and caked blood. His head lolled to one side. But his blue eyes opened and a faint, wan grin played over his mouth.

Jane was crying: "Jerry, what did they do to you?" even as she flew toward the bucket of water that always stood by the edge of the counter. She brought a brimming dipper from which he gulped the life-giving fluid in great, greedy draughts. Then she tore off a piece of cloth from a bolt of cotton, dipped it in the water, washed the blood and dirt from his face, hands and head, daubed the ragged gash she found along his scalp with peroxide from the shelves.

Shannon straightened, struggling to regain his strength. "Thanks!" he said with a rueful grin, elbowing up awkwardly. He felt gingerly of the wound in his head.

"But what happened?" Jane cried feverishly.

"I—I don't quite know," he answered. "I remember getting off the train, wondering why everything was so still and quiet. No lights anywhere; the whole place was pitch-dark. I started down the platform for the village, when I heard voices at the other end. Two men were speaking. I don't know just why I edged quietly away, toward the back street that makes a short cut into town. Maybe it was the eerie feeling of it all, the overwhelming darkness."

Jane leaned forward eagerly. "Who were they, Jerry? Did you recognize them?"

"Sure. Kirkland, the C. R. & R. man, and Zeke Lowe, the teamster. I thought it was a bit funny; those two whispering in the dark like that."

Swift suspicion flared through Jane. "Didn't Kirkland come on the train with you?"

The lad looked at her in surprise. "Why, no, Mrs. Chandler! I was the only one to come this far." He looked at her, went on again. "Anyhow, I groped my way through the alley, aiming for the store here. I thought I'd get a flash, maybe find out what was wrong in town. Just outside the back entrance, though, something struck me on the head. I don't remember anything after that until you screamed."

Jane choked back a little cry. Her wide eyes darted fearfully toward the rear, where the shadows lay in an oily pool. Then the Thing had lurked outside, waiting cunningly. It had struck poor Jerry down, and he had crawled, stunned and bleeding, across the rear threshold, into the store. *That meant the door had been open; that even now, perhaps, the grisly attacker was creeping on silent feet toward them!*

Shannon jumped up from his chair. He was much stronger now. "What's the matter, Mrs. Chandler?"

"Back there," she shrieked through stiffened lips. "Something's coming in!"

Feet thumped hollowly on the creaking boards. Shannon whirled, eyes blazing, freckled face quivering with excitement. His hands fisted into hard knots.

"I'll get that——!"

A man plunged headlong from behind the barricade of boxes. He was panting heavily, as if he had been running. Sweat oozed from every pore on his ashen, fear-stamped skin. His smooth, ruddy face twitched spasmodically. His body twisted backwards, in attitude of deadly terror. He collided with a huge sack of meal, sent it thudding to the floor. He whirled with a gasp of fright, saw the pair in the yellow flare of the lantern, fell back with a scream. There seemed no recognition in his staring eyes.

"Mr. Tracy!" Jane cried out, "it's us— friends. What's wrong?"

The storekeeper jerked his head up, passed a large hand over his face as if to wipe out the memory of a dreadful sight. He came forward slowly. "I—I saw—" he quavered.

Shannon stood, legs spraddled, fists still clenched. "Sssh!" Tracy whispered warningly, with a quick movement of his head toward the girl.

But Jane had heard. Her face was very pale; her heart pounded, but her voice was steady. "It's no use keeping it from me," she said. "Tell me what you saw."

ABNER TRACY groaned. There was remembered terror in his eyes. "I heard strange noises some time ago," he panted. "Like the sound of an army marching, like—dead feet moving along the road. I ran out to see what it was, and—and there was no one! No one in the village, do you hear?" His voice had risen to an insane pitch. "Everything was dark and deserted. Yet the noise of the marchers continued, seemed to flow past me in an icy wind."

He looked at Jane imploringly. "I'm not a superstitious man, Mrs. Chandler. You know that. But I thought then of the demons old Fayre always said haunted the Gap. I was scared, and ran down toward the station. Zeke Lowe said he was going there to meet a man. I—I needed human companionship. But the place was as dark and silent as the rest of the village." Tracy gulped and went on. "By this time, the tramping noise had stopped, and I got my wind back a bit. I was ashamed, too, at having run like an ignorant hill-billy. I started to come back." Tracy's gaze twitched sidewise, as if he were afraid of something out there in the night. He croaked hoarsely: "And God is my witness, I saw him then!"

"Who?" Shannon whipped out.

But Jane shrank back, crying inwardly: "No, no! Don't tell!" She *knew!*

"Everlasting Fayre!" The words thudded in her brain like smashing hammers. "I never was scared of the old fool when he was alive, but now—!" Again Tracy peered fearfully behind him. "When a man's dead, and been buried almost a year, to see him glaring at you in the night, with his beard and hair dabbled with blood—to see him marching down the road, and a great noise of marching Things behind him, when you can't see a living soul—why—why——" He broke down, buried his face in his hands and whimpered softly.

The store was thick with slithering menace. The lamp swayed in the wind, but no light penetrated the thick shadows that leered at them crazily from behind the heaped bales. Outside, the night was a pounding noise of invisible, marching feet. Or was that the racing of the blood in her ears? Jane's spine crawled with innumerable tics. Abner Tracy, ordinarily calm and sensable, had seen—and was turned into a broken, trembling man.

"Poppycock!" Shannon declared loudly, as if he were trying to bolster up a confidence he did not feel. "This is all silly talk—this stuff about ghosts, and spirits and corpses that march."

Tracy raised his head. "I thought so myself, young man, when the others talked. But I *saw!*" He jumped up feverishly, gripped Jane by the arm.

"Listen, Mrs. Chandler," he implored. "You'd better get out of Devil's Gap before it's too late. You and your husband and young Shannon. Zeke Lowe was right; so were the others. There're unholy creatures in the Gap who resent the coming of the railroad. They smashed it once, and sent poor women and children to a terrible death. They laid a curse on your father and all his family—and now you've come back to build it again. Old Fayre has risen from his grave to warn you—to warn us all. They'll get you this time; they'll get everyone in the village."

Shannon took a quick step forward. "What?" he demanded. "Stop building the bridge? Turn and run like whipped curs because a bunch of superstitious fools think they see things! You don't know Kent Chandler, Tracy, if you talk like that."

The storekeeper disregarded him. He clung desperately to Jane's arm. "Please do what I say," he quavered. "I laughed just like this youngster did, but now I know. It'll mean loss of business to me if the bridge isn't rebuilt, and the railroad doesn't run again. I have customers up there in the hills. Zeke Lowe's team's a mighty poor way of shipping 'em my goods. I could sell ten times as much with the railroad delivering. But I'd rather lose every penny I have then see you and Mr. Chandler an' the rest dragged into the Gap by a dead man and his army of the damned."

For one rending moment, Jane wanted to run out into the night, up the road past the station, along the state highway that led away from Devil's Gap as fast as fear-impelled limbs could carry her. Then she remembered and the thought curdled the blood in her veins. Kent, her husband! He had fallen into the hands of the demons! Perhaps even now . . .!

She shook Tracy's hand off her arm. "It's too late," she said unsteadily. "They have Kent already."

Jerry Shannon was at her side, fierce, grim. She had never seen the youngster so aroused before. "They've got the Chief?" His voice was harsh, brittle.

Tracy stared in surprise. He seemed puzzled. "Why, there must be some mistake," he said. "I forgot to tell you, in the excitement. But I saw Mr. Chandler just before I saw Fayre. He was walking very rapidly down the road, toward your house. I called to him, but he didn't seem to hear."

FOR a timeless instant, the universe seemed to have stopped dead for Jane. Then the blood surged in wild leaps through her body.

"Then, then——?" she gasped thickly, "Kent is——?"

"Of course. By this time he must be home, wondering what ever happened to you. But please, Mrs. Chandler—please listen to me! Get your husband to pack up first thing in the morning and forget all about the railroad. Maybe you'd better stay here, and let young Shannon go down to warn him. It would be safer that way."

But Jane was beyond hearing. Kent was alive, and home. Thank God! Thank God! He must have left the house for some reasons, come back after she had gone. What a silly fool she had been, imagining up such dreadful pictures! How Kent would laugh! How he would pat her head and call her a little goose with just the right, tender intonation. Everlasting Fayre? The flickering lights she had seen on Thunder Mountain? Illusions, phantasms conjured up in her fevered brain by the stories she had heard in the village, by the shadows and rawness of her nerves. Shannon had been right. It was all poppycock.

She flew, rather than ran, to the front door. She jerked back the bolts, darted out onto the sidewalk. Her heels made rapid, clicking sounds in the silence of the blank, dead-seeming village. She did not see or hear. All her thoughts were focused on the cottage from which she had fled so crazily only an hour before. Kent would be worried when he came back, and found her gone.

Shannon shouted after her. "Wait, Mrs. Chandler! Wait for me!" But the pounding noise of her heels on stone went on and on. The young man raced for the door.

"Don't go!" Tracy shrieked. "They'll get you too!"

Jane was already a dim, disappearing shape down the road. Shannon cursed and went flogging after her. He did not see the darker shadow dissociate itself

from the tall hedge as he pounded past, trying to catch up with the girl who hurried ahead. He did not hear the swish of the short, black object as it descended straight for the back of his head. There was a dull, smashing thud, and Shannon's knees buckled under him. He crumpled to the pavement, lay there unstirring. The blur of shadow chuckled fiendishly. Other shadows, seemingly part of hedge and walls, floated away from their moorings, clustered around the stricken figure. They bent over him slowly. . . .

CHAPTER FOUR

The Dead Seek the Living!

JANE hurried on, unknowing. The thought of Kent sang in her veins, infused her limbs with the wine of vigor. She was no longer tired; no longer frightened. The cottage—and Kent—waited for her around the next bend. She even laughed happily. The night was no longer filled with rustling terrors, with stealthy Things that moved as she moved. It had been a nightmare, a queer, strange dream from which she was now awakened.

See! The road had swung in its great arc, and there, straight ahead, unencumbered by shrouding trees, was the little three-room cottage. Her heart bounded madly, and she increased her pace.

There was a light shining through the window. A light, where, on her last dreadful journey, there had been darkness and terror. Kent was home, waiting, wondering. The thought of his strong arms around her made her choke with happiness.

She raced up the cinder path, loving the good, crunching sound beneath her shoes. The door yielded to her eager thrust readily and easily. She ran into the living room, calling gladly. "Kent! Kent! I am here. It's Jane!"

The fire was dead on the hearth, but the lamp was a bright, yellow glow. The wick had been trimmed of its char and there was no odor of quenched kerosene. The plans were still stretched on the table, carefully, neatly, nothing out of its place.

But Kent was not in the room. Jane ran for the stairs that led upward to the tiny bedroom under the slanting roof. She shouted again, hopefully. Of course, he had gone up for a minute to get something. Another pipe, perhaps; his smoking jacket. They were still not completely settled in the cabin. They had only come to Devil's Gap the day before. Jerry Shannon was to sleep downstairs, on the couch, until the barracks could be made comfortable for the laborers that were due tomorrow.

Strange that there was no answer! The house was very quiet. Not a sound anywhere. A little fear gathered in her pulsing heart, threatened to grow. . . . She pushed it away determinedly.

Kent was here, had been here. There was no doubt of that. His pipe, the pipe that never left his hand, was on the table, bowl resting against the sleek smoothness of the ash-tray. She ran over, touched it, sobbed happily at the warmth that still ebbed from the briar. It had been recently smoked.

She was being silly again. Kent had worried about her, had tired of waiting. He had gone down to the road. Somehow she had missed him. He would be back soon. She would go to the window, call . . . .

Her eyes froze as she swung around. There, on the smooth, waxed surface of the floor, near the chair in which Kent had worked, a long, keen-bladed hunting-knife quivered like a live, uncanny thing. Its needle point was imbedded deeply in the wood. Its razor-edge was red and sticky.

For the moment Jane did not understand. Just a second before, she had been entirely happy, and now . . . ! Almost uncomprehendingly, her eyes moved dully along the floor. From the chair, in a thin, gruesome trail, it led—a dark red, sinuous trail, as if a man had staggered drunkenly, drip—drip—dripping all the way, shedding his life blood as he moved.

Blood, that's what it is—her staining senses shrieked suddenly to her—the blood of the man you love, done to death by that flung, still-quivering dagger. See how the dreadful trail leads on and on, across the room, out through the door, out into the night, out to where the vengeful Things who inhabit the recesses of the Gap have dragged him with unholy glee!

Terrible sobs racked Jane's slender frame. If only she had waited—if only she had not run insanely to the village—she would have been with him; this would not have happened. It was too late now. This time, Kent was dead, slain by demons who resented the bridge he intended rebuilding over their ghastly haunts; slain by the curse that had been pronounced against Henry Stanford and all his kin.

She moved rigidly toward the door. Vague thoughts whirled through her half-mad mind. She would climb Thunder Mountain; she would descend into the frightful chasm; she would choke bare-handed the Evil Things who had done this to her husband.

Her stiffened fingers gripped the door knob, froze suddenly. The round, smooth knob was turning slowly in the dry palm of her hand. *Someone outside was trying stealthily to open the door!*

JANE clung desperately to the slippery metal. Her lungs whistled with tortured breath; her heart banged furiously against her ribs. The pressure increased from outside the door; there was a faint, scuffing noise. The knob kept on turning. In another instant . . . ! The girl's left hand swung up, slammed the heavy wooden bolt into its socket.

For a moment, she sagged limp and weak against the barrier; then she shrank back from its thin protection. The knob rattled suddenly, loudly. The scuffing noise increased. *Smash!* The pine door quivered on its hinges. *Crash!* The bolt shook violently in its socket; a hinge sagged askew. Another such tremendous blow and the door would be down.

Jane whimpered. The muscles of her larynx were tight with fear. She looked around madly. Where could she hide; how could she escape the menacing Thing outside? She heard heavy thuds as it moved back along the porch. There was a faint, snuffling sound as of stertorous breathing.

Her gaze fell on the window that faced the upper road. A wild hope filled her throbbing veins. If she could climb out, while the eerie prowler had his attention still fixed on the door . . . ! She raced noiselessly to the oblong frame. Her hand twisted frantically at the latch, froze.

A face peered in at her, a face half-hidden in shadow. Eyes bored into her very soul, shrivelling it into tiny bits. There was unutterable hate in those incandescent eyes.

She fell back with a cry. This escape was cut off. Already the heavy *thump-thump* on the porch meant that the next instant might be too late. The other window—the one to the rear! It was her last chance!

Sobbing, panting, she hurled herself across the room, to the recess near the stairs. She grasped the curtain with terror-strong hands, ripped it off. A hopeless moan escaped her pallid lips.

Framed in the narrow section of glass, glowing eerily in the flare from the table lamp, was still another face. Its nose was flattened against the pane; its eyes were twin pits of madness. It raised a long, skinny arm, sent it smashing against the window. Glass shattered.

Jane whirled back into the center of the room, whimpering once more, glaring from side to side. There was no hope, no escape, anywhere! Glass smashed from the other pane. A leg heaved over the sill. Then a great, booming voice sheathed her shuddering limbs in a coating of ice. The door had fallen in a cloud of dust and splintering wood.

A figure moved stealthily into the room. Grey parchment seemed to form its face—parchment grey as the bellies of fish who have long been dead. Shaggy hair and once-tawny beard were stiff with blood and grave-mold; eyes burned like bottomless pits of Hell. Slowly the apparition came for the fainting girl—the corpse who once had been Everlasting Fayre!

Through the shattered windows came other figures, weird and horrible. Through the door, following their Master, crept more and more of them in an endless parade. The dead preacher was upon her now. Stony figures clutched at her waist, jerked her close to the carrion breast. Flesh and blood could stand no more. With a long moan of agony, Jane fainted limply into the monster's arms.

Around her and the Thing that held her, the creatures of the night danced and leaped, mouthing weird, indistinguishable words. . . .

KENT CHANDLER pushed his way slowly and painfully through the brambles that clothed the lower flanks of Thunder Mountain. His left shoulder was a raw ache of fire; blood oozed steadily through his soaked shirt. His legs sagged wearily beneath him, but indomitable will and cold fury at his unknown, unseen assailant kept him flogging onward.

A low-hanging branch whipped against his wounded shoulder, brought a fiery mist of agony before his eyes. His senses reeled with loss of blood; he stumbled, fell heavily heaved himself up unsteadily and groped on again. This was the place where the sinister shadow had disappeared after the knife had been flung at him through the silently opened door.

What did it all mean? First there had been strange, flickering lights on Thunder Mountain. He had seen them through the window as he worked out his plans. Jane had gone to the village, shopping, only a little while before.

His first thought had been the trestle over Devil's Gap, that sinister, almost bottomless slash which separated the village from the upper peak of the mountain. Part had been destroyed by the fanatic, half-crazed villagers after the tragedy. But the supporting arch was still intact, still jutted half way over the gorge. His plans called for utilizing it in the final structure. Suppose those bodiless, yellow flares meant trouble for the trestle?

Kent's mouth had gone grim, but a stiff, scrambling climb up the mountainside had disclosed nothing. The lights had vanished. Only the thunder rumbled in the distance and the lightning slashed across the distant peak, as now. Nothing else. The trestle loomed dark and silent; the depths of the Gap were pools of fathomless silence.

He had returned to the cabin, puzzled, troubled. The lamp had gone out in his absence. He trimmed the wick, lit it again. He scowled over his plans, pipe in mouth. Queer that Jane hadn't returned yet. It shouldn't have taken her so long to do a little shopping. For the first time in his life, Kent felt uneasy, afraid. Premonitions assailed him; the strange stories of demons in the Gap, of the steel cable they had broken with unhuman fingers, of Everlasting Fayre, the fanatic preacher who had died with the others, all rose to plague him. He had laughed at them, but now . . . .

If he had not moved quickly, the knife would have penetrated his heart. As it was, it slashed through his shoulder and fell clattering to the floor.

Perhaps he should go back now. He would never find the Thing that had attacked him on this night-shrouded mountainside. He wiped the sweat from his brow. Lightning flashed ominously overhead, but the thunder had died. His slow progress through the underbrush made a sound loud in his ears. He crawled on and on for what seemed endless hours. He no longer knew where he was or where he was heading. The pain in his shoulder grew more excruciating. Every move was an effort. . . .

STRANGE noises surrounded him in the night, rustled in his back trail. He clenched his teeth, bit his lips to bring clarity again to his brain. He must not get delirious. He must get back to the cabin, to Jane. Poor Jane! She would worry over his absence. He must get back; must—get—back!

The rustlings increased; the darkness grew more and more impenetrable. There were whispers too, voices calling. He shook his head violently. No, no! It was merely the wind, the thunder rumbling once more. If he started hearing things now . . . . But they *were* voices, his shrieking brain insisted. The voices of demons come out of the depths, luring him on to destruction. He, Kent Chandler, had mocked them, denied their existence, invaded their privacy again with bridge and rails and humankind. Now they had him in their power.

Oh Lord, if only his shoulder didn't hurt; if only he knew where he was! He had been a fool to chase a wraith. It had lured him deeper, deeper . . . .

Blue flame leaped madly across the sky, bathing trees and slope with uncanny light. Kent's foot poised for the forward step, jerked back in an instinctive spasm of startled fear. Beneath was emptiness—black and bottomless—The very verge of the perpendicular slash of the Gap. Far below—so far away it could barely be heard—came the thin murmur of the stream that rushed through the bowels of the earth.

Kent trembled violently. Sweat drenched his limbs. Only the sudden blaze of the heavens had saved him from being dashed to terrible destruction. Dread enfolded him in a gruesome winding-sheet. The Things that infested the depths had almost got him. Those murmurs, those voices . . . .

Great God! Was he still dreaming, still delirious? Over to the left, through the intervening network of brambles, came a new sound. *Thud—bump—thud!*

He shrank against the nearest tree, pulse hammering. They were coming for him openly now; they were swarming out of their ancient home to drag this human invader down into the depths.

The noise grew louder. The creaking increased, the thudding became a thunder. Kent pushed his aching body blindly into the darkness. He must get away, must . . !

He banged his wounded shoulder into unseen trees, ripped his face and arms on treacherous thorns, slipped and fell and was up again, running madly down the slope, away from the Gap.

But the noise grew ever louder. It filled the universe with hideous din. Kent crashed into a tree, moaned, swayed unsteadily. He could go no farther. Let them come, let them . . . !

The noise stopped suddenly, close to where he was, almost as close as breathing. There was dreadful, straining silence, in which Kent tried to control the pounding of his blood, the gasping of his lungs.

Then he was hearing things again. Voices, human voices, whispering to each other, not rising above a monotone, as if fearful of being overheard. What were human beings doing here in the remote recesses of the woods, muttering at night?

A strange sound rose high in the air. The whinny of a horse. Kent crouched against the tree, glaring into the darkness. Now he *knew* he was crazy.

Someone said, low but clear: "Shut up, you fool!"

Dim memories struggled in the recesses of his fuddled brain. That voice, that tone! Impossible, yet——

KENT dragged his leaden limbs forward as quietly as he could. His numb fingers parted the underbrush. His shoulder was a huge ache, but he did not heed. Little fingers of electric blue darted across the sky. The dull, black clouds bellied with unshed rain.

Kent pulled his head back quickly. The road was there, the road that skirted the impassable Gap and wound up and up into the hills. The road by which Zeke Lowe trucked supplies into the back country.

And there, quiescent in the rubble-strewn path, was a team of horses, pawing the ground with iron-shod hooves. Zeke Lowe stood beside his wagon, tall and gaunt and greyish in the glare of the quivering sky. There was a snarl of triumph on his black-stubbled face.

Next to him, small and dapper, chuckling in his throat, muttering words that could not be heard, was William Kirkland, representative of the C. R. & R. Railroad!

Kent tried to think, but his thoughts were a grinding torture. What were these two doing here, on the lonely mountain road, heads together in mysterious whispering? What business had they that required such secrecy? His eyes narrowed. He had almost exposed himself, asked for assistance to get back home. Now . . . .

Something rustled behind him—a thin, slithering sound, as of someone parting branches with infinite stealth.

He swung around weakly. A huge, menacing shape blacked out the greyness of the sky. Kent jerked his wounded hand up to cushion the blow. He cried out involuntarily. Far off, as in a dream, he heard startled voices, the thud of flesh against wood, the quick, smashing sound of wheels and pounding, galloping hooves.

Then the sky fell heavily upon him. A white hot iron lanced through his wound. His head flared into coruscating rockets. . .

* * *

The moving air brought dull awareness back to Kent. His head lolled downward, his body jogged up and down in queer motion. He was being carried through the woods.

He tried to move, but his muscles were numb and unresponsive. His shoulder was a great gout of flame; his skull a tearing agony. The Thing that had captured him made crashing noises as it strode through the underbrush. Weird, unhuman chuckles oozed from its throat, sent shivers of dread up and down Kent's spine.

Then, suddenly, the creature ceased its advance. Kent felt his body heaving upward. A branch slashed his face, brought a measure of consciousness to him. He squirmed crazily, swung his head around. A wild scream tore from his throat. He tried to fling his leaden body backward, away from what he had seen disclosed in the lacing network of lightning.

Beneath his pendulous body yawned black, avid horror—the sinister chasm called Devil's Gap! The Thing grunted, dug steel-strong fingers into his aching flesh, swung him struggling out, out . . . !

Kent twisted in an agony of effort. He clawed with hands and knees. Suddenly

the Thing relaxed its grip. Kent's fingers clutched desperately at cloth. There was a rending, tearing sound. Then he was falling, falling into the deep abyss, tumbling over and over in the air.

His blood churned with the noise of the upward-rushing air; his ears filled with the ominous roar of the boulder-strewn stream a thousand feet beneath. A loud laugh, unhuman, terrible, filled the gorge with demoniac echoes. Then he crashed heavily into unyielding rock, and a black wave of nothingness engulfed his body. . . .

CHAPTER FIVE

The Dead Demand Payment!

JANE CHANDLER moaned faintly. The pit of her stomach heaved and kneaded. She was deathly sick. The grey sea in which she weltered seemed interminable. A quiver ran through her slender body. Faint thoughts muddied the blankness of her mind. She tried to move her weightless limbs. They did not budge. Red hot needles stuck in her aching eyeballs, stabbed with fiendish torture into her skull. Her eyelids were lead-heavy as she forced them open.

Where was she, what had happened to her? She looked around in bewilderment, not understanding. Unrelieved darkness surrounded her. Walls hemmed her in with damp mustiness, with the staleness of long disuse. Not a glimmer of light showed anywhere. She tried to move but her tender flesh was bruised against invisible barriers and quivered into painful quiescence.

Realization of the full horror of her situation struck Jane then. She was trussed up like a calf for the slaughter, arms bound rigidly to her sides. Cold, damp stone was beneath her, rasping her skin, congealing her blood with icy bands.

Despair filled her like a cancerous growth. Kent was dead, killed by unholy Things that crept in the night, while she . . . ! A sob swelled the muscles of her throat. She remembered now. The dreadful apparition of Everlasting Fayre, the grave-chill grip of his corpse fingers, the dim-seen leaping, gesticulating figures just before she fainted. Oh God, she moaned, what are they going to do to me, what . . . ?

Something fumbled in the nearby darkness. The sound rasped her eardrums, shrilled its message of fear to her brain. They were coming for her now. The final chapter of her agony was about to begin. Dear God, she could not stand any more. If only she would go mercifully mad, would die before they came!

The darkness grated audibly, and she saw an oblong form open into murky light. Distorted shadows swarmed inside; they danced on the ill-lit walls; they slithered over rusty iron and round-bellied shapes and wheels and sagging leather belts. Outside, the sky was a fuliginous glare, stabbed occasionally with yellow light.

Jane shivered with new-found fears. She knew where she was now. She had been taken to the power-room of her father's abandoned railroad—where the engines had strained and heaved as the great steel cable hauled the line of cars up the terrific slope, and twisted like writhing serpents around the cable drums. Now they were silent and rusted, the haunt of dead men and the sinister denizens of the chasm.

The dim, flickering light suddenly blanked out. A shape filled the panel, moved toward her with clumping, solid steps. Its breathing was loud and ominous. Jane shrank with a strangled gasp against the bruising cords that bound her. Why didn't she die, before . . . !

The figure bulked over her. Huge arms whipped around her quivering form, lifted her up. Her skin crawled at the contact, an ecstacy of terror froze her blood. But the corpse of the preacher smothered her screams against his long-dead bosom, clumped through the door out into the night.

The rushing wind furrowed her bloodless cheeks, whipped through her hair. It howled with demoniac glee. Crash after crash reached her ears, went rumbling with cataclysmic thunder between beetling crags. Incessant lightning sheeted the gash of the canyon with an insane glare, enveloped sky and earth and mountains in a ghastly flame. The demons of the storm blazed over Devil's Gap and Thunder Mountain.

The Thing that had once been Fayre dropped the girl heavily to the ground. With a low moan, she struggled to a sitting position, her back against the wall of the mountain. Dear God in Heaven! Was this the ultimate horror?

CURVING steel rails dropped between precipitous cliffs to the very edge of nothingness. Once there had been a bridge, now there was only the dreadful void. But it wasn't this that made her skull grind into a thousand fragments; it wasn't the wild fury of the onrushing storm that made her throat ache with strangled cries and her skin grow parchment-stiff. It was the huge semi-circle of demoniac forms alongside the rusted rails that exploded her senses into madness.

They screeched with unhuman frenzy at the sight of her. They tossed their skinny arms high into the air, waved torches that flared sootily in the darkness. They brandished knives like that which had sucked her husband's blood; they leaped and cavorted and mouthed unutterable foulness.

The lurid glare of the pitch-pine torches, the jagged lances of coruscating lightning, blurred the hideous obscenity of those pit-born creatures, made them a shrieking, swaying haze to the fainting girl.

Jane knew what they were without seeing. The very thought shriveled her brain with its fiery torment. They were the devils who lurked in the noisome depths of the Gap; they had left their lairs in obedience to the Thing who had lived and died as Fayre.

He stood in front of her, rigid, his face a hideous, frozen mask; his eyes twin jets of hellish hate. His beard did not ruffle in the wind; it stood out straight and stiff and streaked with gore.

"Accursed daughter of an accursed father," he mouthed in dreadful accents, "you have dared return to the scene of his crime. You came with husband and assistant to rebuild what the demons of the Gap had once destroyed in their righteous wrath!"

His voice rose fanatically against the whistling of the wind, the racketing, clattering thunder, the approving shrieks of the swarming creatures along the track.

"It was not enough that your father defiled the sacred haunts of the spirits for his private greed; it was not enough that he mocked and scorned me in life when I prophesied evil on his sacrilegious venture—but in his mad desire for money, he used cheap, inferior steel for the cable."

Jane jerked erect. For the moment fear ebbed from her frozen limbs. The voice from the grave had accused the father she adored of a terrible thing. "It's a lie!" she flamed. "Every inch of that cable was tested for ten times the load it was to haul."

"Silence, woman!" the corpse figure thundered. Its grey mask was hideous in its malignancy.

"Silence!" echoed the ghastly swarm in demoniac chorus.

Jane fell back against the rock. Terror sheathed her limbs in ice again. For one terrible instant, the long line had surged forward, torches high in the wind, as if they would rend her into lumps of bleeding flesh for her audacity.

But the dead preacher waved them back. "Wait!" he said hollowly. "She must hear of her sins, of the curse that has befallen Henry Stanford and all his kin, while she cowers, shrieking and praying for mercy, at the doom that awaits her."

A growl ran through the rank of Things from Hell, a growl choked with gloating expectation.

Fayre's corpse went on in dreadful tones: "Those poor little children, those women who heeded not the voice of their preacher! I exhorted, I warned, I denounced, but they in their folly would go by the hellish steel road to the hills. I went with them, knowing that I held power over the spirits of the Gap. But the cable that Henry Stanford furnished snapped like a piece of rotten thread. Down, down into the bottomless pit they fell, screaming and whirling and bouncing against the unfeeling rock, to be crushed into shapeless flesh and bones. And I, Everlasting Fayre, preacher and man who had walked with God, fell with them."

An eerie wail rose from the crowding demons, a wail that changed instantly into wild shrieks for vengeance against the cowering girl. They surged forward again, hair streaming in savage wildness, torches tossing and waving in the wind of their motion.

Jane cried out desperately: "God in Heaven, save me! Don't let them touch me!"

"God has deserted the tribe of Henry Stanford," the dead Thing shouted. "He has delivered you up to the wrath of those whom your father butchered. He caused you to harden your heart; he caused you to return in your lust for the wealth you thought was hidden in these accursed rails. Even now your husband lies, broken and shattered, in the uttermost reaches of the Gap."

JANE'S skull tightened on the groaning substance of her brain. Her heart stopped its wild pounding, became a frozen lump in her bosom. Kent was dead. Never again would his dear arms held her body against him; never again would his lips seek hers. These demons of darkness and Hell had battered him into a gory mass. The vision of his sightless eyes staring up at a merciless sky—a prey to obscene vultures and the beasts of the night—rocked her reason.

The whole horrible scene—the darkling crags, the rusty steel rails, the blazing heavens, the tossing torches, the Thing that had risen from its unquiet grave, the howling, distorted demons of the Gap—blurred before her pain-swept eyes in a rocking, reeling phantasmagoria of madness.

She was beyond mere terror, beyond mere mortal suffering now. The thread of her being had snapped. Let them glut their will on her fainting body, let them tear her limb from limb, it did not matter any more. Kent, whom she loved more than life itself, was dead!

The voice of the risen corpse pierced her blood-hazed senses. "She is the daughter of the arch-criminal. It is fitting, therefore, that the curse overwhelm her in all its fury. But first, there is that other, the fool who would not go while there was yet time. Let him be disposed of now."

The night became livid with snarls and wordless cries. Unhuman feet pounded and stamped. Dazzling light streaked across the shut eyelids of the swooning girl. Then came another sound, a strange, screeching noise that penetrated her fuddled brain with splinters of new fear; a sound that dulled even the crashing thunder.

It was the unmistakable pound of steel wheels on rails! As if—and the dreadful thought etched like burning acid into her tender tissues—as if a train were rolling along the abandoned roadbed, a grisly train such as the groaning earth had never borne before.

Jane shook her head insanely. It was a mockery, a hideous figment of her disordered imagination. It could not, it must not be! No horror that Hell could vomit forth could equal the gruesomeness of this ghastly train. But the noise grew louder, more overwhelming. The solid rock seemed to quiver with the rolling thunder of the steel. She squeezed her eyelids tighter; she did not want to see what it was. But her shattered senses shrieked the horror to her, conjured up the frightful picture.

It was the train on which a hundred women and children had embarked happily for the promised outing beyond the hills. That train had been packed to overflowing with chattering, laughing humanity. It had rattled across the lightless canyon under the strong, steady pull of a great steel cable.

Now it had come back—a ghostly, thudding Thing—to torture her to utter madness with its freight of gibbering dead, its fleshless skeletons with pitted holes for eyes, its shattered bodies that had once been women and little children. They had all come back to mouth lipless curses against the girl whose father had sent them to their doom.

Oh God, she could not stand it! Anything but that! She tried to crush herself into the unfeeling rock; already she felt, through tight-closed lids, the accusing daggers of those awful eyes.

The shrieks of the demon horde rose to a roar of frenzy. The banging wheels grew loud as the crash of fate, stopped suddenly at her very side. Jane whimpered and huddled low. Soon that awful freight would disgorge, would advance on her with clawing bones and faceless purpose . . .!

"Jane! Mrs. Chandler!"

The startled cry burst through the din with whelming concussions, stabbed her senses as if with slashing knives. That voice . . .!

Jane's delirium fell from her like an outworn cloak; her insane vision fled into vaporous nothingness. She forced her eyelids open. Then she shrieked!

ON the rusty rails, not ten feet away from where she sat, roped and helpless, stood a huge double-wheel of steel. Its one rim hugged the outer rail, its second gripped with shiny luster the inner track. Between the wheels was a concave surface, held in place by the mighty axle. It was the great steel drum over which the cable had twisted when cars were to be hauled up the terrific slope.

But it was not the sight of the cable drum that had brought a scream ripping through her lips. It was the figure of the man who lay extended over the concavity of the inner drum. The man who was stretched in a great, curving arc, like a bow bent for the arrow; whose body was a network of stout, lashed ropes.

The prisoner was Jerry Shannon!

His head was a clotted mass of blood, his face, ordinarily round and freckled, was a tight-drawn mask of pain and suffering. His eyes clung to the wife of his chief with a horrified wideness that Jane knew was not for himself.

His swollen lips moved with difficulty. "Jane!" he whispered, "they have you, too!"

"Jerry," she cried wildly. "Oh, my God! You mustn't die; the curse was not on you. You're just—just—" She choked, turned her head toward the dead preacher. "You must let him go," she pleaded. "Do what you will with me, but let him free. He has nothing to do with the railroad; he is not our kin. He will leave Devil's Gap and never return, I promise you."

In her frenzy, she was appealing to corpses which had no souls, no human emotions, to fallen spirits whom God and Heaven had rejected; appealing to them for mercy!

Jerry reared his head against the ropes that crossed his throat. Fire blazed from his eyes. His voice was strong and vigorous.

"Never, Jane! I do not abandon Kent, or you, or the railroad! I make no promises. Devils from Hell," he shouted, "I defy you! Do your worst! But she—Mrs. Chandler—she——" A spasm contorted his face, strangled the words in his throat. Bright blood frothed from his blued lips. He fell back, head lolling.

The soulless Thing called Everlasting Fayre raised his hand. "It is too late. All must pay the penalty of the curse. Man and woman alike—what do they matter to the dead?"

His heavy tread was thunderously loud in Jane's ears. His corpse-grey arm extended, pushed strongly against the cable drum. It swayed, started to roll down the steep incline.

"No, no!" Jane screamed. "Not that! Great merciful God!"

The wheel turned slowly. The twitching body of Jerry Shannon went with it. Over and up again. His bleeding head emerged, swung upward with the revolving drum. A wan, tight grin colored the waxen pallor of his cheeks. His lips parted. A last fluttering whisper came to the straining, horror-filled girl.

"Good bye, Jane!"

Then the wheel spun again, and his arched body turned over. Slowly at first, with dreadful deliberation, then faster and faster, as the drum gained momentum on the twin rails down the steep descent. Over and over and over, whirling with a pounding clangor of steel against steel, slamming down the abandoned tracks, spinning in a blur of moving parts and shuddering human flesh until . . . !

Jane's skull exploded into a million showering sparks. There, at the very end of the trail, where the trestle had once spanned the Gap, was black, yawning void.

The revolving drum with its human victim thundered to the edge, leaped into space, fell in a frightful flat arc to the fathomless depths below. The last thing Jane heard before she fainted was the fierce ululation from a score of unhuman throats. . . .

CHAPTER SIX

End of the Trail of Terror!

HANDS shook Jane's gelid body. Voices clamored in the grey blankness of her mind. As in a dream, she felt herself lifted. Her feet dragged along the ground. Fingers gripped her arms, propelled her along.

Still dazed, she heard the confusion of voices grow until they beat down the rattling thunder that echoed among the mountains. Returning circulation pricked the numbness of her unbound, dangling legs as if with myriad needles. Dim hope shuddered through her darkened mind. Somehow, she lifted the unbearable weight of her head, opened her eyes.

Two men held her up, were hurrying her along. Two human beings. Her eyes darted unbelievingly from one to the other. The little flicker of hope flared into wild, delirious joy. She recognized them. Walt Eben, flaxen-haired, flaxen-mustached, a farmer who had lived, a sullen recluse, on the outskirts of the village ever since his wife and three children had died in the Gap. And Joel Harris, mountainous and heavy of face, the local quarryman. He too had been a trifle queer since his motherless daughter had been buried in the cemetery.

Jane's heart fluttered like a tiny prisoned bird at the near prospect of release. These were no demons of the Gap, no Thing who should be at rest beneath a graven headstone. They were flesh and blood, even as she. They had saved her from an awful death, from . . .

"Eben! Harris! Thank God you came! Thank God you . . .!"

Why didn't they answer? Why didn't they turn their heads and smile, friendly greetings into her still-tortured eyes? Why, did they grip her arms with brutal, tearing fingers, dragging her along the jagged, flinty rock?

She choked off suddenly, peered wildly from one to the other. The lightning still flared, illuminating the ghastly scene. Their faces were hard and lined, their foreheads wrinkled in grim sneers, their nostrils twitched with queer jerks. Then they turned simultaneously toward her.

Jane felt herself 'cold all over. Her limbs gave way and dragged, bumping and bruising, over the hard, unfeeling ground. These were not the men she had known the year before, the men who had greeted her respectfully as she has passed on the village street. These were strangers, demons in human form.

Hate blazed from their eyes, spittle drooled from their gaping lips. Unintelligible, animal snarls rumbled in the cavity of their throats. Jane's eyes shuddered away from their madness, focused on the dreadful picture straight ahead.

The gruesome horde still lined the railroad track. Torches still sizzled and crackled with burning pitch in skinny hands. But they were all quiet now. They leaned forward with avid eagerness, gloating with insane fanaticism on her slender, dragging body. Jane's mind went dark. She knew now the awful truth.

These demons of the Gap—these creatures of the night who had sent Kent to his death and whirled Jerry into the frightful depths—they were no Things of another world. She knew them, even in the fantastic flare of the torches, even with their madness thick upon them; she knew each one by name and occupation. They were all men from the village, men who had retreated from her as a thing accursed when she entered the single street, long, dim hours before. They were the same men who had strangely vanished when she came out again from Abner Tracy's store.

The corpse loomed before her—the soulless outer vestments of Everlasting Fayre. The grave-grey of his skin made her flesh crawl. The glutted hate of his pitted eyes seared her very soul. His hand was extended upward—like a prophet of evil, like a dead instrument of Hell.

There was no mercy anywhere. The heavens themselves seemed to mock her torment with thunderous laughter. These swarming creatures were men, but no longer sane. Their minds had cracked from long brooding on the tragedy that had engulfed their dear ones. Their madness had grown to fanatical heights under the leadership of the preacher who had died and returned from the grave to spur them on to vengeance against those they believed responsible.

It was too late now to explain. They would not hear; they could not listen. A corpse was their leader, and they were mindless automatons governed by a long-dead mind.

"Behold," Fayre thundered, "the final working of the curse! Chandler is dead, Shannon has plunged to eternity; Henry Stanford will never return to the place that haunts his dreams. Now his daughter, last of the accursed clan, last of those who dared to rebuild the railroad, will follow in their path. No more will steel rails and hellish trains disturb the peace and quiet of Devil's Gap; no more will a bridge fling defiance to the unquiet spirits who lurk beneath. Now and forever will your children's bodies, your wives' wailing souls, my own imploring ghost, rest in their narrow homes, content with the retribution you have exacted. Bind the woman to the wheel, let her follow the others into an eternity of suffering."

JANE was jerked forward. Her eyes widened in horror at the sight of the great steel drum. There it stood on the track, quiescent, yet quivering with a strange avidity of its own. Had it returned from its dreadful journey, had it . . .? But no! She remembered now. There had been two of these drums in the power house. This was the second; the first was twisted steel and ground flesh and bones below.

She flung herself madly around; she screamed, struggled and tore with superhuman strength at the hands that clutched her tight. She would not go to that awful death. Oh God, she cried, why have you deserted me? She begged and implored and shrieked for mercy.

But there was no mercy—could be none—in a corpse; there was none in the wild, fanatic eyes of the villagers. Powerful arms bent her thrashing body over the curve of the wheel; ropes thick and strong wound cruelly over her body.

The horde of crazed villagers streamed back to the line of the track. The torches were sooty, demoniac flares in the wind. Lightning slashed across the sky, died out. A drop of rain splashed into her face. The storm was about to begin.

Nothing mattered now. Soon she would be whirling, a helpless cog on an infernal machine, down the steel rails, hurtling even as poor Jerry had done, into the frightful Gap. A last shriek eddied from her gaping throat, stopped suddenly, even as the dead leader stepped back.

Her madly rolling eyes had detected movement along the outer edge of the gorge. The rocks were piled there in gargantuan blocks. The sooty torches did not penetrate those murky depths. The shadows were thick and ominous.

But a shadow darker than the rest was moving, slithering silently along, merging for an instant with the solid blackness of the faceless rocks, dissociating itself again in the lurid background of the mountain wall.

Harris jerked the last knot tight. It cut cruelly into her flesh, but Jane did not feel the pain. She watched with desperate fierceness that slow, crawling progress. Perhaps, perhaps . . .? She clutched at new hope and spewed it forth again. Despair dulled her limbs. Even if that creeping vagueness were a man, what could he do to help against this hideous babble of crazed men, against a creature from the grave itself?

Harris stepped back, so did Eben. They gloated madly on their handiwork; insane maggots crawled in their eyes. Fayre came forward with heavy, doomful clump. It was all over. In another instant . . .!

A great blaze sheeted the sky. Space seemed a huge cauldron of fire. Jane repressed a shriek that tore at every muscle of her body. The crawling shadow had silhouetted momentarily in that inferno of flame, had lifted its head and stared at her. Then the heaven darkened and blanked him out again.

NOW she knew she was really insane; the unhuman tortures of the night had torn her reason from its moorings. For the face she thought she saw had been the face of Kent Chandler, her husband! Kent, who was dead, whose blood had dyed the waxen polish of the cottage floor, whom the dead preacher had averred lay crushed and lifeless at the bottom of the Gap! This was an apparition from another world, an omen of her own approaching death.

Fayre stood over her, grisly face moveless. His hand extended toward the wheel. A thrust, and . . .

A figure catapulted into the light, crashed into the soulless body. The dead Thing staggered back.

"Jane, darling!"

She opened her eyes in delirious unbelief. Had another hallucination come to plague her in her last moments? Kent was over her, fingers desperate at her bonds. His head was bloody and his hair disheveled, but he was real—alive!

"Look out, Kent, behind you!" she shrieked.

Kent whirled around, too late. Eben and Harris hurled themselves upon him, dragged him back with powerful, pinioning arms. His wounded shoulder cracked with sickening sound; his left arm went limp. Jane saw the agony on his face, tore wildly at her bonds.

Fayre was at the wheel again. His eyes were glaring balls of insane fury. "Now, you she-devil," he gritted between corpse-teeth, "you and your husband both will die. This time nothing can stop me."

He shoved. The wheel tottered, swayed in unstable equilibrium. Above the howl of the storm, the wilder cries of the village madmen, came Kent's despairing curses, the sound of his struggles.

The cable drum started to move. Jane felt her feet going up, her head down. A last, long scream made the tendons of her throat raw. Horror clamped her in a vise. The trail had ended. Kent had been dead and returned to life. Soon he would die again. And her shattered limbs and bones would mingle with his at the bottom of Devil's Gap.

Her head lolled down. Her body was an insane curve. Her feet were up. Nausea griped her stomach. The great drum had started to roll. Over and over. . . .

* * *

Kent's anguished cursing came dimly to her. The leering faces of the madmen who lined the track gloated in their frenzy at the fate which awaited her.

The clamor of their mouthings deafened her ears. She was dizzy now. The wheel was turning a little faster. Everything blurred.

The noise increased suddenly. Thunder cracked, sharp and staccato. The villagers' cries redoubled. There was a new note to them. More thunder. Kent's voice, high, excited, yelling something.

The wheel was going over again. Her body rose into a confusion of wildly tossing torches, of leaping, dashing figures. Weights thudded heavily against the drum to which she was bound. The dizziness became sickness. Her head was down. The wheel had stopped rotating. That meant . . . ? The sky crashed upon her. . . .

SHE opened her eyes to see a remembered form. Arms held her tight.

"Thank God, darling, you're all right." Kent breathed fervently. "For a while I thought . . ."

His shoulder was bandaged and his left arm in a sling. Khaki-clad men, strangers, moved around with winking flashes. Rain splashed her face, but she didn't care. She snuggled closer to her husband.

"But how did you come back to life, my dear?" she whispered. "And what happened to save us just before . . . ?" She shuddered at the memory of that last dreadful scene, pressed against him.

"In the first place," he grinned, "I wasn't ever dead. If you mean the knife thrown at me in the cottage, it just pinked my shoulder. I chased the thrower—Harris has confessed he was the one—up the

mountain, where he outmaneuvered me, and threw me, as he thought, into the Gap. Fortunately, I fell only a dozen feet or so, caught on a tiny ledge. When I came to, I remembered the lights I had seen on the old railroad. The rest of the time I spent in getting here."

"But just before I fainted, everything seemed over," she protested.

A khaki-clad man hurried over. "All the villagers are in custody," he reported. "Two are dead, shot, but the others seem to have come out of their madness. They don't seem to know what happened."

"There's the answer, Jane," Kent told her as the man hurried away again. "State troopers from Meredith, the county seat. They came by special train to Devil's Gap when the call for help flashed through. And here," he continued, turning to two men who stood a bit to one side, "are the ones responsible for calling them. Will Kirkland and Zeke Lowe. They had heard me when I was struck down in the woods, and they had seen enough before to suspect what was taking place." He grinned. "For a while I thought they were the guilty parties. Kirkland is a C. R. & R. man, and Zeke, of course, stood to lose his trucking monopoly when the road was finished. Besides, they were always in conferences."

Kirkland's shrewd, dark face broke into a smile. "I knew Zeke couldn't make a living here after your branch started operation. And Zeke is an old friend of mine. I came to town to make him a proposition to boss a line of motor trucks for my outfit between the river valley and Meredith. He said he'd think it over, and started home. The next thing I heard was that he had gone crazy. Mrs. Chandler told me that. So I went after him."

Zeke grinned sheepishly. "So would you go crazy," he retorted, "if you saw old Everlasting Fayre, who yuh knew was dead and buried, walking down the road, straight for yuh."

Kent's face hardened. "He was responsible for the whole frightful affair. It was he who wrought the villagers to a pitch of madness with his apparitions and his curses. It was he who sent Harris to attack me, and to seize Jane. He wanted to scare us out of Devil's Gap, to stop the rebuilding of the railroad. When he saw he couldn't do that, he decided to kill us off. It was he who cut the cable last year and sent all those people crashing to their deaths. I didn't mention it, but I found the parted strands. They showed signs of a hack-saw. I wanted to investigate the matter quietly."

Jane shivered. "But how could a dead man do all that?"

"Dead man?" Kent echoed grimly. "Look at him!" He arose stiffly, lifted his wife to her feet. They walked unsteadily to where a shape lay, face up, unstirring, in the light of the flashes.

"There's your dead man," Kent pointed. "He's dead enough now."

Jane overcame her repulsion, looked closely. The features were still remarkably like those of Everlasting Fayre, but in places, the thick makeup had washed away under the pelting rain.

It was Abner Tracy!

"I—I don't understand," Jane faltered. "If the railroad went through, it would bring more business to his store, more than he could handle with Lowe's truck."

"That's what everyone thought, and that's what he claimed. But Tracy was smart. He knew it wouldn't work out that way. He saw what happened the first few days the old road operated. The mountaineers didn't stop here; they went on to Meredith for their shopping, where there were bigger and more modern stores. Tracy's business fell off tremendously. That was why he cut the cable the first time. He thought it had settled everything. But when he saw us coming back, he grew desperate. He made up as Fayre to play on the superstitious villagers, to get them to help him in his fiendish plans. This time he was going to make sure that no one would ever think of a railroad again."

Jane suddenly shivered. She clung desperately to her husband. Her lips sought his.

THE END

ATTIC
OF
TERROR

By
H. M.
Appel

*(Author of "Doom Flowers,"
etc.)*

*The leering, monstrous-shaped halfwit whispered foul words to Ray
Greene's wife, and Green thrashed the lewd creature. . . . But had
he known what blood-chilling terror was to follow, he would have
taken his beloved and fled from that horror-infested dwelling where
hell's evil minions leered their unholy greed!*

IT WAS that eerie hour between day-light and dark when dusk hangs its veil of mystery over the earth. Ray Greene felt it, and he knew his wife felt it. As he drove their decrepit car through

the murky tunnel of giant sycamore trees which arched the Raven Creek trail he found himself peering, through gaps here and there, into dim valleys between ragged hills—gloomy-looking ravines which, because of that grey murk of twilight, seemed peopled with strange and grotesque shadow-shapes. From somewhere beyond the sycamores, the wax-white blossoms of many locust trees spread a cloying sweetness upon the air that was somehow reminiscent of funeral flowers.

"The air seems drugged," he remarked, in an effort to break the gloomy silence. "Almost too heavy to breathe. It's depressing. . . ."

"We're almost there now." Gilda, his wife, spoke comfortingly. "Uncle Zac's farm is just beyond the next bend. You're tired—"

"Well, coaxing this ten-dollar wreck from Ohio to Kentucky in one day has been a chore," he admitted wearily. "I hope we like it here—we're out of both gas and money. And these old rear tires won't last another ten miles."

"We've just got to like it!" The words came so strongly that he looked around. Tiny lines had tightened the corners of his wife's full red lips; her hazel eyes looked somber under her dark brown hair. "It was wonderful of Uncle Zac to invite us," she went on. "Our future looked so desperate . . ."

Greene snorted. "I'd have got a job— we wouldn't have starved." Against his will he muttered: "When miserly old Zacchus McNabb gets big hearted and offers to take us in, it looks fishy to me. There's a catch in it somewhere——"

"For shame!" She eyed him hotly, provoked by the cynical curl of his strong, wide mouth, the grim set of his well turned jaw. "Uncle Zac has changed; his heart has softened. Didn't he take in Aunt Sally Otis when she was left feeble and alone? Didn't he send for Uncle Mack Sutton to come and live with him? And poor Cousin Dan McNabb—wounded, mentally unbalanced by the war, yet refused hospitilization—what would have become of Dan except for the kindness of

Uncle Zac? I think you're unappreciative . . ." Her lips trembled, she felt her eyes filling with tears.

"Just the same," Greene said stubbornly, "I'd have found work soon. Other newspapers besides the defunct *Chronicle* need reporters. Say, is this the place?"

They had rounded the bend, and before them stood a habitation—of sorts. A broken gate hung ajar in a rickety fence at the left. Beyond it stretched untilled, briar-choked fields, tumbledown outbuildings. A drab, unpainted, two-story farmhouse reared its ugly bulk from a stony knob. Lights glimmered in several upper windows but the lower rooms were dark.

"God, what a desolate spot!" Ray Greene went on. "Miles from any main road, any town . . . If this is Uncle Zac's conception of 'my old Kentucky home,' he can have it! Looks like a pauper's roost to me."

AFTER grinding along the rutted lane, he brought the car to a jolting stop beside the crumbling verandah. A few scrawny chickens fluttered down from the railing. Two lean hogs rooted under the steps. Beside a dry trough at the well near a rear door, a gaunt, hollow-flanked cow lowed drearily.

Gilda Greene's face lengthened. "Strange," she murmured. "I know Uncle Zac has money. Raven Creek Farm never looked like this when I used to come here. Why, the place has simply fallen into ruin!"

Abruptly, Greene felt her hand clutching his arm, saw her eyes widen with fright.

"Oh, what a horrible face! There—at the window—!" She pointed. "Did you see it?"

He stared at the grimy panes. "No. Are you sure it wasn't your uncle?"

Out of the shadows, like a pointed contradiction, came a burst of idiotic laughter.

It was lewd, menacing, and somehow unclean. The very sound of it made Gilda cringe against her husband's shoulder in abject and sudden terror.

The next moment, in the unscreened doorway appeared a queer figure—squat and bullet-headed, wide of chest, with arms that dangled to its knees. Crablike, it sidled across the porch and approached the car.

Again the loose lips dribbled guttural mirth; and from a repulsive visage, low-browed and bestial, in which what should have been the left eye showed only a red and inflamed socket, it leered with a horrible if mysterious show of cunning.

"It's Toby," Gilda whispered. "I'd forgotten him. Slanderous persons used to say he was Uncle Zac's illegitimate son, but I never believed——"

The idiot—evidently he was no more than that—chuckled. His voice came horribly:

"Toby heard what you said, and you'd better believe if you know what's good for you! Yah, Toby's gonna get everything when the old man dies." He scowled, added complainingly: "Took you long enough to come! Why didn't you hurry?"

Greene snapped: "Where are all the others?"

"In their rooms." Toby pointed upward. "Where else would they be? Can't you see the lights? All in bed—but Toby takes good care of them."

His slobbering grin was hideous.

"Is Uncle Zac ill, too?" Gilda asked. "What's wrong with everybody?"

"Not Zac." Toby smirked. "That old fool is too ornery to get sick. He's back in the kitchen fixing up some papers."

Ray Greene stepped on the starter and heard the motor spin without response. "Out of gas," he grumbled. "If we weren't, I'd head out of this forsaken hole right now."

"You certainly would not," his wife said spiritedly. "With every one ill and only this—" she hesitated—"this boy to look after them, I can't understand why you show so little sympathy."

"Neither can I," Greene retorted, "but I've a hunch we'll soon wish we'd never come."

AGAIN the idiot chuckled. Greene got down and reluctantly lifted their two large bags from the rear of the coupé.

As they entered the parlor they found it pervaded by a musty, disquieting odor, faintly suggestive of things long dead. Toby struck a match and touched flame to an oil lamp on a center table. His shadowy face looked gargoylesque as he bent above the light.

A harsh voice somewhere in the hall beyond exclaimed: "Who's there? Is it you, Gilda? And your new husband?" The approaching tones warmed a little. "I'd about given you up." Then the speaker, Zacchus McNabb himself, entered the room.

"Our car broke down several times, uncle." Gilda hurried forward to kiss him. "We bought it for less than our railway fare, just to make the trip."

Greene, during a brief year of married life, had not met Zacchus McNabb. And Gilda's tales of his niggardliness had made the invitation all the more surprising. With curiosity, therefore, he regarded this thin little old man of sixty whose bald scalp was oddly wrinkled, as were his pink cheeks beneath the stubble of white beard. A certain wiriness of bare forearms and a springiness of step belied the hint of senility in the rheumy old eyes.

McNabb made a vague gesture with a fistful of documents. "I've been doing something nice for you, girl. Life is uncertain at my age and I've lost most of my money, so I've taken out some insurance and named you my beneficiary. It'll pay you a hundred dollars a month after I pass away. All that's needed is the signature of a witness and the papers will be ready to mail."

"You're not going to die, Uncle Zac, for ever so long!" Gilda cried. "But it was sweet of you to think of me." Tears dimmed her hazel eyes and she shot an accusing glance at her husband.

McNabb grunted: "Don't be too sure. The others are bedfast with something that looks like sleeping sickness and I may get took, too. Doc says all they need is rest and nursing, but you never can tell. Here, young fellow! Witness this thing and I'll get it ready for the postman. My other relatives enjoy incomes of some sort, and I want Gilda to have the protection of my insurance. Of course," he continued garrulously, "if she should die, it goes to Toby. That fool will be here when we're all dead and gone."

Ray Greene took the pen and scrawled his name on the indicated blank. Toby, the idiot, looked over his shoulder and grumbled:

"Never nothing for me! Toby does all the work, but he's got to wait till everybody dies." Abruptly, his laughter jangled. "Mebbe that won't be so long."

"Pay no mind to the poor crack-brain," growled McNabb, leading Greene to a desk in the corner. "Address an envelope to The Phoenix Mutual Life Insurance Company at Cincinnati, will you? My eyes ain't so good any more."

THE old man droned on, ramblingly, about the uncertainty of life and death. Toby, across the room, began speaking to Gilda. His tones, subdued but sharp, were audible to Ray Greene above McNabb's monologue.

"Toby gets tired of sleeping with Cousin Dan," he heard the idiot complain. "Dan's feet are too cold. Like ice, they are." He cackled. "Bet you'd never get as cold as him. Mebbe, one of these days, Toby'll try sleeping with you instead."

Greene sprang up, dropping the addressed envelope. In one stride he was across the room and had the half-wit by the slack of shirt front.

"You damned, filthy moron! Another crack like that and I'll break your head!"

Gilda, flushed and trembling, remonstrated weakly: "Don't, Ray. He doesn't know any better——"

McNabb, sensing the nature of Toby's offense although he had not caught the words, gave the youth a stinging slap across the face.

"Out of here!" he raged. "To the barn with you, you good-for-nothing! Always thinking of things you hadn't ought to——"

"Toby's good for plenty!" the idiot squalled, his one eye blazing. "Good enough to take care of them that's lying upstairs. Good enough—" he showed his snags of teeth—"to fix every last one of you and collect all the money. Toby's smart. Toby'll get what he wants."

Another flailing slap sent him dodging toward the door. "Crack-brain!" the old man stormed. "Get out! Go sleep in the barn."

Later, at McNabb's suggestion, Gilda went into the kitchen to prepare supper. Greene, unwilling now to let her long out of his sight, sat upon a stool beside a corner window moodily staring into the night. He was still wishing they hadn't come. Old Zacchus McNabb, he noticed, had busied himself building a fire in the greasy cook-stove, which was cluttered with dirty pots and pans.

"We ain't been much on housekeeping, Toby and me," the old man said apologetically, "what with taking care of the sick folks and all."

"What shall I cook for them?" Gilda asked. She looked askance at the salt pork and potatoes McNabb had just carried in from the pantry. "Do they have a special diet?"

"Eh? Oh, to be sure. But Toby fed them an hour ago. Every one is sleeping now. That's about all they do."

THE meager meal finished, Ray Greene said shortly: "Let's go to bed. I'm tired."

His wife acquiesced. McNabb went upstairs to show them their room. When Gilda inquired concerning the care of the three patients during the night, the old man said carelessly:

"Toby sleeps with Dan. If any of them calls, he'll hear. Of course, I told the crack-brain to stay in the barn, but soon he'll be sneaking back. Come on—we'll peep in and make sure they're all quiet now."

Through the first door, as he opened it cautiously, they saw an emaciated looking old woman, her white hair spread across a pillow.

"Aunt Sally," McNabb whispered. "She's took worst, I reckon."

The next was an elderly man. All that could be seen of him was the back of his iron-grey head.

"And here's Dan's room," said McNabb, pointing within a third dimly lit chamber. "Don't know what to think about him. Toby says he ain't moved a mite since yesterday morning."

"We'd better go in and see—" Gilda began, when her husband snapped: "No! The sickness may be contagious. I won't have you exposed."

"That's right," McNabb agreed. "No use taking chances, I say. Doc'll be out tomorrow. Meanwhile, let Toby look after them like he has been doing."

They bid McNabb their goodnights and Greene, entering the room assigned to them, looked at his wife wryly.

"Bighearted Zac! He invited you down here to be nurse, cook and maid of all work. Cheaper than hiring local help. I wish to God we hadn't come!"

"Not to nurse—you heard what he said," Gilda rejoined, near to tears. "Oh, Ray! Maybe you're right. Something about this place frightens me!"

"That idiot, of course. Blast his ugly hide! We'll stick till morning, but then we're leaving if we have to walk."

They undressed, turned down the light and made ready for bed. When Greene raised the window, his wife said nervously:

"Let's keep it closed. The night's cool, and I'll rest better knowing no one can sneak in. Did you lock the door?"

Standing in a shaft of moonlight which slanted through the panes, Greene grumbled: "There's no lock." At her suggestion, he wedged a chair beneath the knob.

Fatigued, he fell asleep quickly. He didn't know when it was that he awoke. But he awakened with a start—and suddenly froze as he saw that Gilda was gone. Almost in the same instant, from somewhere down the hall, he heard an awful, anguished cry. It was hers.

Dashing out in his pajamas, he glimpsed light through a half-open door. He raced that way, burst into the room. Beside Aunt Sally's bed, hands pressed tightly to her breasts, stood his wife. She was staring wordlessly at the old woman's motionless figure.

"What's wrong?" he cried.

"Ray! For God's sake, look!"

A glance told him the worst. The old woman was dead.

"Queer!" he exclaimed. "Looks as though she'd been dead for days."

Overcoming his instinctive revulsion, he made a brief examination of the corpse. Abruptly he reared up, horrified.

"God! *She's been crudely embalmed!*"

Words rattled on Gilda's dry lips. "Toby!" she cried. "I dreamed he was murdering Aunt Sally; that's what made me come to investigate. But he wasn't here———"

Greene bent to inspect the body again. He loosed a gulp of sheer nausea.

"Look! *Her right hand is gone!* That devil hacked it off at the wrist! In God's name—why?"

Gilda sobbed: "What of the others? Hadn't we better go and see?"

Nerves keyed to the breaking point, they went into the adjoining room. One glance and Gilda, turning her face aside, moaned: "Uncle Mack, too. He's a corpse! And that sickening odor. . . ."

Greene flicked the cover back hurriedly, his eyes encompassing the frightfulness some fiend had wreaked upon the shrunken body.

The abdomen had been opened, then rudely sewn. Red wounds gaped, where veins had been emptied of their blood. And again there was that mysterious absence of the right hand.

"Your cousin, Dan, will be dead, too. Small doubt of that," he whispered.

But the third room disclosed a sight even more dreadful. In this case, both the hands had been amputated, brutally, as with an axe.

Greene's arm tightened about his wife as she uttered a sudden cry of panic.

"Uncle Zac! What's become of him? He must have heard me screaming——"

"I thought of that. We'll find him murdered. Don't forget the idiot's threats."

"You mean—about the insurance? Then, Toby may try to kill us, too!"

"Me, perhaps. But not you—" Green ground his teeth in fury at the thoughts which possessed him. "There's just one thing to do," he went on grimly. "We'll barricade ourselves in our room and wait till dawn. I can handle that moron if I get a fair chance at him, but I don't want him to sneak up on us unawares."

Once more within their bedchamber, he blocked the door as before with a chair, and said: "Crawl into bed. I'm going to dress and stay awake."

He had donned his shirt and trousers and was reaching for his shoes when a sound at the moonlit window made him stiffen.

Someone was knocking there.

HE CREPT close to the glass, keeping well to one side, so as not to be silhouetted against the lamplight. He saw a white hand peck at the pane, then disappear. Again it came, gently tapping, to be as quickly withdrawn.

The rage surged in him. If Toby was perched on a ladder out there, one thrust might send him smashing to the ground— as he so well deserved.

Bracing himself by grasping the handle of the sash, Greene waited. Once more the ghostly hand hove into view and he heaved the glass upward, snatched at the reaching fingers. But only to jerk back the next instant with a great, convulsive oath, dropping the loathsome thing so that it lay on the floor in a streak of moonlight.

For it was nothing *but* a hand—dismembered, shrunken and bony, the flesh dry and ragged about the butchered wrist. And tied to it was a label which read: AUNT SALLY.

Horror gave way to a spasm of fury so intense it left his tall frame trembling. Naturally of high-strung disposition, this final piece of charnel grotesquerie on the part of the witless murderer roused in him a burning desire to mete out punishment. Recollection of the odious creature's lewd remark to Gilda added further fuel to the flames of his anger.

Leaning out through the open embrasure, he studied the ground below. No one seemed to be moving down there. Glancing up toward the roof, a grunt of satisfaction escaped his taut lips. A length of thin white string swayed in the faint breeze. From that, obviously, the hand had dangled. He saw that the string led into an attic window directly overhead.

He closed the sash, blocked it with a curtain rod. From the old-fashioned fireplace he secured a heavy poker. To his wife, who whispered frantic questions from the bed, he snapped:

"Get up! Wedge the door shut after me. I'll catch that half-wit before he either murders us or runs away. I know where he's hiding——"

"No, no!" Springing to his side, barefooted, clad only in her thin nightgown, Gilda Greene flung her arms about her husband. "He'll kill you too——"

Greene raised the poker suggestively. "Let him try it!"

He went out, treading stealthily in his stockinged feet. A door leading to the attic stairs stood open. Cautiously he began to ascend. His teeth were gritted, his weapon was ready. He intended to capture Toby or else brain him at the slightest resistance.

MOONLIGHT streaming along the top of the steps showed that no one was lurking there. Without a sound, Greene crept on. His head level with the floor at last, he peered toward a window in a gable at the farther end.

Only in that narrow central space could a man stand erect beneath the sloping roof. Toby, he thought, must be crouching close under the eaves. He could discern an unlighted lantern dangling from the ridge pole. If that were lit he could drive the idiot from his hiding place.

Moving forward on tiptoe, then pausing again, he listened—heard nothing. Reaching upward with one hand, he pressed a lever, raising the lantern's chimney—his alert glance sweeping the shadows on every side for an expected sudden assault. Striking a match, with one quick gesture he touched flame to the wick and dropped the globe in place. The yellow rays spread across the bare expanse of attic.

No one was hidden there. But a row of hideous objects hanging from nails driven into the chimney held him fascinated. The objects were three severed human hands.

Stepping nearer, he read what was scrawled upon the cards tied to each ragged wrist: UNCLE MACK. DAN, LEFT. DAN, RIGHT.

Perspiration broke forth upon his clammy brow. Unconsciously, he voiced a question which clamored for an answer in his shuddering mind:

"Why? *Why?* What did that devil want with their hands?"

Horror was accentuated by recollection of the idiot's complaint that he had to share a bed with Dan, whose feet were so cold. "God!" Greene thought, revulsed. "He must have been sleeping with that dead body for nights on end. Those corpses were *old!*"

And then, tearing at his overwrought nerves like a tempest, came a despairing shriek from the floor below. Gilda's voice, dissolving in sheer terror.

"No, Toby! Let me go! Keep your filthy hands off——"

In one bound Greene reached the stairs. Like a madman he thundered down them. He had just reached the bottom when a bludgeon thudded against his unprotected skull with a sickening impact and dropped him in a quivering, unconscious heap.

WITH hands lashed behind him to the back of his chair, Greene writhed and moaned as consciousness slowly returned. He could not move; his feet, too, were confined. Opening blurred and bloodshot eyes, he peered about the room. On a low table at his side the oil lamp was burning. Someone had turned it higher.

"Gilda!" he gasped weakly. "Gilda— oh, my God!"

His frenzied gaze had focused on the bed. There his wife lay, unclothed, spread-eagled between the four tall posts, her lovely torso arching high, then collapsing, as she struggled against cords knotting both hands and feet.

A wretched mumble of misery gurgled in her throat behind the towel that gagged her. Toby, the idiot, was nowhere in sight, yet Greene feared that the worst had happened. Why the one-eyed monster had departed, he could not guess.

Desperately he tried to burst his bonds, but made no headway at all until reason returned enough for him to collect his reeling senses.

Then, with the kitchen chair tilted backward and precariously balanced against the wall, he worked his long limbs downward, slowly and carefully succeeding in sliding the ropes off the slender spindles.

But he was still helpless, with his ankles bound tightly together. The oil lamp caught his eye, roused a flicker of hope. Hitching himself around until he faced the table, he swung his feet up to the flat top. Then, with an effort that started beads of sweat from every pore, he hoisted his legs above the lamp chimney and by herculean strength held them there.

The heat seared his skin and he repressed a groan. Then the hemp ignited. He put his feet down and let it burn until flesh and blood could stand no more. Shuddering with agony, he spread his knees, exerted all his remaining strength in one punishing kick. The ropes parted. His ankles were free, but they felt like raw stubs of bone.

He began a desperate struggle with the chair. The inanimate thing seemed endowed with the characteristics of a human enemy. Wrench and struggle as he might, he could not break it, nor loose his hands. At last he fell upon his side. Rolling over, he got the chair beneath his back. By a final joint-straining contortion he passed it under his buttocks and got his hands in front, where he could reach the knots with his teeth. They yielded stubbornly.

Drenched in sweat, panting with anxiety—since any second the idiot might return—he staggered toward the bed.

A sound of measured, thudding blows outside the house made him pause. Glancing through the window he saw the black, misshapen form of a man, working with a pick in the waning moonlight.

"Digging a grave," he muttered. "For one or all of us. That gives me a little time——"

Ripping the gag from Gilda's lips, he pleaded: "Tell me that you're all right. That he didn't——"

"No." Moaning, she shook her head. "But he'll come again. He threatened horrid things. Oh, Ray, untie me——"

ONCE freed, she clutched him in a spasmodic embrace, shuddering with her head against his breast, sobbing her tale of outrage.

"When you started up there, I didn't close the door. Instead, I crouched beside it and waited. I was afraid you might come running, with that fiend in pursuit. You were gone so long! Then—" he could feel her slim body quiver with the memory of it—"someone leaped out of the dark and grabbed me. I heard your shout after I screamed, the sound of your footsteps on the stairs. Toby darted into the hall. Then he came back, yelling like a maniac, and tied me to the bed——"

Greene pressed his palm to her lips. "Listen! I thought I heard——"

Hurrying to the window he saw that the grave digger had disappeared. Coming back to Gilda's side, he whispered: "Toby's coming. He thinks I'm still bound to the chair. We'll fool him this time——"

In feverish haste he snatched two pillows from the bed, posed them on the seat beside the table, draped his coat around the top one. Then he extinguished the light.

"I don't know how that devil kills," he muttered. "My head feels big as a balloon from the blow he dealt me. Perhaps he smothered the others in their beds."

"He said he'd chop off my hands," Gilda wailed hysterically. "That he'd sleep with me after I was dead. Oh, he's crazy! He hears strange voices. He no sooner had me tied than he cocked up his ears and said: 'Hear him out there? Hunting for Toby! Tonight, all but Toby shall die!' Then I fainted—and when I came to, you were sprawled helpless before my eyes. Oh, we'll never escape that monster—" Vainly she tried to stifle her sobs.

"Quiet!" whispered Greene, nervously. "Everything hinges upon surprising him. He's sure to sneak in here soon, and I'll jump him when he passes the window. I don't dare miss——"

Breathlessly, they stood against the wall, where they would be shielded by the door when it swung open. The passing moments dragged, the tension mounted. A muscle in Greene's cheek trembled uncontrollably and his scorched ankles gave him harrowing pain. Were they doomed to suffer in suspense throughout the livelong night? Suppose the idiot, suspicious of darkness, failed to enter?

When a board creaked in the hallway it was almost a welcome sound. Greene could hear Gilda's breath quicken. He touched her lips with his fingers, warningly. Another creak. Then the faint, metallic rasp of a latch, manipulated cautiously. Inch by inch the door opened toward them. A soft ejaculation grated sibilantly:

"Dark! Lamp run short of oil, mebbe?"

SILENCE descended like a pall. Greene thought that soon he must scream if the man did not move. To calm his tortured nerves he began counting seconds, tolled off thirty, keeping his eyes glued to the strip of moonlight which formed a dim path on the floor.

Slowly, a vague shadow began to take shape as the intruder edged forward. With the stealth of a jungle cat he moved toward the dummy on the chair. Greene had counted upon him crossing the illuminated streak, but the marauder kept to the gloom. His figure was still too indistinct to permit launching an assault with accuracy.

A blubbering sob of bloodlust straightened Greene where he stood. Savagely the killer sprang. An axe-blade glittered as it swished through the air. The chair crashed in a splintered heap.

Greene lunged forward. His body collided with the other, and someone blurted a startled oath. Snarlingly he fell upon the marauder, and struggled viciously. With the murderer's fingers fastened like steel hooks about his throat, he gasped, choked, and weakness assailed him.

Then his outflung hand touched the haft of the axe. Seizing it, he drove one knee upward, flung his adversary aside. Springing erect, he whirled the blade about his head and brought it down with all his strength. Blood gushed in a black spreading blot on the moonlit boards.

GREENE was amazed when he noted that the parlor clock marked the hour as only ten. Putting Gilda down upon a couch, he started back with a lamp, to fetch their clothing. But in the same moment he paused, ready to shout with joy. A car had drawn up to the porch outside.

A couple entered unceremoniously, hard upon their knock. A neighbor and his young wife, apparently. The man smiled, said genially:

"We wondered if you folks got here all right. Saw the light when passing on our way home from town. I'm Sam Tate; this is my wife Jessie. By cripes, Greene, you sure look sick enough. White as a sheet! Even punier than Zac said. But,' he added consolingly, "we done what we could for your poor woman, even if you ain't long for this world."

Greene stared. "What are you talking about?"

It was the woman who answered: "About the insurance, he means." She put her fat arm around Gilda's waist in motherly fashion. "Mebbe you'll say it wasn't entirely honest, but them big companies got lots of money. And when Zac told us how sick your man was, dearie, about to die and leave you without a cent, I up and made my husky Sam go in to Fairdale where he ain't known and take an insurance examination in the name of Ray Greene, like your uncle wanted—"

Greene whirled toward the corner desk, snatched up an envelope, stamped and ready for posting. Ripping it open, he studied the printed form with widening eyes. Other mail, arriving that day, interested him, too. Following a hurried glance at the contents, he cried:

"This explains everything! Even the severed hands. Tate, come with me! The devil himself has been here tonight——"

Gilda sobbed: "Toby even killed poor Uncle, who'd given him a home for years."

Greene, carrying a lamp, paused at the door of their bedroom. This may startle you, dear," he said huskily. "That man on the floor was the fiend behind it all."

Gilda screamed. "Why—Uncle Zac!"

"Yes, and Toby's lying there in the hall. Zac struck me down and killed him later, when the half-wit left you the second time. God knows which one murdered the others. That old miser first invited here those relatives who enjoyed small incomes. There's a check downstairs paying Uncle Mack Sutton's annuity, another for Aunt Sally's Civil war pension. He killed them and forged their signatures to continue collecting the money for himself."

"How," asked Gilda, "does that explain the missing hands?"

GREENE explained: "They're not missing. They're hanging up in the attic, each one carefully labeled. And a letter addressed to your Cousing Dan accounts for them. Evidently, he had a small disability policy besides his army compensation. The company, cleverly enough, requires a fingerprint along with the signature when receipting for payments. Their last letter insists that Dan stamp his *right* thumb print instead of his left. Apparently, Zac made a mistake— then feared that a similiar complication might arise in the case of the others."

"But why didn't he bury the bodies," Sam Tate demanded, wiping his clammy brow. "Think of keeping them lying dead in their beds—"

"You were accustomed to seeing lights in each room at night, weren't you? And I'll bet," said Greene, "that he showed you his 'sick folks sleeping,' the same as he did us."

Tate nodded. "He done just so. Zac had it all planned well."

Ray Greene stepped to the window, looked out at a yawning grave. "That was intended for me."

He shrugged. "I'd already signed the policy—as an applicant instead of a witness. With Gilda's body preserved in bed like all the others, he would have told you she came down with the same disease. I would have 'died' suddenly and been hastily buried. Toby simply would have 'disappeared.'

"With all those dead hands grasping for the cash he coveted, Zacchus McNabb wasn't satisfied. But it was greed, you see, which spoiled his gruesome game, when he tried to add still another name to his list of pensioners."

The SCARLET

By Hugh B. Cave
(Author of "Satan's Sepulcher," etc.)

THE fog was a vast grey world of undulating gloom in which the winding Cape Cod road, the gaunt shapes of spectral houses, the massive mounds of stubbled sand that humped down to a vague ocean, were all blurred into a sinister fourth dimension of monstrous distortion. In it crawled the car that carried Mark Andrews and his wife toward their destination.

Mark turned red-rimmed eyes from the drooling windshield and glanced into the white, weary face beside him. Vaguely he said: "Are we nearly there, Judy?"

She nodded without looking at him. Perhaps the evil menace of the fog had

WIDOW

Complete

Terror Novel

Mark Andrews could not understand the curious sympathy which made his wife turn from him to her mother—the strange widow who wore scarlet. He could not understand the dread which gripped that desolate community, nor the horrible creature—neither man nor beast—which haunted the night and the swamp and the dank graveyard, claiming screaming victims for its obscene lust!

crept into her heart, too, as it had wormed into his. Or perhaps she was thinking of that strange letter, from her mother, which had summoned them abruptly from home and caused them to drive all night without stopping. . . .

Perhaps, too, she was thinking of her father, who was dead. The letter had not told much—merely that Paul Bronson had died under mysterious circumstances. Judy had not cried; she had merely become suddenly stiff, pale, and said in a toneless voice: "We must go, Mark. My mother needs us."

Her mother . . . ? During the six months of their marriage and the three mad months preceding, Judy had mentioned her parents not more than half a dozen times, and then only vaguely. They lived in a remote part of Cape Cod. Judy herself had not seen them since leaving home more than two years before. She had written occasionally, but Mark never read her letters.

Strange! He had thought nothing of it before. He had not even realized what was now so darkly obvious—that Judy's silence had not been casual but studied and deliberate. Now he knew and wondered. A disturbing suspicion had for hours been festering in his thoughts, as evil and as sinister as the blur of fog through which the car was creeping.

Something here was evil. The thought squatted like a leering black gnome in Mark Andrews' brain and muttered at him to retreat before his black premonitions took form and summoned some monstrous horror out of the weird world around him. But that was a result of sitting hunched all night behind the wheel, fighting weariness; of peering too often into Judy's tense face and seeing there, in her dark eyes, a nameless dread that had hourly been eating deeper.

Judy, too, was afraid. She was probably thinking of the house they were going to. A house of death, and of——?

Mark's foot swung from gas-pedal to brake, jammed so hard to the floor that both he and his wife lurched forward as the car squealed to a stop. Ahead, a shape had materialized in the fog's grey vapors, which was racing with wild cries of terror toward the car's front bumper.

The machine coughed to a stop. Staring, Mark said through a sudden hard scowl: "What the devil——!" The thing in the road had skidded to a halt, was gazing back with trembling terror into the fog. As it caught between two evils,

it stood whimpering, afraid of the car, afraid also of something else. It was a long-haired Irish setter . . . .

Then Mark saw. Out of the fog came something like a monstrous shape conjured into being by the murk's undulating vapor. Mark's hand tightened on the wheel; he gaped, caught a quick breath of amazement. Beside him, Judy jerked a trembling hand to her mouth and screamed through her fingers.

And the Thing came in a surging rush that resembled the charge of a marauding spider. Formless in the fog, it was a vast, lunging blur that sucked grey murk with it, distorting it into a weird something which was neither beast nor human.

Between it and the car crouched the terrified dog!

The twisted windshield blinded Mark's eyes to what happened next. Out there beyond the smeared glass, all things belonged in some dark creation of their own. In it, the distorted shape of the dog suddenly rushed blindly toward the road-shoulder.

That other Thing—that huge, hurtling shape which seemed to propel itself on all fours with the agility of a great spider —swerved in mid-charge and lunged toward its frenzied prey.

THERE was a sound of frantic bodies crashing through underbrush, a sudden shrill yelp laden with agony, then a low, shuddering, moan and silence—dead, hollow silence that sucked color from Mark Andrews' tense face—which was broken only when Judy reached out a trembling hand and whispered in a voice pregnant with fear: "Mark! Mark— what was it?"

Wire-tight nerves were responsible for Mark's curt reply. "You ought to know. You lived in these parts."

She stared at him, her eyes wide as she caught a breath. "Mark——!"

Then suddenly he relaxed. "I'm sorry, darling. This damned fog, and driving all night——" He stared into the murk where the dog's death-cry had gurgled to silence. Savagely he thrust open the car door. "Anyway, I'm going to straighten *one* thing out! I'm going to see what the thing was, and——"

"Mark, don't!"

"Huh?"

"Don't! Oh, let's get away from here! Please!"

He pulled the door shut again, put the car in motion. "So it's getting you too, is it?" he asked grimly.

She was silent as the machine droned into the weird world ahead. So was he. But the black gnome in his brain was leering again, whispering dark innuendoes that brought all the doubts back to life. And those doubts were blended now in a black blur with premonitions which had suddenly become huge, menacing.

That thing back there in the road had been real—not an illusion spawned by the fog's ever-changing contour. He had *seen* it, had heard the death-yelp of its snared victim. So had Judy. But *what* had they seen? What in God's name——?

And why had Judy refused to let him leave the car? Why that sudden look of terror, of *horror*, that had come into her staring eyes?

He maintained grim silence as the car continued its journey. Twenty minutes later when Judy said suddenly: "There Mark! There's the house!" The sound of her voice cut through a silence thicker than the fog itself and disturbed thoughts which had grown more darkly morbid with each passing moment.

Mark slowed the car to a crawl, stared. He had anticipated something like this. He had vaguely expected their destination to be a huge, unlovely abode as wild and as rambling as the fog-laden terrain in which it reared its uncouth bulk. Reluc-

tantly he turned the machine into the narrow driveway.

Fog swirled around him as he stepped from the car and stood glaring. Into his mind wormed an evil intuition that some monstrous horror had recently descended upon the huge wooden pile before him ... and would come again before long on some new mission of darkest dread ....

"This is where you were born?"

"Yes, Mark. But it has changed—changed so terribly!"

So this was Judy's birthplace! Strange how the thought sent a shudder of revulsion through him as he slowly climbed the steps and pulled the antique bell-knob. Here in this gaunt structure, his wife had first seen the light of day. Here, too, or at least in the nearby woods, her father had been found dead a few days ago. Only her mother was left. The mother whom he had never seen.

He reached again for the bell and the door opened as he did so. Swarthy, Portugese features glared out at him, reaching hardly to his chest. "What you want, huh?"

"My mother sent for us, Pietro," Judy said quietly. Her hand touched Mark's. "Pietro is caretaker here."

The Portugee gaped, spoke the girl's name in a thick whisper of surprise. "Ju-dee!" He jabbed out a grimy hand and Judy took it. And suddenly Mark was rigid, staring past Pietro's stoop-shouldered body at a woman who came toward them in the gloom of the hall.

He knew instinctively that he was looking at Judy's mother, at the widow of the man who had been found dead, days ago, in the woods somewhere nearby. A widow? The word seemed grotesquely incongruous! The woman before him was superbly tall, as pallidly beautiful as a figure carved in wax. And that Junoesque figure was garbed not in widow's black—but in an evening gown of vivid scarlet!

He stared, only vaguely aware of acknowledging introductions, of pacing stiffly into the house and seating himself with Judy and her mother in a spacious living-room. Something about that scarlet-gowned figure confused him. The woman was too attractive; her corpse-like face too deathly pale.

AND then she was talking, uttering low, vibrant words that compelled attention. She spoke of the thing which had brought Mark Andrews and his young wife to this strange, fog-bound abode where nothing seemed normal; where the widow of a man recently dead seemed weirdly linked with death herself, and wore vivid scarlet instead of somber black.

"For two days he was so very strange, so worried and restless about something! Then he vanished. I was frantic! I waited and waited, knowing that something frightful had happened. I telephoned to the village and a searching party was organized. For three endles days they scoured the woods. And in the end they found——"

The woman shuddered, closed her eyes in an agony of remembrance. When she spoke again, her voice was distorted by sobs: "They found him in the swamp near Salt Pond. Only God knows why he went there or what happened. He had been dead a long while. Dead from the bite of a black-widow spider. Oh, God——!"

Judy moved to her mother's side, bent above her. They understood each other, these two. Some strange bond existed between them . . . "But, mother, why must you wear that gown? Why?"

The woman stiffened. "Haven't I just told you? It was a black widow that took him from me! Am I to be a black widow, too? God! All my life I have hated spiders. I warned him a hundred times!

I told him what would happen! And so now——"

She slumped heavily against the chair's ribbed back, stared into space. She had loved her husband; that was obvious. His death had made her a terrified, hysterical creature whose mind ran occasionally to momentary insanity. She mumbled now, almost inaudibly. "When they found him, he was not my Paul. The poison had changed him, and things of the swamp had been feeding on him. God is so cruel, so terribly cruel——"

An alien sound from the hall interrupted her, came as a heaven-sent relief to Mark Andrews' taut nerves. The door had jarred open; a shrill, childish voice was clamoring the name of Pietro, the caretaker.

The woman raised her head, staring. As if speaking to herself she said dully: "That is Pietro's little boy. What does he want?"

Mark was glad of the opportunity to get away, to push himself erect and stride into the hall. But Pietro, appearing from somewhere in the gloomy bowels of the house, was there before him, and a grimy-faced youngster clung frantically to the caretaker's hand, sobbed hysterical words into Pietro's scowling face—Portugese words that Mark Andrews did not comprehend.

He understood, though, the sudden look of alarm that contorted Pietro's swarthy features. And as he jerked forward, the caretaker turned a frenzied face toward him. "He say my wife hurt! Something terrible happen! I got to go quick!"

Evil premonition sent Mark with him, sent them both blundering across the threshold and into the clammy embrace of the fog. Behind them, Pietro's son blubbered in the doorway, fearing to follow.

What had happened? What had occurred to send a seven-year-old boy whimpering through the fog to find his father and sob words of abject terror? Mark did not dare think. Too long his thoughts had dwelt with the macaber thing that he and Judy had encountered back there in the road!

With jerky strides, the caretaker plunged forward, the wheeze of his breath a sibilant sucking sound as the murk undulated around him. He followed a graveled path toward a small, squat building that loomed ahead. The caretaker's house, apparently. And there, Pietro shrilled his wife's name as he blundered to the door.

"Anna! *Anna,* what is wrong? Where are you?"

The door jarred wide when he heaved himself against it. Pietro lurched over the sill, gaped around him, shrieked again: "*Anna!*" Mark shuddered at the shack's uncleanliness, followed mutely as the Portugee stumbled forward.

Then he stopped, stood rigid on the bedroom threshold as Pietro lurched toward a scarred wooden bed that loomed beyond. A black-haired youngster stood sobbing against the bed-end. Something lay in a dark heap on the floor at the boy's feet. . . .

THE shape was a woman, large, near-naked, face contorted in a hideous grimace of agony. Mumbling her name, Pietro staggered to his knees beside her and peered frantically into her face. Slowly, Mark moved closer.

The woman's cheap, cotton dress had been torn from the upper half of her body. Vicious fingers had raked her fatty flesh, gouged throat and breasts. She was groaning in torment. Her big hands clutched the bulging flesh of an inflated stomach, striving to hold back the pain that centered there. The muscles of her chest were contracted. Frantically she fought to husk breath into her lungs. Her arms and legs were purple, bloated to twice their normal proportions.

The truth struck Mark Andrews with sledge-hammer force, hurled him forward. Violently he pushed the woman's husband back. "Get a doctor! Hurry, Pietro, for God's sake!"

But it was too late. He knew it was too late. He had seen victims of the black widow before, and this woman had been bitten horribly. She was on death's threshold, delirious now in that weird, mad delirium that precedes a death of dark agony. Her eyes were wide, gaping up into his own. Broken syllables muttered from her lips.

And as Pietro rushed out of the house, toward that other gaunt abode where a telephone was available, Mark Andrews did what he could to ease the woman's suffering, and listened with increasing horror to the words that croaked from her throat.

"It wasn't nothin' human. God alive, it come at me so fast I couldn't get away! It was big an' hairy—like a spider!"

And again, after a pitiful struggle for breath: "I—I was pickin' beach plums up the road. I wasn't doin' no harm, God knows I wasn't. An' the thing came at me an' knocked me down an' clawed me —an' laughed! Stood there *laughin'* at me while I crawled away. I—I crawled home here——"

The voice rose, shrilled madly through the room's chill murk. "It was a spider-thing I tell yer! My God, go get Mr. Bronson! There ain't no one knows what to do better'n him. He knows all about whatever——"

The words stopped, as Mark had known they would. Stopped abruptly in a hoarse death-rattle that shuddered to silence. Mark stood up, put a consoling arm about the shoulders of the dark-haired boy, led him into the next room, sat there with him, waiting.

Pietro's wife was dead—not from the attack of cruel hands which had torn the clothes from her body and gouged the flesh beneath—but from the poisonous bite of venom-dipped fangs.

She had been attacked, beaten, battered to earth by some monstrous thing which had rushed upon her out of the fog. Yet she had died from the fatal venom of the black widow. How in the name of God could such things be?

Mark shook his head heavily to clear it of the doubts that plagued him. He was wrong, of course. Something more than poison had dragged life from the woman's body. The venom of the real black widow was deadly, to be sure—more so, weight for weight, than the venom of a rattlesnake—but it was normally sluggish, sometimes did not take full effect for more than an hour. This tragedy had happened all too quickly.

And the shape described by Pietro's wife was the same shape that he and Judy had encountered in the road, not far from here . . . !

He stood up, went again into the bedroom and looked down at the woman's contorted body. His diagnosis was wrong, *must* be wrong! Yet he knew better, knew now that his dark premonitions of horror had at last materialized. The horror had struck, had claimed its first victim.

Its first? Mark stiffened suddenly with an evil recollection of words spoken hysterically by Judy's mother, words describing the manner of Paul Bronson's death. Bronson, too, had died from the bite of a black widow! Pietro's wife was not the first! *There would be others . . . !*

CHAPTER TWO

Battle with the Thing!

THE jarring of the shack's front door brought him about with a jerk, and he stood stiff as the caretaker gasped toward him over the bedroom threshold. Pietro stopped, stared, moved slowly on quivering legs and peered into the woman's dead face. After an eternity he lowered himself to the bed and sat there, still staring. Mechanically he made the sign of the cross.

"It is—too late now, huh? I send for the doctor, and it is too late?"

Mark nodded. A shudder shook the Portugee's muscular body; he sprawled forward on the bed and pushed his face into the pillow, lay there sobbing. Silently, Mark tiptoed from the room and returned to the big house where his wife and her mother were awaiting him. . . .

They met him at the door and besieged him with frantic questions. Pietro, rushing in to use the telephone, had blubbered only enough to fill them with dread. Mark told them as much of the rest as he dared. And the effect of his words on Judy's mother was strange. Her tense face, already pale, had gone deathly white; the slender fingers of one hand clutched at her throat as she whispered in a fear-laden voice: "You—you say she was bitten by a *spider?*"

Mark nodded and was utterly unprepared for the sudden violent shriek that welled from the woman's throat. She swayed, would have fallen had he not jerked forward to clutch her arms. Then, moaning brokenly, she twisted away and walked down the hall, her palms pressed hard against the alabaster whiteness of her forehead.

Judy would have gone after her, but Mark's hand stabbed out, stopped her. "I want to talk to you," he said grimly. "I want to see you alone."

"What is it, Mark?"

"I want to know what's going on here! There's something behind all this—something you're hiding from me. Something," he added slowly, "you've been hiding from me ever since I've known you!"

She was suddenly afraid of him. She backed away, tugged her arms from his grip. "There's nothing, Mark, I swear it!"

"Then what's wrong with your mother? What devilish connection is there between the strangeness of this house and the thing we encountered on the way here?"

"I don't know."

"You don't know?" Mark took a sudden step forward, fists clenched. "You *do* know. You know the answer to the whole rotten business! What is it?"

The look of terror in Judy's wide eyes stopped him, made him aware of what he was doing to her. Suddenly he was holding her close against him, horribly afraid of losing her.

"I'm sorry, darling. I must be—going crazy."

She shook her head. "There's something you don't understand, Mark. Something about my father's death." The words came slowly, reluctantly. "When he disappeared, he was not the first. There was another man, a Portugee from the fishing-village. He went, too, and has never been found.

"He has three brothers, and they have been saying horrible things, accusing my father of being responsible for their brother's disappearance. My mother is afraid of them." She leaned her head wearily against Mark's shoulder. "That isn't all, but it's all I can tell you now. You—you'll have to trust me."

He stared, scowling, as she went to find her mother. Alone, he walked slowly to a window and stood gazing fretfully out at the fog. The black gnome in his mind was leering again, mumbling dark innuendoes.

Why was Judy so evasive? Why could she not come out with the truth instead of pleading with him to trust her? Good Lord, she was his wife, not some strange, frightened girl who had never laid eyes on him before!

Yet he realized that the thing went deeper than mere questions and answers. He had been right about the horror that hung over this abode of death. It was real, terribly real. It threatened Judy and himself and perhaps Judy's strange mother.

The jangle of a bell dispersed his morbid imaginings. He peered at the front door, hesitated, walked slowly toward it as the clangor was repeated. When he drew the door open, his lean body went suddenly stiff on the sill. . . .

HE had thought not long ago that Pietro, the caretaker, represented the height of unloveliness in a human being. He had been wrong about that. The three men who stood glaring at him were as uncouth, as repulsive as nameless crawling things that lurked in the depths of the sea in which they made their livelihood. They were Portugee fishermen, residents of the fishing-village down the road. And judging from the similarity of their scowling faces, they were brothers, probably the same three brothers about whom Judy had whispered only a little while before.

Standing his ground, Mark said curtly: "Well, what is it?"

The answer came gutturally from unclean lips. "We want to talk to Mrs. Bronson."

"She is busy."

"Well, you'll do. We come here to find out what happened to Pietro's woman, see? And we want the truth!"

Mark suppressed a sudden desire to step away from that snarling face which was thrust so close. He knew now why Judy's mother was afraid. A middle-aged woman, alone in this big house, had a right to fear three swarthy foreigners who believed her dead husband guilty of a dark horror in which their missing brother was implicated. These men were vicious, sullen, savagely determined. They would not stop at physical violence.

And here might be information—the very information he desired! Abruptly he glanced back along the hall, saw that it was empty. Quietly he stepped over the threshold, drew the door shut behind him and leaned against it, facing the three uncouth visitors.

"I'll trade you information," he said grimly. "You tell me what happened to your brother—all you know about it— and I'll tell you what you want to know."

"Huh?"

"You heard me. I want the truth, as much as you do!"

They gaped at him, exchanged significant glances. They took note, too, of his clenched fists and the determination stenciled in his face. One of them shrugged, leaned against the veranda railing and nodded.

"Manuelo used to come here all the time, see? He done odd jobs for old Bronson. Bronson, he was some kind of a doctor, but he was more'n that. He was always workin' in a room downstairs, messin' with spiders and things."

The Portugee's eyes were narrowed suspiciously, watching every expression of Mark's face. He talked in a low monotone, weighing each syllable.

"Well, Manuelo come here one night and never come home again. Two days later, Bronson disappeared too. We found Bronson all right, but we ain't found Manuelo. And since then there's queer things been goin' on around here. There's a killer been prowlin' around the village, nights, and Ginny Malou's dog was found this mornin' all swelled up and dead from spider-poisonin'. And now Pietro's wife."

"Go on," Mark said grimly.

"That's all. What we want to know now is how Pietro's woman died. Pietro,

he's drunk and he don't remember. And we want the truth!"

Mark exhaled slowly. He must talk or use his fists in a battle which would go against him. He talked slowly, carefully. When he had finished he put a cigarette in his dry lips, stood and watched the three Portugees slouch down the veranda steps and tramp away into the fog's grey murk. Somehow they were like inhuman denizens of the very gloom that gulped them. They were unreal, sinister.

And when he went back into the house, evil thoughts went with him.

Two men had vanished within two days of each other. One, Judy's father, had been found dead. The other, a Portugee man-of-all-work named Manuelo DeSanto, was still missing. And down in the village, at night under cover of fog and darkness, things had been happening to inspire terror even in the stolid hearts of unimaginative fisher-folk.

They were not pleasant thoughts—Not with a fog-laden afternoon dragging away into a night that promised to be as black and evil as the catacombs of hell.

He paced slowly down the hall, stopped with a jerk as the corridor's gloom spawned a scarlet-clad figure which came toward him fearfully.

The woman put icy fingers on his arm, whispered as if afraid of being overheard. "Who were they? Manuelo's brothers?"

He nodded. A sob choked in her throat and she gazed wildly at the door. "Oh, God, why do they come here? Isn't it enough that that other thing——?"

SHE shuddered, turned abruptly and went into the living-room. He would have followed, but he heard her speaking in low tones to his wife and realized bitterly that he was not wanted. Scowling, he paced into an unoccupied room and sat in shadows, sucking savagely at a cigarette.

He sat there a long while. The chamber was dark when he suddenly swung in his chair and peered toward the doorway. Out in the hall, a distant door had creaked open.

He walked silently to the threshold and stood there. It was late now. Lights were burning in the long hall. And as he stared, the scarlet-gowned figure of Judy's mother came out of the gloom at the corridor's end.

The woman was like a red-cowled monk in some dark monastery as she paced forward, mumbling to herself, peering ahead of her. She went to the front door and locked it, retraced her steps and entered the parlor. In the darkness of that room, she went from one window to another, closing and locking them. And Mark realized suddenly that she was deliberately going the rounds of the house, locking every exit, every entrance!

Now that night had descended, she evidently feared a nocturnal visit from the thing that lurked out there in the fog's evil murk!

Mark stood motionless, waiting until she had disappeared into more remote rooms. Then he paced down the hall, seeking his wife.

He found her sitting alone in a dimly lighted chamber at the end of the hall, sitting very still in a large overstuffed chair that loomed grotesquely about her slender body. At the sound of his entrance, she turned, stared at him queerly.

"You've been here alone all the time?" he demanded.

She nodded. "Yes. I knew you didn't want me near you."

He stood glaring at her. "Look here, Judy. We've got to clear out of this. This place is getting both of us. You and I are leaving!"

"No, Mark. My mother——"

"We'll take her with us."

"She won't leave. She can't, until she is sure."

"Sure? Of what?"

There was no answer. There was only anguish in the wide eyes that returned his stare. Again he realized that she was holding something back, that she knew things but would not share her knowledge with him. Again the black gnome in his brain muttered words of black suspicion and made him shrink from the girl he had married only six months before.

A strange creature, this wife he had taken for better or worse. The strange daughter of an even stranger mother. And in the dark secrets shared by mother and daughter, Mark Andrews had no place. They wanted none of him.

Bitterly he strode from the room—and stopped, remembering suddenly the information given him by the uncouth brothers of Manuelo DeSanto.

As yet, he had not acted on that information. Had merely mulled it over ceaselessly in his mind. Now——

Judy's mother passed him as he paced down the hall. She turned and stared, seemed about to follow him, then entered the room where Judy was alone. Fists clenched, Mark prowled through the rear of the house to the kitchen.

An hour ago, the brothers of Manuelo had muttered words about a room in the cellar in which Paul Bronson had worked behind shut doors, far into the dark hours of many an evil night.

He found gloomy stairs that led into the cellar's depths. Grimly he descended, and prowled through darkness, found the thing he sought. It was one of many small chambers in a vast maze where chill dampness filled the dark and the stone floor underfoot magnified the whisper of his intruding feet. Its padlocked door loomed in the shadows of a massive furnace.

With a pen-knife and infinite patience,

Mark picked the lock. Cautiously, he thrust the door open. There was a light-switch here, undoubtedly, but he could not find it. He struck a match, held the sputtering flame high and peered ahead of him as he advanced. Above a work-bench at the side of the room dangled an electric flood-light. The bulb had been removed.

The match burned to Mark's fingers and he dropped it, struck another. In that eerie glow, the chamber was a place of weird illusions. Laden shelves lined the four walls; an immense table stretched from corner to corner along the rear. On the table, in a glass box perhaps two feet high and four long, something alive, disturbed by the light's flickering glow, moved furtively as Mark paced forward.

With a shudder of revulsion, he stiffened.

Small air-holes had been drilled through the cabinet's upper surface that the imprisoned monsters might live. They *were* monsters, tiny, but deadly as serpents. More than a dozen of them glared out at him through the glass panels as they scurried about in dread of the light. . . .

SPIDERS! Black-widow spiders, known to science as *Latrodectus mactans!* Deadly, hideous little creatures, each of them jet black with shiny bulbous abdomen and long slender legs—and red warning signs, twin triangular spots of carmine roughly resembling an hour-glass, on the under side of the belly.

Shuddering, Mark backed away. The match in his fingers burned low and he dropped it, fumbled for another. Behind him in the shadows of the doorway the darkness was suddenly alive as a hunched, crouching shape slithered over the sill. Heavy feet, naked, whispered on the stone floor. Mark whirled.

Blood jellied in his body as he leaped sideways, avoided the intruder's furious rush. He had seen that uncouth shape before. Judy had seen it, too. And Pietro's wife had described it in her death-agonies. It was the *Thing*—the nameless monster against which Judy's mother had closed and locked every window in the house!

And Mark fought it, using fists and knees and feet in a frantic effort to free himself from its vile embrace. Blindly he staggered back, crashed into the table, reeled clear and thudded into rows of shelves that lined the wall.

His clenched fists flailed the thing before him, smashed against heaving, hairy flesh. Into his brain came the mad, numbing realization that the uncouth shape he was fighting was not human!

He was down, then—down in a contorted heap as his groping feet tangled with a stumpy three-legged stool and splayed out from under him—down in a horrible darkness as of death, with a fuming, snarling monster on top of him, tearing at him, seeking to bury drooling fangs in the flesh of his throat.

Spider-fangs! A shriek retched from Mark's gaping lips; abject terror gave him strength to lash out with feet and fists, to batter at that venomous maw until it snarled upward, away from him. He rolled, flung his twisted body over and over on the floor, crashed into the legs of a table and clawed himself erect.

And the Thing—the monstrous hairy Thing that was not human—leaped at him again as he gained his feet.

Only a huge spider could move with such uncanny speed. Only a spider could stand so still one minute and hurtle through space so rapidly the next! But this thing was no spider! In form, it was human. Its half-naked body was clad from the waist down in damp, evil-smelling garments designed for a human being!

Mark staggered back, pawed the table in passing. His raking fingers found the neck of a thick glass bottle, raised it and hurled it wildly.

But the bottle missed its mark. It hit something else. With a splintering crash it struck the edge of the long table and shattered the glass panels of the box that loomed there. Even in darkness, Mark knew what had happened, realized the hideous consequences!

The Thing knew, too! In mid-charge it froze to rigidity, jerked about and uttered a hoarse sound more human than any other sound it had yet spilled forth. Snarling, not with rage but with fear, the hairy shape rushed forward, flung Mark aside, sped with frantic speed across the threshold—and was gone into the cellar's gloom!

Mark swayed, clutched the wall and sobbed for breath. His wide eyes stared into the room's darkness, seeking the venomous shapes, jet-black and deadly, that he knew would be there. With numb fingers he fumbled for a match, struck one as he lurched to the doorway.

The yellow glare streaked floor and table, revealing the broken glass cabinet. The box was empty now of the monster-shapes that had been imprisoned within it. And on the stone floor, dark shadows were crawling forward rapidly . . . .

One of them leaped with fantastic quickness toward the sputtering match in Mark's hand. With a hoarse cry, he stumbled over the threshold, slammed the door shut. Then, trembling, he struck another match and pushed himself through the huge cellar toward the stairs by which he had descended. Of that other shape— that hairy Thing out of the night—there was no sign.

Just once he turned, stared back at the shut door of Paul Bronson's laboratory. And he knew then that he had flung the door shut too late. At the edge of the match-glow, where the stone floor was a narrow passage between coal-bin and furnace, black bulbous shapes sped quickly back into gloom as the matchlight flickered out to embrace them. Some of the room's frightful occupants had escaped!

With a hoarse sob, Mark turned and ran. . . .

TERROR was like a leering old man of the sea riding his shoulders as he lurched through the kitchen upstairs. He was afraid, and knew it; afraid of the nameless hairy Thing that had sought to destroy him, and of those other things, not nameless, which were scuttling about down there in darkness.

How many of them had escaped? It did not matter much. Liberated from their glass prison, the others would soon find their way out of the room itself, through cracks, crevices, even through the very walls! God alone knew how long they had been imprisoned without food. They would find their way upstairs now —savage, venomous little monsters seeking sustenance, vengeance. And then . . .

Staring with red-rimmed eyes, Mark stumbled along the hall to the room where he had left his wife and her mother. He knew the answer now. There was only one possible answer left. Lurching over the threshold, he planted himself wide-legged before his wife's chair.

"Get your things. you and I are leaving this house *now!*"

She gaped at him, at his soiled, tattered clothing and the livid welts on his face and arms. But for the mercy of God, she might be gaping at something more hideous—at gouged flesh and a bloated, writhing body contorted by evil poisons— but she did not know that. She stared helplessly into the bewildered face of her mother, then back to Mark's scowling features.

"Mark! What happened? What have you *done?*"

"Never mind that now," he said grimly. "We're leaving."

She stared until a convulsive shudder shook her slender body. Slowly she swayed her head. "I—I can't go. Oh, *why* won't you try to understand?"

"You mean—you refuse?"

She stood erect before him, her hands clutching his arms. "Mark, you said you'd trust me. You promised."

Mark had no answer. There *was* no answer, unless it lay in the fleeting smile of triumph that seemed to move across the face of Judy's mother. He groaned, closed his eyes in defeat, knew that his wife's love for him was not so strong as the mysterious bond existing between mother and daughter.

He shrugged, sank helplessly into a chair. Moments passed before he moved or spoke; then he said dully: "I'm half starved. How about some supper?"

CHAPTER THREE

The Mad Ghoul

IT WAS a strange evening during which each hour dragged to an interminable nerve-racking length. They sat in the living-room, Mark Andrews, Judy, and the scarlet-gowned woman who was Judy's mother. The big house was a huge, leering pile wrapped in its winding-sheet of chill fog and darkness, filled with furtive whisperings that filed Mark's nerves to the breaking-point.

Twice, associating vague sounds with what had happened down in the cellar's gloom, he paced into the kitchen, turned on lights and jerked open the stairway door, peering down into darkness. When he did that the second time, something small and black moved on the stairs below him and he flung the door shut, backed fearfully from it.

Judy and her mother noticed the abnormal paleness of his face when he returned to the living-room. Again they sought to drag from him an explanation. Again he evaded their questions, knew what the truth would do to them.

And then Pietro came—drunk, staggering, wailing of the death of his woman and demanding money for more liquor, that he might forget. He had to be sobered and sent back to the squalid shack where the mangled body of his wife still lay. And he did not want to go, though terrified children were awaiting his return, afraid of the thing that had been their mother, dreading the night and the darkness and that other Thing which might return . . . .

An evil, unholy business, all of it! And yet Judy refused to go away, and Judy's mother continued to mumble to herself and stare into shadows . . . .

If he told them of the horrors that lurked downstairs, would they yield to his wishes then and go away with him? He did not think so. And telling them would only increase their terror.

In the end, the scarlet woman said wearily: "You two had better go to bed." She showed them to a room upstairs, near her own. And Mark was glad that at last he no longer had to sit staring at her. He could be alone now with his wife. Perhaps she would listen to reason.

He was wrong about that. He argued, and to all his entreaties her answer was the same. "We can't, Mark. You must believe me, trust me. We can't go away!"

He felt, when he donned pajamas and climbed into the antique four-poster beside her, that he was doing something wrong. She was no longer his wife. He was glad when she turned away from him and slept.

He himself lay awake, staring at the vague blur of ceiling above him. Eternities ago, when he had first ventured into this strange bleak house of shadows, he had entertained dark premonitions of impending evil. Now, again, he felt uneasy. He feared to sleep.

All around him, the big house whispered and muttered with weird voices of its own, yet those nerve-chilling sounds merely made the silence more intense, more pregnant with evil. Somewhere in a room nearby, Judy's mother had locked her door and retired.

And suddenly, at Mark's side, the warm body of his wife twitched in sleep and turned restlessly against his own. Breathing heavily, the girl uttered low, moaning sounds that became words. And Mark was rigid, every nerve alert to catch the syllables that groaned from her lips.

"Oh, God, I can't tell him! I can't! He wouldn't understand . . . or believe me. . . ."

The words droned to a whisper, began again as Judy twitched convulsively, tossing the bedclothes from her shoulders. "They'll tell him it was murder. But it's not true. It's not! He . . . killed . . . they say he killed . . . my father . . . *I can't leave now, Mark! Why won't you trust me? Oh, God, why : . . I love you so . . .*"

Again the words became incoherent, ceasing altogether as Judy relaxed, lapsed again into normal sleep. But Mark was staring, thinking thoughts not good for a man to dwell on. Damp sweat oozed from the pores of his body, chilling him.

Murder! What had Judy been trying to say? *What did she know about her father's death?*

Suddenly he was rigid, listening to other sounds. Beyond the locked door of the room, someone—something—was prowling furtively along the hall.

He shot a quick glance at his wife, thrust his face close to hers and saw that she was asleep. Silently he swung his feet to the floor and took lithe steps to the door.

Noiselessly he turned the key, drew the door open and stood staring.

A night-light burned in the corridor wall near the stairhead. Beneath it, an all-too-familiar figure was turning to descend the stairs. A tall figure, clad in the macaber scarlet of a vivid evening gown!

SLOWLY, Judy's mother descended, clinging to the bannister. When the gloom of the stairwall had gulped her from sight, Mark toed forward, closed the door behind him and followed. And the woman did not turn to see that she was not alone.

She turned left at the foot of the stairs and paced rapidly along the lower hall into the kitchen. A night-light glowed in that room, too, and Mark saw that the woman was afraid. The waxen flesh of her bosom rose and fell with labored breathing; her hand trembled violently as it opened the door that led to the cellar.

Then she was gone into the cellar's inky blackness, and Mark, staring after her, was suddenly rigid with remembered horror.

Later, long later, he tried to diagnose the numbness that crept over him at that moment and sealed his lips against the warning cry that welled against them. Only he and that nameless hairy Thing from outer darkness knew the horror that lay in wait down there in the cellar's gloom. Yet he did not cry out.

The cry shrieked within him and died there, why, he was never afterward certain. But that scarlet figure had gone into the cellar's black peril, and he did not shout at her to come back. Standing there at the head of the stairs, his hands gripping the sides of the door-frame, he stared into darkness and listened to the scuffing of the woman's slippered feet as she paced across the cellar floor. And his own dread was smothered under a surge of savage determination.

Fists clenched, he forced himself down the stairs, following in the steps of the woman who might reveal to him, through her actions, the secret of this hell-house of horror. And he fought fear as he went. Perhaps those venomous black insects were asleep. Perhaps not. If they were on the prowl . . . .

At the foot of the stairs he stood rigid, as a match suddenly flared in deeper darkness ahead. Flickering light showed him the woman standing there before the door of her husband's laboratory, staring at the padlock which he himself had opened hours ago.

She pushed the door open and paced over the threshold. Again a scream of warning jarred against Mark's teeth, and again, because of the dark hell in his heart, he was silent as he prowled forward. He would chance even life itself now, if need be, for an answer to the nameless thing which had come between himself and his wife.

When he reached the doorway, the woman was at the far end of the room, staring at the broken glass box which had imprisoned those black death-crawlers. Shuddering, she turned away. A lighted candle was clasped in her outthrust hand, and the room was dim with yellow shadows that went with her as she prowled.

She was seeking something and she had not found it. In the end she turned away—and suddenly stopped, stared down at the floor. Stooping, she scooped something into her hand. And the thing she picked up glittered dully in the glow of the candle.

Mark scowled. He himself had explored this room, had seen nothing of significance on the floor. In his battle with the monster had he torn loose some small object of wearing apparel . . . ?

The woman clutched her prize in trembling fingers and stared at it, then turned, with sudden madness in her face, to peer again around the room. Almost too late Mark jerked back from the doorway as she swung toward him.

She was muttering to herself as she strode into the cellar. Pacing past the huge furnace, she stopped to gather up a heavy spade that leaned there.

Her destination was not the staircase but a short flight of wooden steps that angled up to a bulkhead. And she was no longer afraid. From the very erectness of her body Mark saw that she was obsessed now with some mad desire that lured her on!

She thrust open the bulkhead and climbed up into darkness. Cold, damp air chilled the sweat on Mark's face as he followed. Then he was outside, standing in ankle-deep grass beside the frowning wall of the house itself; ahead of him, the woman was striding determinedly through fog-laden gloom, toward the road that curled past the front of the building.

Trailing her then was easy, yet it became a nightmare task that thickened the blood in Mark's veins. For the woman, reaching the road, continued straight across it, following a footpath that snaked over stubbled ground and ended, some hundred yards from the house, in a small fenced-in enclosure which was a cemetery.

She stopped then, stood like some macaber ghoul exuding a scarlet radiance against the undulating greyness of the fog. Slowly she pushed open a gate in the fence, walked forward through damp grass and halted beside one of the few stone slabs that reared their heads in the murk.

THIS, Mark realized, was a private cemetery, probably jointly owned by a few scattered families who dwelt in the isolated district surrounding it. And the grave before which the scarlet widow stood was the newest mound of them all —undoubtedly the last resting place of her husband.

What horrible thing did Judy's mother intend to do?

The fog hid him from her as he crouched close to the fence, watching. And suddenly his eyes bulged, a wave of revulsion welled through him. For the woman had begun to dig!

She used the spade awkwardly, frantically, as if afraid of being interrupted. Through the murk came a soul-chilling sound of damp earth sucking at the iron blade that sought to dislodge it. And another sound—a low, hysterical sobbing from the woman's own lips.

Numb with horror, Mark stared. . . .

He and she were alone, alone with the dead man whose grave she was violating. Yet a chill sensation stabbed through him that other eyes, malevolent and vindictive, were watching. The scattered stone slabs of the cemetery returned his gaze, and the fog itself had eyes, had cold wet tentacles that reached out to curl around him. And the woman who toiled there on the mound was something less than human, something weirdly horrible out of the night itself.

Mark Andrews wanted to lurch erect and run, but terror held him motionless as time crawled on with blood-freezing slowness. And then at last, the evil suck of the spade changed to another sound, to a dull sound of iron scraping on wood. The woman hunched forward, half hidden by the sodden mound of earth that loomed at the grave's edge.

And suddenly Mark Andrews was staring beyond her.

They came out of the fog's grey maw, slowly, like gliding ghosts distorted to weird proportions by the murk that swirled about them. Two of them: two silent, slow-moving shapes that advanced toward the grave, stopped and stood watching.

The woman saw them. Convulsively she stiffened, stared into the evil glare of two pairs of malevolent eyes.

Mark Andrews had looked into those eyes before, on the veranda of the gaunt house that loomed a hundred yards distant in darkness. They belonged to the brothers of Manuelo DeSanto, who had disappeared and not been found.

Grimly silent, the two Portugees advanced to the grave's edge, peered down into the pit and stared evilly at the woman who stood holding an earth-clotted spade in her white hands. Then, with sinister intent, they moved toward her.

For seconds only she stood her ground, rigid because her body was numb with terror. Then suddenly she found her voice. The cry that shrilled from her lips was a wild, mad shriek of fear—of something deeper and more terrible than fear.

She whirled, dropped the spade and ran screaming toward the house. And the Portugees did not follow. Seemingly bewildered, they stared after her, then peered again into the pit that yawned before them. They mumbled words that Mark did not catch. In a little while, they went away and were gulped in the grey murk from which they had come.

Mark pushed his aching body erect and dragged air into his cramped lungs. He knew now what he had not before been sure of—his wife's mother was mad. That settled it. There was only one course left open.

Grimly he turned, strode back to the madhouse where he had left his wife asleep. . . .

CHAPTER FOUR

Daughter of Madness

MARK was not surprised, when he hammered on the front door for admittance, that it was his wife who opened it to him. Clad in the same silken pajamas in which he had left her asleep, she stood like some slender, ethereal ghost in the gloom of the hallway. There was terror in her wide eyes as she gaped at him.

"Mark, what is it? What has my mother been doing? Oh, God, she came in here just now and rushed to her room as if ——" Her own voice broke with hysteria and she stared again like a small frightened child as Mark kicked the door shut. "Where have you been?" she sobbed. "I woke up and you were gone. I was frightened!"

"Your mother is in her room?"

"Yes, but——?"

"I've got a few things to say to her," Mark said grimly, "and I want you to hear them. Come."

She went with him reluctantly, fearing the savage scowl that made an angry white mask of his face. Upstairs, she shrank from him as he thumped on the closed door of her mother's room. When the door opened, Mark stood between Judy and her mother—the first time, he thought bitterly, that he had been able to come between them.

They seemed to realize it, too, and the look that the scarlet woman sent at Judy was a look of supplication. But Mark ignored it.

"Now listen." The words were pregnant with pent-up emotion that threatened to break from control. "For what happened just now there's only one explanation. I'll tell *you*——" he swung to his wife—— "what that is! Your mother is mad. Do you hear? She's stark, rav-

ing mad! And we're getting out of here before *we* get to be the same!"

Judy's answer was a low moan. She moved closer to him and put trembling fingers on his arm. "Mark, please tell me what happened. Please!"

"I'll tell you when we're out of here."

"But I can't go. I can't!"

His temper would have burst its bonds, then, if he had not thought suddenly of the words she had mumbled in her sleep. No, she could not go. She and her mad mother shared a secret that was stronger between them than a bond of steel. Judy was no longer his wife.

"Very well," he said stiffly, "you've made your answer. So have I. If you refuse to leave this damned house with me, then I——"

In the hall downstairs, the jangling clamor of a doorbell interrupted him, turned him on stiff legs. Into his mind flashed a vision of the two Portugees who had vanished into the fog. Slowly he descended the stairs, paced along the lower hall and jerked the door open.

Pietro, the caretaker, stood like a shaggy black-haired beast on the veranda, glaring at him.

"Listen." The caretaker's voice came in a drunken growl. "Me and my kids are leavin', see? We're clearin' out!" He swayed, thrust his stubbled face close to Mark's own, and his voice rose shrilly. "That damn' thing is prowlin' around again! I heard it twice! It's lookin' for someone else to murder, and me and my kids ain't stayin' here to get what Annie got! We're goin'!"

Rocking on bent legs, he shrieked again, luridly: "We're *goin'*! And we ain't comin' back to this cursed place ever!" Then violently he lurched backward, turned and went noisily down the veranda steps.

Slowly, Mark pushed the door shut.

Judy and her mother, standing at the

top of the stairs, had heard every word. As he climbed toward them, Judy's wide eyes searched his face; she put out a trembling hand. The drunken voice of old Pietro had effected her strangely. She refused now to meet her mother's stare of supplication.

It was as though she had suddenly seen the truth and was fighting to free herself from the vile embrace of clutching tentacles.

"All right," Mark said quietly, "we're leaving. Come."

He drew her toward the door of their bedroom, and this time she went with him, though he felt that something within her—something that was a vital part of her—was savagely holding back. Her mother was a macaber, rigid figure in the gloom of the landing—glaring, taciturn.

Without wasting words, Mark closed the bedroom door, flung a suitcase on the bed and began packing. Moments were precious now. Judy was still only half-convinced, and if she changed her mind now it would be the end.

SHE stood stiff, nervously gripping the end-board of the bed. Neither he nor she heard the door inch open behind them or turned to see the groping hand that slid through the narrow aperture, noiselessly withdrawing the key from the lock. The door closed. The key grated from the outside.

Too late, Mark jerked around, caught a quick breath and lurched forward. The door was locked. The girl's mad mother, realizing defeat, had found a cunning method of turning defeat into victory!

After that, Mark Andrews knew the meaning of rage. It came at him in a viscid wave, ungulfing him, while he stood wide-legged and reviled the name of the mad woman who had tricked them. His temper burst its bonds in a crimson torrent, driving a rush of blood to his face.

It was a long time subsiding, and even then Judy watched him with large eyes, afraid that it would return. But he was calm now and sullenly determined. With a snarl he flattened against the door and crouched there, listening.

Moments passed and he heard the slow tread of the mad woman's footsteps as she paced down the hall, descended the big staircase. Then he drew from his pocket the same pen-knife with which he had picked the padlock on the laboratory door down cellar.

Picking a lock was not hard if you knew how. Grimly he went to work. Five minutes later he had forced the key out of the slot, on the outside, and ten minutes after that he had the door open.

He turned then to Judy—and knew at once that he had failed.

The expression on her face was all too familiar. Her pajama-clad body was rigid against the bed-end; her wide eyes stared straight at him without blinking.

She said almost inaudibly: "I can't go, Mark. I—can't—go!"

He had a wild desire to open his mouth and let a hoarse jangle of insane laughter shrill out of it. He restrained himself only because he saw that Judy was afraid of him. Terror was in her eyes, in the cringing attitude of her body.

And she was prepared to fight him! Beneath the filmy silk of her pajama-jacket, her breasts were hard and inflated with sucked-in breath. Her arms were rigid, her slippered feet braced against the floor. Funny feet, he thought foolishly. A dozen times he had played with them, tickled them, even kissed the little glass-eyed bunnies on the toes of her slippers. God!

"I can't go with you, Mark." She spoke the words slowly in a low voice that ate to his innards. "I belong here. I *must* stay here. You'll have to go alone."

He took a step toward her, stopped. His hands, reaching out and up, were trembling. "Judy, dear!. Oh, God, what's wrong? What's happened to you since we came here?"

Her answer stunned him. Like a slender, sinuous cat she swayed toward him, glaring at him with eyes that glittered. It was not his wife who stood there; it was some strange, angry creature who hated him with a hate beyond measure.

"Nothing has happened to me! Nothing at all, except that you stopped loving me and trusting me. You want to go away from here. All right, *go! And don't ever come back!*"

She should not have said it. Already his nerves had taken more punishment than the nerves of a human being were intended to bear. The black gnome in his brain had leered too long.

He sucked breath until his big body was bloated. "Trust you?" he snarled at her. "How in the name of God can any man trust a mad woman? You're mad, you and your mother both! This whole house is a madhouse! I'm *leaving!*"

He slammed the door behind him, was a madman himself as he strode down the stairs. He heard the door open again and heard the low, sobbing voice of his wife as she called his name, but he did not stop.

In the doorway of the living-room, the scarlet-clad woman stood staring at him, but she made no attempt to stop him. Violently he yanked open the front door, paraded down the veranda steps and along the driveway to the car. He did not see his wife standing in the open doorway, with both arms extended helplessly toward him as he sent the machine roaring down the drive.

In his brain, that black gnome of hell was beating a huge, noisy drum of madness, cackling with insane mirth. The car lurched drunkenly to the road, swung into a swirling grey murk that sucked the house from sight.

It was neither sudden remorse nor sud-den sanity that made him realize what he had done. It was chance alone that made him peer down the stubbled slope as the car growled forward. Down there his gaze encountered the tenuous white fence that surrounded the little graveyard. He braked the car to a squealing stop. . . .

AFTERWARD he was not sure why he did it, except that deep within him lurked a vague, dull desire to try again —once again—to bridge the gap which had widened between himself and the girl he loved. He left the car in the road and prowled down the slope, and for the second time that night invaded that silent, fog-ridden cemetery which might contain the answer to all things unanswerable.

Standing there above the newly opened grave of Paul Bronson, he stared down. Black desire seized him, lured him forward. Muttering to himself, he descended into the pit, tugged with both hands at the wooden box that lay there. Here in this violated grave might lie the answer he had so long been seeking. . . .

Sobbing sounds tightened his throat; his lips were bloody from the bite of clenched teeth before he succeeded in wrenching the wooden box open. Then, by the light of sputtering matches, he gaped down at the enclosed horror.

What had Judy's mother said? The body had been found in a swampy section of the woods, where it had lain for days after the poison of a black widow had stifled the life within it. Deterioration had been rapid. Things of the swamp had fed on the corpse . . . ?

It showed it. Little had been done to make that emaciated form less frightful. More than likely, it had been interred hurriedly because of its appearance. Mark swallowed a thick blackness that welled in his throat. Slowly he pushed himself out of the pit, turned and stared at the looming bulk of the Bronson home. The sight of Paul Bronson's dead body had driven some of the madness from his brain.

And into his narrowed eyes came a glint of determination—of dark resolve induced by the thing that lay in the pit. Abruptly he jerked forward, but not toward the car that stood in the road. His destination was a small, strange room in the bowels of the big house before him. Bronson's laboratory!

He went slowly, because the lead-heavy darkness was a tangible, sinister force that whispered of menace ahead. There *was* menace in that looming pile—not alone the peril of tiny black, crawling things, but of something macaber and monstrous. He should know for he had already encountered it.

There were lights now in the upper level, one of them glowing in the room where he had left the mad creature who was his wife. His—wife! The word rang queerly in his brain.

A little while ago, he had been on the verge of going away, leaving her to whatever fate might await her. God! The evil atmosphere of that abode of horror had affected him as much as it had her. He, too, had been temporarily mad!

But he was coolly deliberate now, his eyes narrowed, his mouth drawn in a thin firm line that presaged danger for any person or thing that attempted to thwart him. He made no sound as he prowled to the rear of the house and descended the bulkhead steps.

Darkness sucked him into the cellar's evil depths, and he shuddered. Somewhere in this well of gloom, a dozen or more tiny black monsters lay hidden, perhaps sleeping, perhaps hellishly awake and alert.

Ahead, near the frowning bulk of the furnace, the laboratory door was open, revealing the yellow glow of the candle which the scarlet woman had left burn-

ing in the room beyond. No one had come here, then, since the woman had left on her grisly mission to the graveyard. No one suspected . . .?

Mark stopped in his tracks, took a sudden side-step into deeper darkness. Somewhere nearby, a door had creaked! He stared, every nerve wire-tight and alert. The sound came again, and this time it had direction; it came from the top of the stairs that led to the kitchen. And something was slowly descending into the cellar's gloom!

Motionless, Mark stood with one hand flat against the wall, his heart thumping hollowly. In that subterranean gloom, he could see nothing: could only hear. The stairs creaked dismally, ceased creaking when the intruder reached the cellar floor. There was a whispering sound then of cautious feet pacing toward the laboratory. And suddenly, into the ocher glow that emanated from the doorway, crept a slender pajama-clad figure! Judy!

Mark's eyes bulged; only with great effort did he refrain from uttering her name aloud. What was she doing here? What was there in that room of mystery which made it a loadstone for her, too?

He stood stiff, watching as she went timidly over the threshold and vanished into the room beyond. Silently, then, he toed forward.

And suddenly, remembering the broken glass box on the table in that room of death, and the things which had been imprisoned within it, Mark went rigid. Terror came at him in a numbing wave, blinding him.

Judy did not know! She had gone into that room without knowing of the hell that lurked there! And he had let her do it!

A scream jangled up from the depths of his numbed body as he lurched forward. His wife's name shrilled from his lips and shrilled luridly through the cellar's silence.

And the scream was smothered by another cry that came at him from the room ahead. His own cry was nothing, gulped up and absorbed by a terror-shriek that retched in red madness from the depths of a woman's soul. In that room something was happening! Some black horror was threatening the woman he loved. . . .!

CHAPTER FIVE

The Scarlet Widow

HE HAD been mad before, but the madness that surged into him now was a seething, tangible force that lashed him forward. He was not conscious of hurling himself through the yellowed doorway. Fists clenched, chest heaving with great gulps of breath, he hurtled over the sill and blundered against a table in the room beyond. Then he saw, and his eyes became horror-rimmed pools.

Judy stood flat against the wall, her body jammed hard against the wooden partition as if seeking to escape through it. In that ocher glow, she seemed almost naked as the light penetrated the filmy silk of her pajamas. And she was not the room's only occupant!

On the far side of the chamber, facing her in a half-crouch, stood a thing that seemed savagely, hideously aware of the girl's near-nakedness. The *Thing!*

Judy was not screaming now. Stark terror had stolen her power to utter any but low sobbing sounds—sobs that sounded weirdly like insane laughter. She was waiting for the monstrous Thing to make its attack so that she might know which way to hurl herself in fleeing its outthrust arms.

Hairy arms . . . terminating in curled fingers that twitched hungrily for the pale flesh of the girl's body! And in the room's eerie light the rest of that uncouth form was blurred in gloom.

Yet it was human, because it had arms and legs and a torso; because it was garbed in rags of clothing which had belonged to a human being. The rest was horror. The head that bulged above those knotted shoulders was shaggy and malformed, with drooling lips spread in a vile grin and deep-sunk eyes glowing through a matted tangle of hair.

Staring in horror, Mark thought suddenly of the black crawling things which had escaped from the glass cabinet. And then the monster moved!

It moved with incredible speed, timing its rush to the split-second interlude when Mark's alertness wavered. And when it charged, it *was* a spider! With a shrill whine of exploding breath it hurtled straight at the girl's body.

Screaming, Judy leaped frantically to one side. She flung herself at Mark, and a sweep of Mark's corded arm sent her stumbling past him toward the open doorway. And then, with madness in his heart and a scarlet haze blurring everything before him, Mark was fighting— fighting for his life and hers—fighting, for the second time, with that hairy, half-human horror from some black outerworld of evil. . . .

IT WAS the end. He knew it precisely as the Thing's arms lashed out to embrace him. Granted an even break, he might fight the monster to a standstill, might even defeat it—but not before those filthy claws ripped into his flesh.

Before him loomed a vision of Pietro's wife, bloated and dead from the venom of those same claws. But with certainty of annihilation came a fatalism that brought reckless abandon. Judy would escape, anyway. Before he went down beneath that hairy mass of hell, she would have time to get away in safety! **She** would have to go alone. This was the penance for his failure to trust her.

Desperately, he fought to keep his contorted body between the Thing and the doorway. His fists raked out, crunched against the drooling gargoyle that came at him. And those other hands, open and twisted, took their toll, clawed frenziedly at him in their violent efforts to drag him down.

Blindly he fought, staggering from the Thing's spider-like rushes, always moving, always retreating. Death did not matter now. He had been fighting for hours, for eternities. Judy had had time to get away, to flee from this house of unholy horror. Nothing else mattered. She would know now that he loved her.

And suddenly, the thought of death was a chill horror that engulfed him, put a glare of red hate in his bulging eyes. He wanted to live! And this hairy, half-human fiend meant to destroy him!

With dark fury, he beat back the monster's uncouth bulk, hurled himself forward with such force that the Thing reeled away from him, gasping. The victim had become the aggressor.

He used fists and feet in furious assault, snarled with bestial satisfaction as his blows took effect. The Thing's contorted bulk crashed against a table, rebounded. Then, matching his own fury, it hurtled forward in a headlong rush. But Mark's wild gaze had encountered something else —had fallen on the broken glass box which stood there on the table.

His hand shot out, gripped the iron frame of the cabinet and swung it clear. Then, staring, he lurched back.

On the table's dark surface, two bulbous black shapes had stirred to life! Two venomous crawling things had been asleep beneath the shattered cabinet!

Wide-eyed, Mark backed against the wall and stiffened there, momentarily safe from the fiend's attack. No living crea-

ture would dare advance past those twin death-dealers! And in order to advance at all, the monster *had* to come past them, through the narrow aisle between wall and table.

Rigid, one fist gripping the broken cabinet, Mark sucked breath, thought himself safe. And he was wrong.

With a madman's laugh of triumph, the Thing lunged forward. One bloated hand raked along the table-top, curled forward with fantastic quickness. That hand, naked, unprotected, whipped over the table's surface, scooping the death-monsters into its cupped palm as if snaring flies!

And then the hand lashed out, hurling the deadly prisoners straight at Mark's body!

He had no time to sidestep; he was too utterly astounded even to move in his tracks. One of the two spiders missed him, struck the wall and fell stunned to the floor. The other made sudden frightful contact with his leg, raced up his rigid body toward the bare flesh of his throat!

A lurid scream jangled from his lips. Frantically he raked the thing aside before its hairy legs reached flesh. But that moment of madness was the moment his cunning assailant had been awaiting. With hellish quickness, the Thing shot forward, arms outflung to murder.

Mark had no chance. Just once he swung the broken cabinet and smashed its shattered glass against that gargoyle countenance. Then he was down, hurled in a writhing heap on the floor, with awful fangs seeking his throat.

Death leered at him from the fiend's sunken eyes. Hairy hands descended to rake flesh. And from the room's doorway, a white, pajama-clad figure—a frantic shape which had never once moved from that same doorway—rushed forward and fell upon Mark's assailant.

Judy! Wildly he gaped into her colorless face and shrieked her name, screamed at her to go back. But she had already flung herself on the shaggy hulk above him, had seized that thick throat in her hands and dragged the drooling maw away from him.

THE move was madness. As before, those beady eyes sucked in the pale beauty of her near-naked body; those gleaming fangs hungered to bury themselves in her flesh. With desire blazing high, the monster flung itself around, forgot Mark and centered its attack on a girl who had no hope of defending herself.

She staggered away as the thing turned to seize her. Screaming, she reeled across the room, crashed against a table and sank to her knees. And Mark saw something else.

The room's doorway had spawned a macaber, scarlet-gowned shape that stood rigid on the threshold. In one outthrust hand, the woman held a revolver; above the gun, her wide eyes were laden with horror—with something else that was deep and mad and indefinable.

She took a stiff step forward as the monster swarmed toward its sobbing victim. The gun in the woman's hand jerked high, belched a lurid roar of thunder. As if struck by a battering ram, the monster halted, turned on quivering legs and reached a hairy, twitching hand to its chest. The gun roared again—and again. Like an undermined tower the great beast took two lurching steps and crashed headlong.

Judy's mother, sobbing in sudden hysteria, staggered forward and sank to her knees beside the body of the thing she had killed. Collapsing upon it, she buried her face in its shaggy chest. And she moaned dully: "Oh, God, what have I done? Paul! *Paul!* There was no other way . . .!"

Moments passed before Mark Andrews could sway forward. His arms went out and enfolded the trembling form of his wife. Together they stood and stared down at the two strange shapes on the floor—one, a hairy malformed monster which now, in death, seemed less uncouth; the other, a scarlet-clad woman who was wretchedly sobbing the name of her dead husband.

Her—husband! That hairy half-human thing on the floor . . .!

It was Judy who put trembling hands on her mother's shoulders and drew her erect. And Mark, knowing the danger of crawling things that still lurked in the room's gloom, made haste to lift that shaggy dead thing in his arms and follow his wife and her mother through the cellar.

In the living-room upstairs, where a warm glow of lamplight dispelled some of the horror in his heart, he lowered his burden to the divan and stood over it, staring. This—this dead thing was Judy's father!

He turned then, peered at the girl's mother who had sunk, sobbing, into a chair. Damp clay clung to the woman's shoes—clay from the newly opened grave in the cemetery. No need to ask questions; the answers were obvious. Judy's mother had followed him from the house, had trailed him to the graveyard and watched him open that interred coffin. And she herself had investigated what lay within it, learning its secret.

He, Mark Andrews, had only guessed. Judy's mother had recognized the truth.

But why had she not known before, when the body in that coffin had first been discovered? Vaguely he knew the answer to that, too. The body, then, had been a bloated horror, unrecognizable. Endless hours in the grave had resulted in a collapse of bloated flesh that had produced something more nearly normal.

The body in the grave was that of a Portugese—undoubtedly that of the missing Manuelo DeSanto. And this thing on the divan—this thing which in death more nearly resembled something human, though naturally thick-set and hairy—was Paul Bronson.

Mark shuddered. The eyes that stared up at him were almost *not* human. Dully he wondered . . .

But Judy's mother was talking, and the words she uttered were significant enough to cut through his dark thoughts.

"God is so cruel, so very cruel at times. I told Paul that. I warned him, but he argued. He said it was a way to compensate for the shadows that lay behind him. And then he told me something of what he was doing."

A shudder ran through the woman's body as she continued. She talked of how the Cape woods were infested with deadly black-widows, of how Portugese workers had died in agony while picking cranberries and grapes, of black bulbous things that had invaded some of the shacks down in the fishing-village. And so for months, Paul Bronson had experimented, seeking a serum that would counteract the black-widow's deadly venom.

"He used his own body to experiment on. He thought I did not know, but I watched him change slowly, terribly, as he let himself be bitten again and again and drugged himself with serums that he obtained from the spiders themselves, and from the blood of poisoned rats . . .

"I pleaded with him and he would not listen. And then one night he sent for Manuelo and took Manuelo to that room downstairs. Manuelo never came out of that room. I dared not ask questions. For two days Paul was so strange and worried and restless. And then—he disappeared."

QUIETLY Judy interrupted. "There is something Mark ought to know, mother. I have never told him." She turned, held herself very straight as she looked into Mark's bewildered face. "My father was a doctor, Mark. At one time he was the head of a private hospital. He was a good doctor and a good man, but he became involved in the deaths of two patients. He was innocent, but his name was blackened and he was forced to retire. He came back here to live in solitude. That was over two years ago."

Moments passed before Mark realized the full portent of his wife's words. Then he understood, why, during the six months of their married life, she had almost never spoken of her parents.

"And now you know—" the voice of Judy's mother was low, almost inaudible— "what must have happened to Manuelo. My husband had reached the end of his great research. His own body was so laden with poison and serums that he could no longer experiment upon it. He used Manuelo. He must have. Perhaps, because Manuelo's own father died from the bite of a black-widow, he even volunteered for the test."

Into Mark's mind came a blurred vision of Paul Bronson carrying a dead body deep into the woods, changing garments with it, working over it to make the alteration of identity complete, and then planting the corpse in a swampy spot where decomposition would come rapidly and nullify any remote chance of failure.

The man had had no other choice. With the discovery of Manuelo's death would come a return of that other shadow on his life. And then—prison!

But Paul Bronson, even then, had been a walking specter, so laden with self-administered poisons that his wife had already noticed terrible changes in his appearance, his temperament. Without doubt, he had clung to life only through the constant use of drugs and serums.

And so, under cover of fog and darkness, he had prowled back to his laboratory, fearing to be discovered but needing the drugs that meant life. And Mark Andrews had driven him away, sent him back to the gloom of the woods to prowl in torment as the black virus in his blood ran unchecked, making of him something less than human.

Perhaps there had been something more. Perhaps, knowing what he was and would be, Paul Bronson had gone mad, had believed himself to be no longer a human being . . .

"I suspected the truth," Judy's mother moaned. "Perhaps it made me a little mad, too. You and Judy must forgive me. I tried so hard to keep you from learning. And then, in the laboratory, I found this and knew——"

Her outthrust hand held a tiny silver locket, the thin chain broken. "It was his. I gave it to him long ago, and he always wore it. It was not on the body they said was his. And when I found it on the floor down in that room, I knew that he had come back."

Mark stared, stood up, then, and drew his wife close. "We've got to leave here. You and I and your mother. We've got to go now, before those creeping things find their way up into the house. Later we can 'phone the police."

He stared again at the thing on the divan. Stared dully, as Judy clung to him and her mother went silently from the room. It was over now—all over. But this house was a strange abode of shadows, and the darkness outside, crowding against shut windows, was a vast fog-laden blur that leered with sinister knowledge, as if possessing dark secrets of its own.

And as Mark kissed his wife, he vowed silently to banish from their lives, forever, those haunting doubts. . . .

THE END

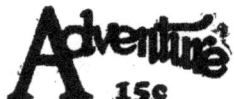

The Child Who Lived With Death

By Wyatt Blassingame

(Author of "Dark Child of Doom," etc.)

Paul Reece stared fearfully at that innocent-looking, three-year-old child. . . . Was the grey shadow of Death really peering at him in that guileless gaze?

THE first thing I noticed was his eyes. They stared at me out of the small, grimy face of a three-year-old child—and yet they were the eyes of an old man, a man who might have been cursed in infancy and thus made to carry terror, suffering and death with him always. Nor was it only pain which lay in those eyes, but fear—a fear I did not then understand, though I felt its presence, dark and horrible, like a shadow beyond shadows in the depths of his steady, unwinking gaze.

Paul Reece rocked the child lightly in the crook of his left arm. "How do you like my kid?" he said grinning.

I looked at Reece and smiled. He did look humorous standing just inside the door of our cottage with the brat in his arms. Reece was a tall, dark, handsome man who, even while taking a bachelor's vacation in this little Florida town, wore his clothes like an actor.

I said: "Already? And we've only been here two weeks!"

"It wasn't the stork," he said. "I found it in a hollow stump."

"I'm old enough," I said. "You can tell me the truth."

"Honest to God," he protested. "I was walking down by Soldier's Bay. There's not a house for miles. And I found this in the middle of the path. From the looks of him he must have been there a day or two."

I stepped closer, and as I reached out an awkward finger toward the child I felt once more the strangeness of his eyes.

"Did you get lost, Sonny?"

He just lay there in Reece's arm, watching me. His face was black with grime, but from his eyes, as clear as tropic seas, I got the uncanny impression that he was knowingly pitying me, looking through me at some monstrous horror I could not possibly avoid.

"He won't talk," Reece told me then. "He hasn't said a damn' word since I picked him up. He looks as if he ought to be old enough to, but I don't know." He shook his handsome head, and grinned that sudden flashing smile of his, all his teeth gleaming between his red, healthy lips.

Somebody laughed out in the yard and the sound of it almost shook the windows. "There's Ed," I said. "Wait until he sees what you've brought home!"

A moment later Ed McDonald came in. The three of us had come down from Birmingham for a month's vacation and had taken this cottage on the Gulf Coast. There wasn't a house closer than the little town of Palmetto, about two miles away. Ed looked the way his laugh sounded. He was over six feet and weighed around two hundred. His face was big and square and good natured beneath a mop of tousled blond hair. He couldn't talk or laugh without being heard a half mile away—and he was generally doing both.

AS he noted the child, which Reece was still holding in his arm, he stopped short, staring. And then he flung back his big head and let out a burst of laughter. "Where in the name of sin did you find *that*?" he asked.

Reece, remarking that sin had had nothing to do with the discovery, explained.

"And you haven't fed the kid!" Ed howled. "My God!" He twisted his head toward the back of the house, yelling: "Essie Lou! Come here!" And to us: "She'll know where the brat lives."

There was a mumbling from the vicinity of the kitchen, a shuffling of feet, and a moment later Essie Lou, the old Negress who cooked and looked after the cottage for us, appeared in the doorway.

"What you—" And then she saw the child in Reece's arms, and her words clicked short.

Her eyes grew wide in her face. The pupils contracted to such pin points that the whites looked enormous, and her thick, kidney-colored lips fell open. Her whole body shook; as she stumbled back against the doorsill she seemed to shrink into herself in sheer terror.

"Oh Lawd!" Her voice, starting as a

mutter, rose to a scream. "Git dat—dat *thing* outa here! Oh Lawd, Mistar Paul, take hit out *quick*!"

And with that she was gone. From down the passageway we could hear her moans slobbering through the semi-darkness, washing about in the silence of the room where the three of us stood motionless, staring at the empty doorway.

Ed's booming voice shook our momentary terror. "Now what the hell is wrong with that old girl, I wonder? You'd think she saw a ghost."

I said: "I'll go ask her."

Ed started with me, while Reece stood where he was, the child cupped close to him. "I'll stick here with the kid," he offered. "I don't think he and Essie Lou like each other."

We found the old woman cowering in a corner of the kitchen. Terror showed even through the ebony of her skin, leaving it the color of cold ashes. When she saw us, she flung back against the wall and called out in a voice that was high and shaking.

"Don't! Fer Lawd's sake, don't bring dat *thing* in here. Oh Lawd!" The last words drooled from her lips as she went down on her knees, her big black hands covering her face.

What was strange was the way that woman's fear affected me. If someone had told me about the situation, I think I would have thought it funny. But seeing it wasn't funny. It made the flesh along my back break into tiny prickles. You see, I kept thinking about the eyes of the child.

But evidently it all struck Ed McDonald as nothing but humorous. He flung back his big head, and again his gargantuan laugh roared out. "What the hell's wrong with you, Essie Lou?"

The old woman let her hands drop slowly. But she stayed on her knees in the corner. "Hit ain't me," she said. "Hit's dat—dat *thing*!"

Once more I noticed the intensity with which she pronounced the word thing! Ed noticed too, for the smile left his face, at last. "What do you mean?" His voice was quieter, the first hint of seriousness in it.

I was standing with my back to the kitchen table, watching the old Negress. I didn't know what she was going to say; yet I was not surprised by the story she told. It seemed that from the moment I had looked into that child's eyes, I knew horror and death had come into the cottage.

FIVE years before, Essie Lou began telling us, the child had been born to a couple living in Palmetto.

"But that kid can't be five years old," I interrupted. "Why, it's just a baby!"

She merely shook her head. "Hit's five years. Nigh onto six."

The child was three when the woman's husband learned it was really the son of a neighbor. The husband had been inordinately fond of his wife, and the news drove him crazy. He killed both her and the man, and would have murdered the child too if some people, hearing the racket, hadn't arrived in time to prevent him. They took him to the asylum, and as he went he cursed the child horribly, saying it would lead a life worse than death and that whoever protected it would die.

After that—so Essie Lou's story ran— the child ceased to grow, though nothing happened for a long while, to the family which adopted it. More than a year later the murderer-husband hanged himself in his cell at the asylum.

It was then that things started to happen. Two days later the woman who had adopted the child was found with her neck broken. The child went to the orphanage. Later the superintendent fell off his horse and broke his neck and the woman supervisor who took his place was killed one night with several persons around her.

"Dere was a storm and de light went out," Essie Lou explained. "De folks could hear de *thing* comin', but dey couldn't see hit. Den de woman yelled and run and she hit de wall and when de lights come on her neck was broke."

After that, said Essie Lou, the child had disappeared. At the orphanage they explained that it had run away, but everyone knew it had been pushed outside the gates and forced to leave.

When the old woman quit talking and there was only silence in the room, I became aware that my fingers were pressing hard against the kitchen table, even as the edge of it pressed across my hips. Then I heard my own voice saying: "And how —how has it lived since then?"

The room suddenly shook with Ed McDonald's laughter. "By God!" he cried. "You must believe the yarn!"

Essie Lou kept her eyes fixed on mine. The pupils were still only tiny dots as she answered: "Hit's jest—jest lived around, tha's all. I don't know how. Now 'n 'en folks seen it—out in de bushes. But dey jes . . . ."

"Good Lord!" yelled Ed. "You mean they let that kid, that baby live like an animal? I bet it hasn't had a good meal since—" He turned, bellowed into the hallway. "Reece, bring that brat here. It's hungry."

"Oh Gawd!" cried the old woman. "Don't! Don't! Hit'll kill y'all. Hit'll break yo' necks. I ain't——"

She was on her feet now, coming toward me. "Mistar Dave, fer Gawd's sake don't let 'em keep hit. You know what'll happen!" She pawed at me, blubbering in terror, the saliva drooling from her lips.

I didn't move. I just stood there, fingers digging into the table, thinking.

I couldn't believe that story. It wasn't possible that a man could carry his revenge beyond the grave, could come back from the dead to murder those who protected a child he hated. And yet, I couldn't forget the look in that child's eyes. And I couldn't forget the utter sincerity, the utter terror in the old woman's voice.

I SAID: "The man didn't kill those persons, Essie Lou. It was just a coincidence that similar accidents happened to them." I knew I was talking as much to myself as to her, that my voice sounded strained and shaky. Ed McDonald started once more to laughing.

"Well, here we are," Reece said from the hallway, cheerily. He came into the kitchen still carrying the child.

"Oh Lawd!" moaned the Negress. She went backward two slow steps. Her lips hung slack and trembling. Her eyes bulged. Then her hand, groping behind her, found the knob of the back door and she was gone. We three stood in the room, silent, looking from one to another.

Ed McDonald chuckled uneasily. "I'll be damned—she does take it seriously!" He pointed toward a hat hanging on the wall. "She was bragging this morning about that new hat, and here she's gone and left it. But she'll be back."

Paul Reece shook his head. His thin, handsome face looked sober. "She won't be back," he said. "I was out in the hall and heard her story. She won't come back while we keep this kid—and I don't intend to turn it loose in the bush again."

"What the hell are you going to do with it?"

"Keep it here until we go back to Birmingham, then find a home for it. Any objections?"

Ed grinned. God, no. But Dave might have. I think he lines up with Essie Lou on that ghost story."

Reece turned his dark eyes toward me, and deep within them I saw the shadow. It was only a flicker, gone that quickly.

But it had been there, and I knew that he too felt the weirdness of the child's gaze; felt, deep within him somewhere, the shadow of subliminal fear.

He said slowly: "Do you mind?"

I tried to laugh, shake off the absurd dread clinging to me. "It's your neck," I said. "You're the one brought him in." After that we set about cooking a bowl of oatmeal, and fed the youngster.

* * *

Nothing happened that afternoon or night. We rigged up a pallet for the child and curling up on it like an animal he went to sleep. But twice after going to bed I awoke suddenly, sitting bolt upright, staring through the window into the moon-filled night. The next morning I felt ashamed of my fears.

Before lunch I drove into town trying to get a cook to take Essie Lou's place. It was no use. The story had spread and I couldn't get a Negro of any kind to come near me. I went back to the cottage. "We'll either have to get rid of the kid," I said, "or do our own cooking."

Reece's dark face set. "We'll do the cooking," he said.

Ed burst into laughter. "Your cooking will soon get rid of him—and us too probably."

THE storm began to blow during the late afternoon. The wind was from the southwest, across the gulf, bringing with it a driving rain which swept along almost parallel to the ground. The clouds were black and low, making for an early, furious darkness, split now and then by jagged terrific streaks of lightning. To wild bursts of thunder, and white streaks flashing out of darkness, the night shut down, pressing tight and hard against the earth.

Then rain beat in at the windows, and from the center of the kitchen ceiling a steady drip-drip of water fell, in a grow-ing puddle, to the floor. The wind roared down the drafty chimney so that we had trouble cooking supper. Also, beneath the howl of the wind, and the creaking of the old house, came the steady, constant sound of the surf. I got the weird idea of it being a bodiless voice, shouting out there in the darkness, shouting over and over some terrible, furious message I could not understand.

The storm was getting on Paul's nerves. I noticed that while we ate supper. Once he stopped with his fork halfway to his mouth and sat as though listening to some voice from the darkness. In the unsteady glow of the lamp I could see the fork trembling in his hand.

As for Ed McDonald though—not even the child could affect his nerves. I don't think he really noticed the kid sitting across the table from him. But I could not forget the youngster. I could hardly take my eyes from its face.

It sat there, bent over its saucer, holding a spoon in its fist the way children do, dipping up its food. And then, slowly, deliberately, it would raise its head and gaze toward one of us with that same look in its eyes, that look of terror and pity, and a knowledge of some ineluctable horror in the black shadows beyond death.

For a long second it would gaze toward us, sometimes looking straight into my own eyes, while I sat there stiff and cold, watching it, seeing that horror in its eyes, and feeling fear, dark and furious, gathering in my chest. Then, slowly, it would look downward to its plate and begin once more to dip the food.

Feeling such terror groping about me, I tried to shake it off. I tried to keep from looking at the child; to laugh and joke with Ed. But I couldn't eat; my hands shook whenever I used them and my appetite was gone. I stuck a cigarette in my mouth, struck a match. My fingers jittered so that the flame winked out. I leaned over and lit the cigarette from the lamp.

Reece was watching me. He said: "You're not eating tonight?"

McDonald was on his third fish. "Leaves more for me," he offered flippantly.

"You and Blue Boy, the prize hog," I said, and tried to laugh. The sound was so shaky, even Ed looked up.

Reece's dark eyes narrowed. "I think both of us would like a drink," he remarked. He went to the cupboard and, coming back with a gallon jug, handed it to me.

I poured out half a glass. "Nothing like corn whiskey," I said as I downed it.

"Why not use the jug if you're going to drink it all?" came from Ed. Reece didn't say anything. He took three quick drinks. Each time he lifted the glass I could see that his fingers were tight around it, yet the liquor sloshed from side to side.

The house creeked under the battering of the storm. The rain lashed like whips against the windows, and under and beyond it all was that voice shouting in the darkness, the eerie cry of the surf.

After supper Reece put the child to bed and carried the lamp into the front room. I followed with the jug.

THAT air of tense expectancy, of waiting for some horror we did not understand, nor know where to look for, filled the small living-room. Perhaps even Ed McDonald felt it, perhaps it was only the silence of Reece and myself. At any rate Ed quit laughing and sat with his big fingers fumbling the leaves of a book. We couldn't read well by the lamp, but all of us sat around the table, holding books, saying nothing. I was hardly conscious of the one in my own hands; sitting stiff and straight in my chair, I was just—listening.

There had not been much thunder before. But now, all at once, there came a vast cannonading. The whole house rocked and shivered. For one long minute the wind hung still and waiting, while the sky burst in explosion after explosion, while low and soft and frenetic under the thunder came the sound of that voice shouting in the darkness, the sound of surf surging onto the beach.

Then the thunder stopped and the wind struck the house again. The timbers creaked. The glass rattled in the windows. The lamp flame flickered to a dull yellow, and shadows gathered in ghastly silence in the room's corners.

Yet the sound of that voice shouting its warning came steadily with the wind. I knew it was only the sea—nonetheless I could have sworn it was a human voice, screaming against the wind, trying to warn us of some horror gathering slowly and inevitably about the cottage. My head had twisted to one side, as I sat listening, trying to make out the words howled along the wind.

"I won't put him out! By God! I won't put him out in the storm!"

I whirled, coming to my feet half crouched. The breath stopped in my lungs, the words beat about me.

Paul Reece was standing beside the table, gripping it with white fingers, his dark handsome face drawn into a corded mask of horror. The book he had held was sprawled on the floor.

"I won't!" he cried again. His hands shook the table.

Ed McDonald moved fast for so large a man. In one stride he had come out of his chair and reached Reece. His big hands clamped hard on Paul's shoulders, though his voice was almost gentle.

"Steady, kid. Steady. Now what's the trouble?"

The life seemed to go out of Reece. He dropped into his chair, put his face in his hands and sat there without moving.

I was still standing. My book had fallen to the floor, but I didn't know it. I could feel the sweat coming out on my forehead in small, cold drops.

After a moment Reece looked up. His face was still white and drawn, but he was trying to smile. "I'm sorry," he said. "My nerves seem to be running away with me. It's this damn' storm."

He lifted the jug of whiskey from the table, forefinger through the handle, balancing the jug across his elbow, and took a long drink. Putting the jug down, he made a face, then wiped his lips. "At supper I kept looking at that damned brat," he said. "I kept thinking about that story and listening to this storm. It—it sort of got on my nerves. And the way that sea's booming out there, sounding like somebody shouting . . . ."

"You've noticed that?"

Reece swung toward me. His long fingers were stiff on the chair arm. "Noticed what?"

"The surf. The way it sounds like—somebody."

ED'S laugh burst in the room. "You damn' fools!" he said. "Not a cat's brain between the two of you. Scared as children hearing a ghost story." He flung back his big head and laughed until the lamp quivered. The sound made both Reece and me feel better. It was good to have an unimaginative, stolid, common-sense fellow in the room. I felt ashamed for having been frightened.

Reece grinned. "I know I'm crazy."

"What we all need is a drink," was my own heroic contribution.

"Your first intelligent remark tonight," said Ed, reaching toward the table. But it was while he was still reaching, that the thing happened.

Thunder burst like a concussion above the house. Wind shook the windows. The light flickered high—and went out.

And with that, the thunder was gone. With that the screaming surf faded so that there was no sound, no motion except the grip of the wind holding the house.

No sound, that is, until the child began screaming.

Remember, he had not made a sound since Reece found him the day before. Yet now, starting so gradually I never knew when I heard the first cry, he began to scream, the soft whimpering getting louder and louder, growing high and shrill, dominating the darkness, holding us motionless, breathless, while our nerves tautened, our bodies tensed, our muscles grew stiff and hard. And still the cries rose higher, to an absolutely weird shriek. And then stopped.

So that once more there was, except for the wind, silence in the house. Even the sound of the gulf was gone, leaving a vast hollow in the darkness.

And then that other sound came gradually. First, from far off, in the great emptiness left by the surf. Then growing louder, nearer, crawling toward us through the darkness.

A board creaked. Another. There was a long while in which that dark silence whirled furiously around and around and around until I almost screamed and yet my lungs were aching because there was no air in them. Panic tore at my throat, but made no sound.

The board creaked again. It was right at the doorway now. There was no doubting any longer! *Someone had come down the hallway and into the room!*

In the utter darkness Ed's voice sounded strange and harsh. "I'll get the lamp. . . ."

I heard his fingers fumbling with a match box, heard the tiny sound of matches striking together. A board creaked not five yards away.

"I'll get . . ." Ed said again. A match

scraped. Flame spurted, yellow and red. I could see Ed's big fingers gripping the match. Light flickered out across the floor, across the spot where the board had creaked, and soaked into darkness. There was nothing but empty floor.

The board creaked again, right under the light. The match guttered with a choking sound, and went out. Darkness stormed the room.

"Oh God!" It was a scream of breaking nerves and utter panic. Paul Reece sobbed deep in his throat. His shoes cracked the floor. A chair crashed over and suddenly the wind was once more howling about the house. I heard Reece strike the wall— hard. Then there was the soft, feminine sound of his body crumpling.

Down the hall the child screamed again, on a flat, high note.

IT had happened in three seconds. I felt a breath tear my throat as I sucked in deeply. Then, half mad with terror, I was floundering after Reece, striking out into the darkness, whirling my fists through empty space.

The wind drew back and the house was still. A match flickered dully, and disclosed nothing. There was the small click of a lamp chimney being replaced, and the light spread out across the room.

I stood in a half crouch, my hands in front of me. To the left Ed McDonald's face showed white above the lamp chimney. Near the wall on the right, dim in the shadows, lay Paul Reece. His face was turned upward, strangely. Even before I reached and knelt beside him, I knew that his neck was broken.

For a half minute I knelt there, my hands above the body, not quite daring to touch it. The wind had struck the house again, shaking the windows, howling about the eves. But somehow it seemed far away now and detached. Moreover, the voice of the sea was in the wind once more, howling through the darkness.

And all at once I knew. The voice was the same as before: Death had come to this cottage—but he had not left, and the sea was still screaming its warning.

I tried to tell myself it was only the sound of the waves breaking. But Paul Reece had heard that sound—and died.

I did not see Ed McDonald as he crossed the room toward me, did not hear him. Then he was kneeling beside me so that, looking up, I saw his face. It was as pale as his tousled, ash-blond hair. His nostrils were pulled wide, and quivered when he breathed.

It was Ed McDonald who first touched Reece's body. He rolled it gently onto its back. The head wabbled, and I saw there was a smear of blood on the forehead. Ed unbuttoned Reece's coat and shirt and put his hand over the heart. He drew in a long breath then, and the muscles in his arm went rigid. He adjusted the clothes, and stood up.

I got to my feet and stepped back to the table. Somehow I wanted to be near the lamp, in the very center of its light; although I couldn't take my eyes from the shadows near the wall and the white blur of Reece's face.

And suddenly there was a voice in the room, a voice so cracked and high that I could not recognize it as my own, saying: "It was the child killed him! His neck is broken like all the others. If he hadn't brought the child—" But there was no more breath in my lungs and the words clogged. I stood there, gripping the table behind me, swaying.

Ed McDonald turned slowly. His eyes showed dark and large in the paleness of his face. There were beads of sweat on his forehead. But his big jaw was set hard, his mouth pulled thin. I knew what he was about to say, and I was afraid. I wanted to get out of the house, away from that child. I leaned toward Ed and my voice shook with panic.

"If we don't send him away, he'll kill *us!* He killed Reece for protecting the child. He'll kill us! Listen to the ocean, it's——"

For just one moment Ed McDonald stood there, head turned to one side, body taut. I knew he was listening to the surf. Then his shoulders squared. He said: "We're letting our nerves run away with us. We've got to look at this thing sensibly."

"But Reece——" I stared at the dead face, showing like a pale flower of terror in the shadows.

ED'S voice was strained, but steady. I could tell he was as frightened as I— but he was fighting against his fear, refusing to recognize it. His nerves were stretched to an edge, but he held them. "We've got to look at this thing straight," he said. "No ghost killed Reece. That's impossible. There hasn't been anybody in the house except us, and the kid. Yes, I know—I thought I heard footsteps too. But listen now . . . you can hear the same sounds. It's only the house creaking in the wind. Reece lost his nerve and ran across the room and struck the wall with his head. You can see the bruise. That's what broke his neck."

I stood there, gripping the table behind me, fighting my nerves in order to steady them.

What Ed said sounded reasonable. Of course that was the way Reece had been killed. It was impossible that anything else had happened. Impossible. And yet. . . .

"Somebody's got to go for the undertaker and the sheriff," Ed went on. "We can't let . . ." He paused and I heard him suck a deep breath through his nostrils. He and Paul Reece had been friends for years. He added: "You drive better than I do, and it won't be easy in this storm."

I knew what he meant. Somebody had to stay with the kid; driving into town and coming back with the sheriff and undertaker would give me a chance to steady my nerves.

I said: "All right." Then I went into the back room for my slicker and hat. Passing the door to Reece's bedroom, where the child lay, I kept my neck very stiff and straight.

In the front room once more I looked at Ed McDonald. His face was still white and drawn, but his jaw was set as hard as ever. His eyes looked deep-sunk under his wide forehead and mop of blond hair.

"Why don't you come with me?" I suggested. "We can be back in half an hour."

The line of muscle along his jaw bulged. "No, I'll stay here with the kid—and Reece."

For the first time I realized how much his friend's death had meant to Ed. Not one word of sorrow had passed his lips— yet he was willing to face death to sit there by the body. I said: "I'll be back soon," and went out.

The wind struck like a giant hand, blowing me halfway across the porch. The rain lashed my face. Off to the left, the surf crashed against the shore and howled like some torture-ridden soul. Despite the slicker I was soaking wet before I reached the car.

We had lashed a tarpaulin over the hood before the storm began: the motor caught up almost at once. And all the way to Palmetto, fighting the wind and the narrow, water-filled road, I kept thinking about what had happened.

The surf was not audible now. Nothing but rain, and darkness, and wind. There had been something strange, something almost human about the storm before, but now it seemed ordinary enough. I felt ashamed of the fear which had clutched at me, ashamed of the belief I had put in a story which could not possibly be true.

I reached Palmetto. The jail there is a small, square building. As I arrived before it, only one dim light showed in the front room. I left the car in front, plunged across the rain-swept sidewalk and pushed open the door.

IT was a small room, bare of furniture except for a long table and a chair. A small bulb hung on a dusty cord from the middle of the ceiling. Stretched on the table, snoring loudly, was a fat, bald-headed man. A large bunch of keys dangled from his belt.

"Hello," I called. The man's snore rose high, then sank to a gigantic whisper.

Stepping nearer I tapped him lightly on the shoulder. "Hello," I said again. His snore changed into a shrill whistling.

"Hey! Wake up!" I shook him, and the bunch of keys jangled. The snoring became hoarse and plaintive.

I was grinning now. The terror which had haunted me all night was forgotten. "Somebody could take your keys, let out the prisoners—if there are any—and lock you up and you'd never know it," I said aloud. I grabbed him by the shoulders and began to shake.

He sat up suddenly, swinging around, eyes blinking, unable to focus. "Hey, hey, What——" He sputtered.

"Are you the sheriff?"

He rubbed fat knuckles across his eyes. "Nope. I'm the jailor. Sheriff's gone over to Sandy Ridge. Been a killin' of some kind."

"When's he coming back?"

He sighed sleepily, pulled out a great nickel-backed watch, and looked at it. "Jest 'leven o'clock now. Should be back most any time."

"Where can I find an undertaker?"

The jailor quit rubbing his eyes and looked hard at me. "Ain't no undertaker here but the coroner, and he's with the Sheriff. How come?"

"We've had an accident. In that cottage out near French Bay."

The man's body began to stiffen. He kept sitting on the edge of the table, but he leaned his pudgy shoulders toward me. "You one of those fellows from Buminham rentin' that old Elders' cottage?"

"Yes."

"Y'all got that—that child out there?"

Every muscle in my body jerked. I felt the wave of cold fear surge through me again. I said, "Yes."

Then tenseness went out of him. His bald head nodded slightly. He slid back across the table and sat there like some fat frog, looking at me.

All at once I was angry. Angry with this man, but more so with myself. It was evident that he put utter faith in the story of the child. He was the sort of person who *would* believe such stuff—a fat, slovenly, half-witted countryman.

And I had believed the story too. So that was the kind of brain I had, right on a par with his! I cursed myself for a fool. Ed McDonald had explained how the thing happened, but I had still been afraid. I had left Ed there alone with the child while I had run away.

Well, the least I could do was go back, show that I wasn't going to act like a baby any longer.

"When the sheriff and coroner return, send them out," I directed. Then I turned, not waiting for an answer, and left.

For more than half the way back I cursed myself as an idiot. Yet by the time I turned into the small side road leading to French Bay, I'd left off cursing.

The rain and wind had not slackened. The night was like pitch, beating the headlights back against themselves. The rain pounded on the windshield and piled up in streams along the wiper as it moved from side to side. The palmetto at each side the road, barely visible in the head-lights, jerked and swayed. I rounded a sharp curve and the lights flattened against the bleak, rain-swept walls of the house. I swung the car into the front yard, stopped, and cut off the motor.

EVEN as I opened the car door and stepped out into the rain, the eerie feel-ing of terror came over me. It was like the blood in my veins, frozen in every pore, yet moving round and round, cease-lessly. I said aloud, "You damned cow-ard!" and the wind snatched the words from my mouth. Off to the right the surf screamed its hollow warning.

All at once I noticed that the light in the living-room was not burning. I stopped dead, the rain, as it beat into my face, making little clicking sounds against the slicker, and I stared at the dull blackness of the house.

"He's gone into the back," I whispered. "Maybe he's gone to bed. Ed would do that." The words were not audible under the noise of the wind and the surf. The blood in my body began to grow as cold and thin as the rain.

Slowly, the feeling of terror gathering, deepening, becoming more and more in-tense inside me, I went toward the house. My shoes clumped wetly, soddenly up the steps. The doorknob was cold to the palm of my hand.

I twisted it, opened the door, stepped in-side. Wind and rain came in after me with a howl. It took all my courage to close the door. The sounds of the storm faded then, leaving only the echoes which shook through the house, and the creaking of timbers.

"Ed," I called out. My voice almost broke. "Ed!"

No answer except the gnawing of the wind, the far off screaming of the surf.

"*Ed!* Where are you?"

I started forward, hands outstretched in the darkness, groping. My left foot struck something big and rubbery. I could feel myself falling, rolling through the dark-ness, plunging down through a long eter-nity before I struck the floor. I shouted, but the clogged muscles of my throat, I knew, emitted no sound.

How I got to my feet I don't know. I remembered pawing at the living-room table, at the lamp, muttering to myself: "Steady, don't turn it over." And then the shadows swayed back against the wall and the lamplight was mellow in the room.

Paul Reece lay where we had left him.

In the hall doorway, big head twisted grotesquely to one side, eyes wide open yet staring up at nothing, lay Ed Mc-Donald.

"Oh God!" I said aloud.

I wanted to run, and couldn't. My muscles quivered and ached. There was a vacuum in my chest; my ribs were being sucked in, cracking. I stood there, holding to the table, half twisted so that I could see the two bodies, for the space of a dozen slow heart-beats.

A certain amount of calmness came over me, all at once. I had not moved from my position at the table, nor looked about the room, nor stepped to Ed McDonald's side. I knew he was dead, that his neck was broken. But as my muscles quit shaking, I seemed to see myself as I saw the others —to stand off to one side and watch my-self, there by the table. It was the part of myself which stood detached and able to think, which told me what to do. There was only one way I could save myself. I knew that now.

Get rid of the child.

I SLID my hand across the table, found the lamp, picked it up. Holding it high I went out of the room and down the hall. Without hesitating I turned into the room where Reece had put the youngster to sleep.

The lamplight glided across the room, the table, the cot where Reece had slept, the small pallet on the floor.

"I'll be damned!" It was the part of me standing to one side, which spoke.

The child was gone.

I began to search the cottage. And as I went from room to room without finding any sign of the boy, my courage returned. "He must have gone out into the storm," I thought, "after—after—" I remembered Ed McDonald's big face staring up into the darkness. Well, at least that meant he was out of the house. At least I was safe. I turned back toward the front room.

I must have known it, *felt* his presence —before I saw him.

I still had the lamp in my hand, moving toward the table. The light was sliding along the floor, swelling out into the darkness, making the room come into view gradually, as invisible ink does when held over a flame. And then, half way to the table, I stopped so short the kerosene slushed in the lamp. My body went as cold and still as a marble statue. For one long second there was utterly no feeling in me.

Very slowly my eyes started to raise, my head to turn. I could see the table in front of me, then one edge of it, the floor beyond, the chair in which Ed McDonald had sat earlier in the night. I didn't want to look in that chair. I tried to turn my eyes away. But I could no more check them than I could check the shadow of a cloud across the sun. The next instant I was staring at the child, cuddled in the chair.

The light of the lamp flowed mellow and golden about him. It showed his face, small and pale; reflected lambently in his eyes, making them shine the way a cat's eyes shine in the dark. The glow caused that look of terror and pity in his gaze to leap like a flame. And in the center of it— I could see the death that was coming toward me.

Perhaps my nerves shattered then. Perhaps it was the sudden wild screaming of the surf, as a giant wave broke on the shore. I heard myself shouting, felt the pain in my throat as the sound tore through. I saw the lamp falling, turning over slowly, saw my hand, nerveless, still suspended in the air before me. And in that last flicker of light I saw the child's eyes, and heard his scream come terribly through the darkness.

It must have been a full minute longer before I became conscious of the silence. I could feel the house shiver under the impact of the wind; I knew that outside, in the night's darkness, the sea was crying its eternal warning.

But in the room, in the utter darkness which crowded like a hideous animal against me, there was no sound. There was not even the sound of my own breathing.

"I am as silent as the dead ones," I thought. "It's like the grave before even Death comes into it."

And then a floor board creaked in the hall!

I HEARD the slight squeak as it straightened again. I felt myself moving, but I made no sound. I was half crouching, turning slowly, endlessly, as one moves in a dream. And at last I was facing the hall door. I knew I was facing the door and the sound, though it was like moving deep under a sea of pitch, with only blackness pressing hard against wide open pupils.

It came again, the slight squeak of a step. It was like a tiny knife blade of sound striking through the darkness. And yet underneath it, invisible, without sound or motion yet always there, was the terrible roar of meaning—of what came with that sound: *the dark and heavy breathing of Death!*

And once again the board squeaked. Just inside the room this time. To continue my long eternity of waiting. For though I wanted to run I could not. Though I wanted to scream I couldn't do that either—there was no air in my lungs.

Finally the board squeaked from a spot not three yards away. And then the thing *touched* me . . . .

I don't know what happened after that. Perhaps I did cry out, for a thin sheet of sound burst up through the darkness. Then I was on the floor, writhing. My neck was bending backward. My spine creaked. The very ligaments seemed to scream in pain one second before they tore loose.

Long darting arrows of light slashed the room, beat at my head, whirled around and around with my terror. Then I must have fainted.

* * *

Two men were rubbing my wrists. One wore a large star on his coat. The sheriff and coroner, they said, but at the time words meant little to me. They put the bodies of Ed McDonald and Paul Reece in my car and the coroner drove it away. The sheriff took me with him, but he left the child behind. He pretended not to see it, and I said nothing.

"I can't put in the records that ghosts killed those men," he said as he drove back to town. "I can claim they got panicky, ran against the wall, and broke their necks. And yet . . . ." He sat silent for a long time.

"What about me?" I asked.

He said, "That's what I was wondering. You were lyin' on the floor, havin' a fit when we came in. But——" I could hear his breathing above the throb of the motor, the beat of rain on the top. "But—there's the marks of ten fingers on yore neck. And the marks are bigger than yore own fingers."

They did not believe Colonel Holmquist's fantastic tale. . . . At first, they thought it a gigantic hoax, but the gruesome happenings on that storm-bound estate changed their bravado to whimpering fear—for a ghastly creature of the Arctic was stalking them, murdering them horribly, one by one, and there was no escaping its insane lust for blood!

"YES," Colonel Holmquist said, "I'm going back—back to hell!" It was shocking, the way he said it—not as a jest, but grimly, soberly, bit-terly—and the look on his face was that of a man who had indeed some dreadful knowledge of the place. We all knew, of course, that he was referring to the far

THE ICE MAIDEN

By John H. Knox

(Author of "Dead Man's Shadow," etc.)

*A Novelette of
Deathless Hate*

north. His explorations in the Arctic had made his name a by-word long ago. But there was no zest in his announcement now, only an unhealthy fever in those great steel-colored eyes, a sort of mania in the set lines of his long, angular face.

There were five of us about the table, assembled at the Colonel's invitation. He had promised to reveal something startling. I suspected that he wanted money from us, money for his forthcoming expedition. That was why, with the exception of myself, he had chosen men who had been connected with his work in past years.

"An apt word, Colonel," said Julian Eubanks. "Hell really got its name from the frozen North. Wasn't it the Scandinavian demoness, *Hel,* who carried dead souls to a realm of fireless darkness?"

Eubanks, whose books on the Arctic had made him famous, had accompanied Colonel Holmquist on an expedition ten years before. He was a tall man, with a dark, saturnine face and a cynical manner. His small, attractive wife, who sat beside him, smiled proudly at his erudition.

But Colonel Holmquist did not smile. A look of almost angry impatience crossed his haunted face. "You didn't stay in the North long enough to learn not to laugh at it, Julian," he said grimly.

Edmund Benedict, fat, complacent, thrust forward in his chair. "I say, Colonel," he remarked, "you really seem grim about it, not keen for it at all. Why go back if that's the way you feel?"

Colonel Holmquist looked at him a long moment before replying. Benedict had been his chief radio technician on that expedition ten years ago. He had since made a tremendous fortune with an electrical invention. No one would have guessed, looking at his present air of sleek prosperity, that he had once been an adventurous spirit.

The Colonel's eyes narrowed; something like pain cast a swift shadow over his hollow cheeks. "I'm going back because I have to, Edmund," he said. He turned to the silent figure behind his chair. "Joe, get the glass case from my study."

We stared uncomfortably about the shadowy room. It was long, low-ceiled, paneled in dark wood. A fire glowed in the deep hearth, sending out ruddy streamers of light that contrasted strangely with the ice-bound, twilight landscape visible through a wide window. Snow was falling. I began to wish that I had never come up to this lonely mountain retreat. There was a good chance that we'd all be snow-bound here.

Why had the Colonel rented this great, stone lodge anyway? Was it true, as he said, that Arctic winters had made him

unfit for the life of cities, or . . . ? My thoughts flew to the mystery which had surrounded his return from his last expedition—the strange coffin-like box he had brought with him packed in ice, the evasive answers he had given about its contents. That was the reason I was here tonight. He had promised me a story for my newspaper. And, I must confess, I was anxious to get it and be gone!

The man called Joe came back into the room on noiseless feet. He was a burly giant, with the face and build of a prize-fighter. He had been the Colonel's confidential servant for years. He carried in his hands a large cube-shaped something covered by a white cloth. He laid it upon the table before Holmquist and went out.

A BREATHLESS hush fell over the room now. The Colonel's sunken eyes, with their queer, crawling light, roved from face to face; the fingers of one lean, muscular hand drummed on the table top.

"I'm glad I have this thing," he said finally, indicating the covered case, "for otherwise you would not believe what I have to tell you. My friends, *I am a haunted man!* Don't look at me as if you thought me crazy; I'm not—yet!" He turned to Julian Eubanks. "Hasn't it ever occurred to you, Julian, that these myths you laugh at may have some basis in fact? Why are they so similiar in every northern land? *Hulda,* the Norse demon of winter, the monster *Erleursortok* of Greenland, who leaps upon dead souls to devour them; the frightful *Cheenos* of Nova Scotia, the Frost Giants of the Scandinavians, and so on. . . ."

"But, Colonel," Edmund Benedict sputtered, "you're not seriously suggesting . . . ?"

"I am *stating,*" Colonel Holmquist snapped, "that there is an original, a mould, a pattern, from which these ghastly myth-demons are drawn. Man-monster or demon, I do not know, but I do know that his race persists there in the far North. That he can assume a form that is structurally similar to that of man, I have absolute proof. I will not say that he is limited to that form, for his powers, occult as well as physical, are as far above ours as ours are above the ant's! But this abysmal *Thing*—I call him the Ice-Beast —has learned to hunt men as we hunt rabbits. He has not yet invaded our warmer climes and our cities. But if he should—God help us! And he has already found a bait to lure him here."

"And what is that?" I asked.

"Our women!" said Colonel Holmquist. "The Eskimo has already found that out. The white man will learn!"

"And how do you know . . . ?" Julian Eubanks began.

Colonel Holmquist glared at him. "I know," he said, "because one of these grisly horrors has followed me back from the North! He is here now, in or about this house, hovering, listening, waiting . . . !"

A sharp, choked scream broke in upon the low rumble of the explorer's words. It was Myra Eubanks. Huddled against her husband, she was holding the back of one hand over her mouth while her wild eyes were fastened on the window.

We stared at the window too. "Just the fog," Julian Eubanks muttered.

Yes, it was just the fog. It had come up suddenly and was pressing its grey, featureless face against the pane, then writhing past in grotesque convolutions. But somehow, it shut us in with an almost ponderable weight; I felt it against my chest, restricting my breathing. I was glad to turn away.

Myra Eubanks was apologizing for her fright with a half-hysterical laugh. "I thought I heard a muffled crash somewhere in the house," she said. "Then I looked at the window, and that awful fog there. . . ."

"I heard nothing," Colonel Holmquist interrupted. He was frowning now, and something like fear was twitching at his mouth. "I suppose it was Joe Lechner moving about." His hand was on the cloth covering of the case now. He lifted it, and we rose from our chairs with gasps.

Under the square glass case lay a skull. But such a skull! It was huge—as large as a medium-sized pumpkin—yellowed and discolored with age, somewhat crumbled on the facial plane, but in a fair state of preservation. The great teeth between the grinning jaws were as large as the teeth of a horse. The brain cavity in the cranium seemed enormous!

WITH a feeling of awe, we drew nearer, stared breathlessly. The tint of the glass case threw a greenish patina over the thing. It was awful to look at. Julian Eubanks was the first to speak. "Great God!" he swore. "Where did you get that?"

Colonel Holmquist grinned now—unpleasantly. I noticed that his hands were trembling. "I found it," he said, "on my last expedition. This time I shall take it back. I don't want it."

"Take it back!" Edmund Benedict shrilled. "Why, the archeologists of the world would give their necks for that, Colonel!"

"I may give mine, too," Colonel Holmquist replied, "but not willingly—not if I can help it!"

"And this is why the—the *Ice-Beast* has followed you?" Myra Eubanks asked tremulously.

"Perhaps," the Colonel said, "but I think not. I think it is because of the other—the thing I brought back packed in ice."

"What's that?" three of us chorused.

"You shall see," Holmquist replied.

"I'm going to show you now. I have an idea the *Ice-Beast* will not be pleased, but you shall see it anyhow." He got up, stepped to the door and called, "Joe, Joe! Bring a light and open the basement for us."

There was no reply; the echoes of his voice volleyed weirdly through the empty rooms. The Colonel's shaggy brows knotted, he bit his lip. "Joe, Joe!" he called again. Then, a trifle weakly: "We'd better look for him."

Candles were lighted. We went from room to room through the sprawling stone house. The man was nowhere to be found. We called from the doors, but the carpet of undisturbed snow at each entrance proved only too clearly that he had not left the house.

We came to the basement last of all. The Colonel stood at the head of the dark stairway that led down and called again. We huddled behind him. Nobody expected an answer now. It was bitter cold; my hand holding the candle was blue around the knuckles. But there was a deeper cold that lay against our hearts, heavy, oppressive. Myra Eubanks' teeth were chattering.

We went down slowly. God, but it was cold! We reached the cement floor. It was like ice. The Colonel was fumbling at a locked door; the brass key shook and wavered in his hand. He pushed the door open.

Did you ever go into an ice vault in a packing house—one of those places where the red, raw carcasses hang on hooks along the walls? That was the smell that came out of that place. We realized, then, I think, that horror awaited us beyond the sill of that shadowy doorway. We knew, and wanted to draw back, but the Colonel was taking a faltering, forward step.

Myra Eubanks shrieked first. It registered on me vaguely, along with Julian's hysterical muttering as he caught her fainting form, tried to revive her. The candle dropped from Colonel Holmquist's hand, fell sputtering in some red substance upon the floor. Something like a cough burst in the old man's throat. That was all; but I glimpsed his frozen, glassy eyes as I pushed past him with the candle.

There was no corpse there—only the fragments of a corpse! The floor was littered with pieces of that broken body. It was indescribable. The bursting of a high explosive shell in that small concrete vault might approximate the ghastly havoc. For the body of Joe Lechner had been literally shattered. If it had not been for the ghastly head, with the skull cracked wide open like a nut, the horrid remains of what had once been a human body would have been unrecognizable.

What could have done it? What nameless, unheard-of power had wrought this unthinkable mutilation? My stunned brain could not grasp it; my fevered imagination could evoke but one picture—the picture of a giant madman, slowly and methodically tearing a doll in fragments, pinching and breaking the brittle members between huge fingers.

It was Eubanks' scream which caused me to turn then, and I saw a grey, imponderable something move swiftly in the shadows beyond the stairs. At the same instant, my nostrils were assailed by a peculiar, musky reek. An instant only, and it was gone again, but my brain retained the fleeting impression of a vast and shaggy shape, of two beastial eyes that had stared for an instant with hate and hunger!

When we finally mustered sufficient courage to creep back toward the stairs, the *Thing* had vanished utterly, leaving no trace except the shadow, the echo, of its nauseous odor, still lingering in the air. . . .

CHAPTER TWO

The Thing in the Ice

I WAS thankful for Edmund Benedict then. He was the coolest one of the lot. Without his cool sanity, I'm afraid I should have run out of the place like a yammering madman. Eubanks was carrying his limp wife back up the stairs. The Colonel still stood like a smitten creature, and I was quaking with terror. It was Benedict who snatched the candle from my hand and went into the room.

His face was grim but composed. He stooped, picked up one of the ghastly fragments and then dropped it quickly. "Cold!" he exclaimed. "Colder than ice!" He backed toward us, turned. "Let's go back up."

Lord, but the warmth of that open fire felt good when we were back in the long, dim room. Eubanks, pale as a ghost, was forcing a drink between the lips of his wife. Colonel Holmquist slumped into a chair. Benedict and I went for whiskey.

There was a little color in Benedict's face when, after downing a couple of stiff ones, he swung about suddenly and squared off in front of the Colonel's chair. "Now!" he said grimly. "Maybe you'll give us some explanation."

Colonel Holmquist lifted a haggard face. "So help me, God, Edmund, I know nothing except what I have told you."

"No?" Benedict's eyes narrowed. "You were always a sly one, Holmquist. I suspected that you got us here to bleed us, but I never expected quite so grisly a game."

"But, God in heaven, man!" the quavering voice of Holmquist protested. "How could I have done it; how could any *man* have done it? I've got to take the things back, I tell you—the skull and that other. Nothing else will appease this monster!"

"He's right, Edmund!" It was Julian Eubanks who interrupted now. He came stalking over, his thin face a sick lemon-yellow, his long, wax-like fingers trembling as he gestured. "He's right about it not being any human agency." His black eyes glittered as he fastened them on Holmquist's face. "It's the curse, Colonel, the curse that rests on you for leaving McArtney to die there on that barren ice floe!"

Holmquist's slumped form straightened; he rose upright, kicked back the chair. His gaunt face had gone apoplectic. "You damned liar!" he bellowed. "You ruined me with that story—that damned slander—putting it in that cursed book of yours. And you, too, Edmund Benedict—you spread the rumor, too. That's why I can't get the funds I need now. Damned skulking liars, both of you! That kid McArtney was practically dead when we left him. And it was done to save the worthless necks of the rest of you. If it was a crime it was your crime as much as mine!"

Edmund Benedict laughed sourly. "See how the hatred crops out, Eubanks?" he said. "I told you we shouldn't have come out here. He's hated us for years because of that. Now I'm going back to town."

It was Holmquist's turn to laugh now. "I don't think so, Edmund." He waved a big hand toward the window. "The snow in the pass will be about four feet deep by now. To try to cross it in a car would be —well, just shoot yourself, if you're too yellow to face it out here."

Benedict was silenced for the moment. So were the rest of us. We were staring at the window, against which the huge snowflakes were fluttering like white moths. It wasn't a pleasant thing, knowing we were shut in there, whether we liked it or not, shut in with something unimaginable and monstrous. My eye fell on the great skull gleaming there in its glass case, and I turned to pour myself another drink.

Benedict was facing Colonel Holmquist again. A sour smile twisted his thick mouth. "Very well," he said, "we'll stay then. You have guns on the place, Colonel, plenty of guns?"

"I have guns," said Holmquist, gesturing toward a rack on the wall, "that will kill an elephant. Help yourself. They'll do no good."

BENEDICT went over and lifted down a large-caliber repeating-rifle. He emptied the magazine on the floor, picked up the steel-jacketed bullets, examined each carefully and replaced them. He smiled. "I'll face anything that breathes with this," he said, slapping the gun. "Now, Holmquist, I want to ask you about that locked room down there where we found the—the remains. Any other entrances to it?"

"The door on the other side," the Colonel said, "had a padlock on it in plain sight."

"Where did you keep the key to the first door?"

"In my desk," Holmquist said. "No one but Joe and I knew where it was."

"Is there another key to that lock?"

"Old Hidge has a duplicate, I suppose."

"Who's old Hidge?"

"Caretaker of the place. His cabin is behind this house."

"What do you know about him?"

"I was given a letter about him by the agency from whom I rented the place. He seems to be a quiet old fellow who minds his own business."

"Then the first thing," Benedict said, "is to see about that other key. Nobody picked that heavy Yale lock. I want to see Hidge, Colonel."

It was plain by his manner that all he wanted from Hidge was a confirmation of his suspicion with regard to Holmquist.

"You'll probably find him in his cabin," Holmquist said. "Shall I go with you?"

"No!" Benedict snapped. "I'll go alone." He snatched up his overcoat and hat and stalked out, gun in hand.

"Quite the hero, eh?" Holmquist growled when the door had closed behind Benedict. "Quite the little hero, our Edmund. You know what I've always suspected, Julian? I've always suspected that young McArtney was the real inventor of that electrical gadget that made Edmund his fortune. McArtney was working on something like that, I know—had the plans with him out there. I've always wondered if our Edmund didn't slip a little something into McArtney's food. Now he storms about leaving McArtney on the ice!"

A shudder passed through Julian Eubanks' frame. His eyes kept probing the shadows of the room and then returning to the figure of his wife. "That other thing you were going to show us, Colonel," he said huskily, "that thing in the box packed in ice?"

"Ah, to be sure," said Holmquist. He turned to me. "I imagine you're impatient, too, Mr. Gage. I promised you a story. Well, you shall have it, if you feel equal to going through that room down there."

Nothing short of my gnawing curiosity could have dragged me back into that abattoir, but I nodded that I was ready.

"And I," Julian Eubanks chimed in.

Holmquist frowned. "I'd not advise leaving your wife here alone, Julian," he said. "You'll understand, when you've seen. . . ."

"And I certainly won't go down there," Myra Eubanks' voice broke in. "But go ahead, Julian. You might hand me one of those guns, though. I can shoot quite well."

Holmquist started to protest, I think. But Eubanks was already reaching toward the gun-rack. His wife took the heavy rifle which he handed her, and we left her holding it firmly in two slightly unsteady but competent-looking hands.

I led the way this time, holding the candle before me. They seemed glad to let me go ahead. I heard the Colonel take a deep breath when we stepped into the first room. My stomach retched at the faint, sweetish, sickening smell; I set my teeth and picked my way carefully across the hideous débris. Eubanks was sidling along one wall, stepping gingerly, like a skittish colt.

The second door was heavier than the first, crossed by bands of iron and fastened with a formidable padlock which Holmquist opened with some difficulty. He gave it a shove then, and stood a moment peering in uncertainty.

LIGHT from the candle flickered weakly into the dark interior, wagging red tongues of fire against the icy darkness. The room seemed to be empty. The Colonel took a breath of relief, stepped in. I followed, with Eubanks at my heels, and the door was closed behind us. It was then that I noticed the odd structure at the far end of the room. It was a huge, iron-barred cage such as a circus might use to hold a ferocious beast. A sheet hung over the front of it, hiding its contents from our eyes. I listened as we moved nearer, but there was no sound except Eubanks' harsh breathing which he seemed unable to suppress.

"I fancy the *Ice-Beast* could break those bars if he tried," Colonel Holmquist said in a low voice. "I don't know why he hasn't. I'm sure he'd like to get into that cage."

"Into it?" I echoed in bewilderment.

"Yes," said the Colonel, "for I have stolen this thing from him. I know it now." He had reached up, was pulling the sheet away.

I do not know what I expected to see, but certainly not what actually burst upon my eyes. It stunned me so that my senses swam for a moment. For if the thing was horrible, it was beautiful, too—more beautiful than anything my eyes had ever rested on before!

In the shadows, at the back of the cage, barely touched by the candle's feeble glimmer, was a huge cake of ice. It must have been, roughly, nine feet high and three or four feet wide, but of irregular shape, so that the ragged edges, struck by the light, glistened green and blue like a diamond. And in the center of that cake of ice, locked in a cold and crystal casket, was—a woman!

There are no words to describe the awe, terror and fascination which the sight caused me. I heard Eubanks cry out sharply, but it scarcely registered on my consciousness. She was beautiful beyond words—a vision, a dream. The cold fire of a northern sun was in the honey-colored hair that fell over her white shoulders. Her lithe, tall body—the skin like some pale snow-flower—stood there as if in life, with one knee thrust forward from beneath a skirt of iridescent sea shells. Her hands drooped nonchalantly like white lilies; she almost seemed to be walking, walking toward us out of that ice, and her clear blue eyes were open, staring, as if she had just awakened from the dreams of a thousand Arctic winters.

It was Holmquist's voice which brought me out of a wild dream of awe and terror and half-formed, hopeless yearning.

"I found her there," he said in a low tone of reverence, "in a cave of ice, a sort of shrine. The skull was there, too. Where did she come from? For how many ages has she stood in that frozen sepulcher? No man knows. I would say she is the daughter of some Norse chieftain, stolen away by those primordial ice monsters, worshipped by them in that crystal shrine. If that is true," his voice quavered, seemed to echo the hopeless passion that must be in the heart of every man who gazed upon her, "if that is true, she has been there for centuries. Think of that!"

Eubanks was clutching the bars of the cage with convulsed fingers. Now he jerked away, stared at us with vacant eyes that still held the marvel of that dream in ice. "God!" he said weakly. "I fancied for a moment she was alive! Isn't it faintly possible, Holmquist, isn't there a remote chance that she might be, well, revived? I've heard. . . ."

Holmquist cut him short. "Would you risk seeing that beauty crumble to corruption?" he asked. Then he sighed "It doesn't matter, anyhow, Julian. She's going back, back to the shrine where I found her. She has her guardian, never fear." He frowned into the surrounding dark. "What I can't understand is why he has permitted you to see her. I rather expected. . . ."

The rest was never said. For at that moment the sharp report of a rifle volleyed down from the silent house above us. Crack, crack, crack! Three times. Then a shrill scream, a woman's scream, squeezed from fainting lungs by mortal terror: "Julian! Julian! Help! It's got me—it's. . . ."

The cry trailed off into silence—horrible, empty, maddening. . . .

CHAPTER THREE

Monstrous Carnage

JULIAN EUBANKS sprang past me, almost knocking the candle from my hand. I followed close behind him. We left the Colonel in the dank cellar in our mad race up the dark stairs. Eubanks reached the living room first. I heard his wild cry of alarm:

"Myra, Myra! For God's sake, answer, Myra!"

He had spun about, was facing the door as I entered. Except for him, there was no one else in the room! The gun was on the floor near the couch upon which the woman had lain. Nothing else in the room had been disturbed.

"She's gone," Eubanks kept repeating, "she's gone!" There was a look of numbed idiocy in his eyes, as if he couldn't quite understand. Then he whirled about, snatched a gun from the rack on the wall. "By God, it's that damned Benedict!" he shrilled. "He hates me. I gave him a black eye in my book, too, the sneaking fiend! He's planned this thing to kill us all, he. . . . By God, if he's touched Myra . . . !"

I caught his arm as he staggered past me, jerked him about. "Steady," I grated, "steady! Keep your head, fellow. Don't rush out that door. If there are any tracks we want to see them."

I stepped ahead of him into the hall, strode to the front door and opened it. A biting blast of wind howled in, driving a swarm of the huge snowflakes in our faces. I pointed to the foot-deep bank of snow that had piled up against the door.

"See," I said, "there are no fresh tracks. That one set—the ones Benedict made when he went out—are almost covered!"

"Myra!" Eubanks howled into the face of the storm. "Myra!"

I shut the door. Turning about, we met Colonel Holmquist coming up from the dark of the back hall. His great, bony figure was slumped, there was an air of sleep-walking about him.

"Mrs. Eubanks has disappeared," I told him.

He looked at me dully. "Ah!" he replied and turned into the fire-lit room.

I followed him. "Ah!" I mimicked. "Is that all you've got to say? Do you realize what's happening—in *your* house?"

He had slumped down in a chair, buried his long face in his hands. "I am an old man," he mumbled. "God, but I'm an old man tonight!"

I left him. Eubanks was already at the back door. But the snow was undisturbed there, too. We searched every room, looked under every window. There were no tracks. I dragged Eubanks back into the library and forced a drink into him. It brought some color back into his face. He still had the gun gripped in his white-knuckled hands.

"Is this loaded?" he asked Holmquist.

Holmquist looked up. "Yes," he said, "but it will do no good, Julian. No good at all. I told you not to leave her. . . ."

Eubanks started for the door.

"Where are you going?" I asked.

"I'm going to find her!" he blurted. His teeth were chattering. He had the look of a stunned, terrified child. "I'm going to find her—and Benedict!"

"I'll go with you," I said. I knew it wouldn't take long to get lost in that blinding snow. I slipped on a coat, took a thirty-thirty rifle from the rack and carefully examined it. Then we left the Colonel slumpd helplessly in his chair. I looked back just as we passed through the door. I wanted to see if he had moved, if he perhaps might be acting a part. But his crumpled figure did not stir. I followed Eubanks to the door.

THE night was like a tangle of grey veils about us. The wind came through the pines with an eerie whistle, driving the huge snowflakes like blind, mad creatures in a demented ghost dance. The fog rolled and billowed and trailed past us—a host of incorporeal phantoms, wind driven and tormented. The cold, unearthly light which came from no visible moon or star was like a phosphorous emanation rising from the dead corpse of the world itself. And it was cold, bitterly cold. Our boots crunched in the snow with a gritty sound.

For a few yards we followed Benedict's tracks. Then, as the glow from the lighted windows faded, the half-filled pits in the deep snow were no longer visible. Eubanks paused, and his head jerked nervously from side to side like, like a blind man.

"Hear something?" he asked. "Footsteps, heavy, slow?"

"Damn you!" I grated, "go on! The cabin—Benedict's there." My own nerves were in no condition to tolerate the man's uncertain terror. For something more cold and terrible than the grip of that icebound darkness—something that clutched at me with every violent throb of my heart—was struggling to beat down my last reserves of courage. I, too, had seen strange shapes, huge, monstrous, moving behind the thin, deceptive film of light. "The fog," I had told myself, and I continued to say it over and over under my breath.

A splinter of light floated in the waves of churned mist ahead—a gleam from beneath a curtained window. We steered toward it. The black bulk of the cabin loomed out of the swirling greyness. I pushed ahead to the door, knocked.

At first, I heard nothing but the wind's *swish* in my ears. Then a feeble moan, low but distinct, filtered through the closed door. Eubanks heard it, too; something like the whimper of a frightened dog escaped his lips.

I grasped the doorknob and pushed. The door came open a few inches. Warm air and the light from a glowing bed of coals in a fireplace played over my face. I shoved again. There was a sharp moan from the floor. I pushed gently then, and edged my body in.

A man's head had blocked the door. He lay face down, a tall, raw-boned figure, and the position of his body seemed to indicate that he had been trying to reach the door when he fell. Then I saw the pool of blood in which his face lay.

Eubanks had edged in and stood shivering behind me. "Give a hand," I snapped, "let's get him to the bed."

We lifted him with difficulty, laid him on the bed at one end of the room. His eyes, closed at first, had opened now, and he stared at us stupidly. He had a lean, leathery face; a short, grizzled, grey beard, now stained and clotted with blood. A thin stream was flowing again, trickling from the corner of his mouth. The wound seemed to have been made by a bullet.

I got a pan of water and bathed his face with my handkerchief. He started to speak two or three times, but the blood seemed to choke him. I thought he was dying. Then I saw that the bullet had simply torn through the corner of his mouth and shattered a couple of teeth.

"You're Hidge?" I asked.

He nodded.

"How'd it happen?"

The man's torn mouth quivered; he cleared his throat; blood ran down over his chin. "I don't know," he answered haltingly. "Somebody knocked. I went to the door . . . nobody was there. Then I saw it—God. . . ! Enormous, grey, shaggy. . . !" He spread his arms wide; his eyes were big with fear. "It was off in the fog a ways. I started to turn back. The bullet struck me . . . I fell, must have fainted. . . . Later I crawled to the door, closed it. . . ."

"Then——" Julian Eubanks stammered, "then you didn't see Benedict? A man didn't come?"

"Who! Benedict? Don't know him. I didn't see any *man!*"

EUBANKS' hand gripped my arm. "You see; you see?" he shrilled. "It's Benedict! God! And he's got Myra!" He flung to the door, opened it and began to yell her name into the foggy darkness. The vaporous maze swallowed his voice, the hissing wind mimicked him.

"I'll kill him!" he shrieked. Then he was out the door, plunging into the fog like a swimmer into the surf.

I sprang out after him, calling over my shoulder to Hidge that I would be back. Eubanks was floundering about like a madman, cursing and brandishing the gun as he ran. "Stop, you damned fool!" I yelled.

He stumbled then, and it was a good thing. He had been heading toward the woods with no more sense of direction than an inanimate mechanical toy. He would have died there in that fog-choked maze. I plowed through the snow to his side, grabbed his arm as he staggered up.

"Pull yourself together, Eubanks," I snarled. "We've got a fighting chance to live through this night—but no more than that. If Benedict is at the bottom of all this, as you say, the most obvious conclusion is that he won't stop until we're all dead. There are three of us left now. Together we can beat his game with a little luck. But if you're going to run amok like an idiot. . . ."

He nodded, seemed to get a grip on himself, and followed me back to the house. We found Colonel Holmquist just where we had left him. When I told him about Hidge, his eyes narrowed. "And Benedict?" he asked.

"Benedict had not been there," I said.

"Ah," he mused, and this time the syllable had a quite definite meaning. "If I could believe . . . !"

"Believe what?"

"That some human agency is behind this." There was a flicker of hope in his face; the old adventurer seemed to be emerging once more from the wreck. I knew now that he was not afraid of flesh and blood; but that the terror of unknown powers had sapped his courage. He got up now. "And what do you suggest?"

"We'd better make a thorough search at once," I said. "Whether Benedict's at the bottom of it or not, somebody or something has been in this house and has carried Mrs. Eubanks off. There are no tracks at any of the entrances. That indicates that there is some secret entrance to the house—some tunnel, or something of the sort. There's no other way to explain where the monster goes. How about it, Colonel?"

It seemed as if his steel-grey eyes had been veiled for an instant. Something of that impression lingered in his voice when he said: "There's nothing below but the two rooms I showed you. I don't see where. . . ."

"But you've only been here a couple of months," I pointed out. "There may be a lot you haven't found out. You rented from an agency; I suppose you don't even know who owns the place. For all you know, Benedict may own it."

"But really, Gage!"

"Sure it's far-fetched!" I broke in impatiently. "But what the hell? The whole mess is far-fetched, isn't it?"

"Yes, and we're going to search, too," Eubanks broke in belligerently, "whether you like it or not! We'll tear the damned house down."

"Just as you please, Julian," Holmquist replied dryly. "Perhaps we won't have to tear the house down, though. Where shall we start?"

"In the basement," I said. "We've searched the upper part of the house pretty thoroughly before."

WE ALL three carried guns this time, and a lantern, instead of a candle, lighted us down the dark stairs. Eubanks had stepped out ahead; I followed with the lantern, and the Colonel trailed in the rear. We held our guns ready, like hunters.

Before we were half-way down the stairs it seemed to me that I could smell the bloody reek of that closed room, and another smell, too—a faint, musky odor that made my flesh creep. But it was a comfort to remember that Hidge's wound had been made by a bullet. To fight against something tangible, even if it happens to be a homicidal maniac armed with a high-powered rifle—and God knows what other strange and formidable weapon—is bad enough; but to fight against something unseen and monstrous like the half-mythical demon of Holmquist's haunted brain is infinitely worse.

The door was locked. I noted that, even in his excitement, the Colonel had not forgotten to lock that door. He pushed it open now, and Eubanks stepped in with his gun half-raised. There was a pause while I swung the lantern forward to light the way. And then Eubanks was stumbling back toward us, a wild cry of horror on his lips.

"What is it?" I jerked out, pushing into the room.

Eubanks staggered against me. His teeth were knocking together like rattled dice. "Look!" he shrilled. "My God! Look! There are two of them now—two heads!"

I saw it then—the other head—and strangling coils of horror knotted about my body. It was more horribly broken than the head of Joe Lechner. It was as if a coconut had been crushed in some giant fist and dropped in a shattered heap. And the rest of the body was the same—not mashed or mangled or cut, but *broken!* It lay in a hundred fragments, grotesquely mingled with its ghastly predecessor—stumps of limbs, ragged-edged chunks of flesh with the blood glowing hard and bright as amethyst in the exposed veins, all cold and hard as if petrified, so hard that when my toe kicked accidentally against a piece, it rolled and rattled like a rock on the concrete floor!

But we knew whose body the ghastly thing had been. As with Lechner's body, there was no scrap of clothing to identify it, but the stiff red hair that bristled weirdly on the chunks that had been a skull, was the hair of Edmund Benedict!

CHAPTER FOUR

Beauty and the Beast!

AFTER that first swift glimpse in which our shocked eyes took in enough of the details to make the grisly horror clear, we drew back and huddled, speechless, in the dark doorway. Not the ghastliness of the sight alone, but also its frightful implications, numbed and froze us. All the neat theories, built up to insulate our minds against the raw hideousness of Holmquist's fantastic explanation, had collapsed. There on the floor lay what had been Edmund Benedict. Then who, *what* . . .?

The picture we must have made there during those awful moments in which our minds plumbed unfathomed depths of terror has often flashed across my memory. You have seen ants pause in their nervous scampering to examine the mangled body of a comrade which some human foot has crushed. We were like that, and the *Thing* which had passed here and left the mark of its violence in this inexplicable carnage was to us, as to the ants, something monstrous beyond comprehension.

Colonel Holmquist spoke first and his words were a dry rattle in our ears. "You see, you see now? We'll all be like that!"

"And my wife?" Julian Eubanks whimpered. "You think . . . ?"

"He'll not kill her," the colonel assured the frantic man.

Eubanks' mouth was twitching; the gun w a v e r e d crazily in his tight-clenched hands. "But I've got to find her, I've got to . . . ?"

"He'll come for the rest of us soon enough," the colonel intoned. "The wise thing would be to wait for him—not to allow him to pick us off one by one. I have a notion he may be afraid of fire. We

might have some chance against him if we stick together and stay close to the fire."

I looked at Eubanks' face. Stark terror had reduced him to an unresisting pulp. He nodded in agreement. I made no objection; there was some sense in what the colonel said.

We lost no time in getting back to the library. We piled the fire high with logs till it roared like the devil's own furnace and smeared the walls of the long room with banners of red light. We made sure that the windows were locked; we barricaded the double doorway that gave on the hall with a waist-high breastworks of furniture. Every gun was taken down from the rack, examined, loaded, and laid ready to hand. Then we divided the night into three watches. I took the first one, while Eubanks and the colonel lay down to rest.

The colonel seemed to sleep, but Eubanks tossed and twitched. I sat in an armchair with a repeating shotgun in my lap and never took my eyes from the shadowy doorway.

During the first hour, the suspense was terrific. With each queer-shaped shadow that leaped or wavered in the hallway, I would sit up with a start and raise my gun expectantly. Waiting like that is a horrible thing; it seems to eat a man's nerves away, cell by cell. I found my eyes avoiding the glass case on the table in which the monstrous skull, splashed grotesquely by the red firelight, grinned and leered suggestively.

But nothing happened. The clock on the wall ticked on; an occasional board creaked somewhere in the dark house; the whistle of the wind came, muted and melancholy, through the sealed windows, the shadows danced their ghostly saraband on the plastered walls, and my thoughts turned with a morbid fascination to the beautiful, dead creature in her casket of ice below the stairs.

I tried not to think of her; I knew that it would not be good for me, but there was no helping it. The golden fire of her hair, the white flame of her beauty still burning with a strange, unnatural fire in that frozen sarcophagus, lured and tempted my brain to mad and impossible imaginings. I remembered the story of the inventor of a powerful lens who had discovered a living women in a drop of water, yet had been forced to see her perish before his eyes. I felt the same agony of futile yearning stir in my heart. "You fool!" I said, "You fool! The thing is a corpse, a dead thing from which the life and soul has flown, perhaps a thousand years ago!" I tried to think of how that body would look if only a little warmth should strike it—a ghastly carrion! But it did no good. Then I began to be afraid of my own thoughts.

I CAME out of a mad whirlpool of dreams with a start. I looked at the clock. It was fifteen after one. I awakened Colonel Holmquist, whose turn it was to take the next watch. He took up his position in the chair and I lay down upon a pallet near the fire.

I couldn't sleep at first. It wasn't the fear of the nameless monster who blasted human bodies as if they were china dolls. That was real enough; but another obsession had engulfed and swallowed it. The woman with the golden fire in her hair, the woman in the ice! There was fear of that too, a curious creeping fear—a hollow, indefinable dread. For she seemed to have taken possession of my mind. Like some poisonous, terrible growth, she had attached herself to my brain, sucking both reason and soul from my body.

When I did fall asleep from sheer exhaustion, it was only to meet her again in dreams—strange and terrible dreams in which beauty and horror, passion and loathing were blended like vivid, unearthly colors.

I dreamed that I heard her calling, heard her voice, plaintive and wild, coming up from the dank, abysmal depths beneath the house. I dreamed that I was creeping out of the room on hands and knees, crawling down the cold hallway, descending the dark steps, feeling the horrid reek of that abattoir rise up about me, feeling the great wings of wintry monsters fan over me in the gloom, yet crawling on and on, through endless vaults of darkness.

That faded and it seemed that I was lying on my pallet, watching the red reflections of the light, and listening in an agony of cold paralysis to footsteps moving in the darkened hall, moving nearer and nearer. And I knew that they were her footsteps, coming up from the gloom below, coming up to me. . . And I wanted her and I did not want her. For she was not a living thing, but something that had been dead for ages!

Then she seemed to be there in the room, standing between me and the barrier at the door. I wanted to scream then but I couldn't. Something choked my throat, and I could only lie paralyzed while my eyes traveled in terror over the whiteness of her body, so real, so indescribably lovely, with the light striking glints from the sea-shell skirt, gleaming on her marble skin, changing the yellow glory of her hair to burnished copper.

But I was afraid, horribly afraid. I wanted to scream: "Go back, go back! I didn't call you!" For I knew that what comes up from the grave is not lovely, not even though it comes in a body like hers! I flung myself away from her then, flung myself toward the hearth, some primordial instinct driving me toward the fire for protection. My hand, thrown back to protect me, struck something wet and sticky there, something that clung to my fingers, something that gleamed crimson as I jerked a shaking hand into the light. I screamed then, for the stuff on my hand was blood. I felt it, saw it, smelt it, and though the white, motionless figure still stood between me and the door, *I knew that I was not dreaming at all!*

She was real, yes, but with the realness of a thing come up from death—a *revenant!* The horrid words shrieked through my brain. Perhaps that shell of beauty from which the soul had fled ages ago now housed the very monster whose ghastly carnage had made this gloomy house a shambles! I snatched up the gun, raised it in frozen, shaking hands . . .

She screamed then, and the sound of her voice pierced me like a dagger of ice. But it sobered me; for there was the warmth of human blood in that cry, and fear in the startled movement with which she shrank back from me. The gun in my hands jerked down; I scrambled to my feet.

"You're alive?" I shrilled, "alive?"

"Heavens, but you frightened me!" Sudden relief had flooded the whiteness of her face with color. She moved toward me now.

"What about me?" I barked. I was still uncertain, still incredulous, still half-inclined to think it was a dream. "What are you, what's the meaning . . . ?" No question I could frame seemed adequate. "You were down there, in the ice?"

SHE was near me now; I reached out a tentative finger, touched her.

She smiled at that, drew near the fire, shuddering. "It's a mess," she said, "a ghastly mess. I'm through with it. Where's Colonel Holmquist?"

For the first time now, I stared about the room. Both Holmquist and Eubanks had vanished. There was only the ugly and significant pool of blood on the pallet. "Maybe you know!" I said. "They were here when I went to sleep. What's this business about anyhow?"

"I'm beginning to wonder myself," she replied. "Colonel Holmquist told me it was all a harmless joke. But now . . ."

"Harmless joke!" I echoed. "Two or three murders a harmless joke?"

"Murders?" Her eyes were wide with amazement and horror. "You don't mean someone's been murdered? Oh, my God! What have I done? Tell me . . .!"

"You do the telling first," I insisted grimly.

"I'll tell you all I know," she gasped. "I'm Ellen Warner, an actress. I was forced to take this job; I was broke and hungry. But Colonel Holmquist said he only wanted to play a little joke on some of his friends. That wasn't really ice, you know, that I was in. It was glass, two blocks of it that fitted together with a space hollowed out to fit my body. I was to slip into that whenever I heard anyone coming. There's a tiny little room behind that cage where I had a fire and where I stayed between the acts of the farce. So help me God, that's all I know!"

"Good God!" I swore. The whole thing had dawned on me. I knew that the thing was no mere joke, but a deliberate, cold-blooded scheme of Holmquist's. It was all clear now. He had brought me into it for the publicity he needed. What a story that would have made—the woman in the ice, the monstrous skull! That damned skull must be nothing but a cunning job in plaster of Paris. If he had succeeded in fooling us, he'd have gotten all the money he needed for his expedition! But . . . ?

It was the rest of it that puzzled me. Why these ghastly murders? What was the motive in killing the rest of them? Perhaps the man was raving mad after all!

"Look here," I said to the girl, "this Holmquist is a fiend—a madman perhaps. Are you sure you're telling me all you know?"

"I swear it," she said, "I . . . !"

The rest of her words were broken off short by my sudden movement. A sound in the hall—a sound of footsteps—had reached my ears. I shoved her aside, darted toward the barricaded door. I stopped there to listen, peering cautiously into the dark. Then I saw him. He was crouching, ape-like, on his haunches in the shadows, and his face, limned faintly by the flicker from the fire, was like nothing human. With glassy eyes and bared teeth, it was the face of a snarling dog—a mad dog!

It was Colonel Holmquist!

Without an instant's hestitation, I raised the gun and fired.

There was a crash that blended with the gun's explosion, and through the clearing cloud of smoke, I saw something which my eyes at first refused to believe, something which set my blood churning in wild convulsions. For the figure of Colonel Holmquist had collapsed, not as a living body falls, but with a crash like the shattering of some huge thing of glass. And there, before my eyes, the head fell from the shoulders and rolled like a croquet ball; the arms snapped off like brittle twigs, and the dismembered corpse fell forward and broke in two as it struck the floor!

I pushed the furniture which barricaded the door aside with a frantic heave, staggered into the hall. The hideous truth had struck my horrified brain like a thunderclap. Holmquist had been already dead when I fired, his body frozen stiff and brittle to the bone.

Almost simultaneous with that discovery, a new terror dawned, a terror which I did not have time to fully digest. A curious shuffling scrape on the floor behind me—a peculiar musky smell—caused me to swing about toward the shadowy depths of the hall. And what I saw there melted the joints of my bones and sent my brain reeling with incredible horror.

The thing was huge, a horrid greyish bulk. Half-veiled by the gloom, it was shuffling toward me, with the swinging, ponderous movements of a gorilla. It seemed to be covered from head to foot in white shaggy fur, to which icicles clung like the spines of cactus; a whitish mist rose from it like steam. Even at a distance I could feel the biting cold which enveloped the thing. But no human face was discernible—only a pair of vicious eyes, blazing with horrid malevolence.

I tried to scream, to warn the girl, but the words froze in my throat. Desperately I dived for the doorway where I had left the gun. But I was too late. Like a swirling column of snow, the grey thing was upon me.

I ducked, but huge, strangling arms swung out, closed around my body with a grip which no amount of struggling could loosen. Choked screams of mad terror and pain gurgled from my throat. My face was being pressed into the hideous, frozen pelt. With my free hand, I pounded frantically against the huge bulk, but the icicles with which the thing was covered cut and bruised my knuckles, and the monstrous body seemed to absorb my blows like rubber. Then something that was like the impact of a racing locomotive struck my skull, and I went down in a burst of crazy fireworks which the inrushing dark swallowed with a roar. . . .

CHAPTER FIVE

Crucible of Doom

I WAS hanging head down by my bound ankles; the knuckles of my half frozen hands touched a cement floor. It was all a surprise to me, to feel anything at all, because it had seemed to me that I was dead and had been dead for a long time. Perhaps it was the cold that did that, for my body was numb with it.

Then I saw the others, and the whole hideous nightmare that was reality came back to me. There was something wrapped in a blanket in one corner of the large, concrete vault. A face peeped out, pale and stiff, seeming dead. It was the face of Myra Eubanks. Her husband's body lay across her feet, as if thrown there carelessly. Blood had oozed from an ugly welt on his head, and lay in a frozen puddle on the floor. But his eyes were open, open and staring in a delirium of terror.

White billows of steam were coming from somewhere in the room. I saw another blanket-covered figure now, a figure which the pale streamers of fog had at first obscured. It was the girl—Ellen Warner—and terror clawed at my numbed body when I saw that her eyelids were closed, that a strange pallor lay over her lovely face. Was she dead? In that awful instant, I forgot the terror of my own predicament. A sort of rage mingled with my fear. I knew then that I loved her, had loved her even when she lay in that sarcophagus of simulated ice. It was as if she had come back from the dead to life, and then been snatched back to make my torment more exquisite.

A harsh laugh that seemed at once human and inhuman broke in on the dismal chaos of my thoughts. Jabbing at the cement floor with one hand, I swung my body about, stared at the weird upside-down scene that met my eyes. A pair of monstrous, shaggy legs stood like hairy pillars a few feet away from me, and a strong odor of musk came from them. Beyond that was the source of the steam clouds. It was a huge tank of some gleaming metal, and its rim stood perhaps two feet above the hole in the floor in which it stood. The fog of mist was rising into the air from its invisible contents.

My eyes fastened on the ponderous legs and rose fearfully upward along the great body. The white ice-covered fur still encased it, and it was plain that heavy padding gave the thing its massive gigantic

appearance, for the shape beneath was human. Fearfully, I lifted my glance to the head, and gasped with sudden amazement. The leering brown face which stared out from beneath the thrown-back hood was the face of the man whose wounded mouth I had washed in the caretaker's cabin. Strips of tape covered the wound now, and the short grey beard was still stained with the blood.

"Hidge!" I gasped.

He stared at me with a horrid, insane grin. "No," he said, "not Hidge—McArtney! I had to kill poor Hidge in order to step into his shoes and plan my little reception for the Colonel. I was all ready for him when he came."

"McArtney!" It was the voice of Julian Eubanks which echoed that revealing word. He had lifted his hand weakly and was staring with groggy eyes at the fur-clad giant. "No! You're not McArtney—you can't be! McArtney was five years younger than I . . ."

"McArtney *was* five years younger than you," the voice of the fiend replied. "But that was before you and the rest of them left me to die upon the ice. Did it ever occur to you that a man may age ten years in a day, and maybe twenty-five in two days? No, it never occurred to you, nor to Holmquist. And naturally you never thought of the remote possibility that I might be rescued. But I have a constitution of iron, and I lived, and was rescued. McArtney is dead, in personality as in appearance; there is left only a machine of venegance!"

"My God!" Eubanks whimpered, "you intend . . . ?"

"I intend," said the madman, "to give you a little taste of real cold. Only I'll be more merciful than you were. It won't take days for you to die—only a few moments. In that time you'll be a solid chunk of brittle ice, and I can break you to pieces with a hammer like I did the others. I especially enjoyed knocking Edmund to pieces. He almost got me with the gun before I grabbed him and shot the hypo in his arm." He gestured toward the steaming tank. "Know what that is, Julian? That's *liquid air,* and it's so cold it will freeze mercury. Nice little bath you'll have tonight, Julian. You won't look pretty either, when you come out. It freezes the death-agony on your face!"

"Oh, my God, McArtney!" Eubanks moaned. "It wasn't my fault." He choked with fear. "But let my wife go and you can do what you please with me."

McARTNEY laughed till the icicles fell from his suit of fur. "Don't worry," he said. "I shan't kill the women—yet. When Holmquist invented his little fable to gull you, I decided to give him a real monster—just the sort of monster he described. His monster, you recall, had a weakness for women. Well, so have I. A man gets that way in the North."

Curses drooled from Eubanks' lips, and he tried to struggle up. But McArtney kicked him back. "Don't be in a hurry, Julian," he said, "I'll put you in the tank soon enough. I'll give you a little demonstration first to make the pleasure of anticipation more complete." He looked at me. "This fellow will make a nice subject!"

"Damn you!" I swore. "What have I ever done to you?"

"You got in my way," he replied. "You don't think I could very well let you go now, do you?"

I saw his point. All arguments, all pleas for mercy, I knew would be futile. I was looking into the grisly face of death, and it was only a few feet away. I'm no coward; I could have faced it, but it was the thought of the girl—the girl I wanted for my own—left in this monster's hands that made my body quiver.

The blood, already heavy in my throbbing head, beat at my ear-drums like pounding hammers. Already McArtney was reaching out with a long pole that had an iron hook on the end. He was reaching toward the chain that bound my ankles. I understood his intention. For the chain was tied to a rope which ran from a pulley set in the ceiling. From there it ran through another pulley and down to the iron anvil which acted as a counter balance. With the hooked pole, he would drag me out and over the steaming tank of liquid air! And he would keep himself well out of the way; I couldn't possibly reach him with my hands.

The hook connected, the pulleys creaked, and the anvil rose into the air as my swinging body was pulled over toward that bath of horror!

"You see," McArtney crackled, "this little contrivance simplifies the thing. When you're frozen stiff, I can just release you and let the weight drag you out again. One man could literally freeze an army this way. I may even use you for target practice. That was neat the way you cracked old Holmquist to pieces after I had set him up there to tempt you."

His gloating words faded out in the swirling tides of horror that seemed to be washing my reason away in their mad currents. The cold mist was billowing about me now, stinging my face, freezing the hot tears that trickled from my eyes. I spun and jerked and writhed, but it was useless. Inexorably, the long, hooked pole was pulling me over the tank of death.

Then I ceased to squirm. I was directly over the vat, looking down into that opaque liquid, blinking against the biting mist. In a few more seconds, it would envelop me in a cold so intense that it would freeze the life from me in an instant. It was all over now, all over . . . .

I lifted my eyes for a last glimpse of Ellen's sweet face. Then I gave a violent start. Her eyes were open; our eyes met and suddenly her body jerked forward. Her hands and ankles were tied, but she was wriggling like a snake across that frozen floor, moving straight toward me.

A bellow of mad laughter came from McArtney's mouth. He knew that it was futile, and he was taking a cruel pleasure in the sport. She would try to grasp my body, and he would pull her with me into the bath of death.

And then she stopped. Instead of coming to the tank's edge, she was rising to her feet. McArtney saw it too late. He was on the other side of the tank. Still holding his end of the pole, he sprang toward her.

But she had already jumped up lithely, a flat-footed jump that carried her tied hands to the anvil swinging from the ceiling. She grasped it, clung, and the weight of her body jerked me back so swiftly that the pole slipped from McArtney's hands.

What occurred next happened more swiftly than it can be described. The released pole, still hooked into the chain at my ankles, swung down toward my face. I grasped it even while I was swinging into the air, and yanked it loose from the fiend's grip. Then, with one wild sweep, I struck McArtney on his fur-clad legs. The blow neither stopped him nor threw him off balance, but the hook caught in the fur suit. I jerked then, jerked with all my strength and a prayer on my lips.

A wild howl of terror burst from the man's lips as he tottered on the brink of the tank, swinging his arms in a frantic effort to regain his balance. But the weight of my pull was too much for him. The air was filled with curses for an instant. Then a great splash threw the churned liquid against walls and ceiling, and McArtney vanished beneath the surface. When his head bobbed up amidst the steam, no cry escaped his lips, for they were frozen, frozen stiff and brittle like the bodies of his victims.

WE were soon out of that frigid place of awful vengeance. Carrying the still unconscious body of Eubanks' wife, who was still under the influence of the hypo McArtney had administered to her, we groped through the gloom of a tunnel and came into the house by a cleverly concealed opening in the wall, beneath the basement stairs. The death-chamber had been beneath the caretaker's lodge.

It was half an hour before Myra Eubanks revived. But by that time, we were sufficiently recovered to start back to town.

Perhaps you'll wonder about Ellen and me. Well, it could end only one way. We're to be married next month. We're going to spend our honeymoon in the South Seas. We want plenty of tropical sunlight to wipe the memory of that night of cold terror from our minds forever.

THE END

THEY DID NOT NEED A HELL!

By
Robert
Newman

From the Infinite Sink beneath that mouldering, fog-bound graveyard—through the weird evil of the Anti-Christ's black magic—the Presence transported itself to that lonely cabin on the hill—and there, in thralidom to the Unknown, Charles Colton and his beloved Tessa faced the ghastliness of a thing undead!

CHARLES COLTON pulled the door shut behind him, turned, and walked down the steps to the road. The wind wailed loudly. and he buttoned his coat high around his neck. A sudden shudder ran up his spine. It wasn't the wind alone, dank and cold as it was, that caused the shudder. It was the eerie scene below him.

The fog had covered the whole Connecticut Valley. Now it crept slowly up the hill like some grey monster, some amorphous, evil entity surrounding him as an amoeba does its food. The graveyard, just below the top of the hill on which the house stood, was almost covered by the tenuously thick mist. Most horribly covered, too, because this was the time when the graves were drowned by a few inches of fog and the white tombstones thrust up through it like imploring hands, hands whose bodies were already becoming one with the foul and mouldering stuff underneath. . . .

He shook his head savagely. He must learn to control that unbridled imagination of his! It made for great writing but . . . it also made for madness!

He started down the road into town. It was three quarters of an hour's walk to Silverside Tavern. There would be a fire there, people, drinks. He had no right to go, really. He had no right to spend a cent on anything that wasn't absolutely necessary. Tessa was in New York now, trying to beg or borrow a few more dollars to keep them going through the winter, to keep them from starving until he could finish his book. And here he was going into town to spend some of the little money they had left—going there because . . . because . . . well, say it . . . because he was afraid! Afraid to be alone! Afraid to spend an evening by himself in that ramshackle house on top of the hill when the fog was creeping up!

Damn that night when he had stood at the window and tried to analyze his fear of the fog. He had figured that it wasn't the fog itself he was afraid of, but the feeling that it was a shadow or the symbol of a shadow! A shadow cast by something so horrible that he couldn't force his mind to think what it was, a Thing, which had crept up the hill before just as it was creeping up now, surrounding him as the fog surrounded him . . .

That analysis had been more frightening than the formless fears he had known previously. He had laughed at his own fears before, but he did not feel like laughing now. He felt like . . . screaming! Yes, like running, screaming through the fog until he saw lights and knew he was safe. He felt so much like doing that, that he gritted his teeth and actually forced himself to walk, slowly.

He was passing the graveyard now. The fog was knee-high. He was walking into it, deeper and deeper, like a man following a will o' the wisp and sinking, always farther, into the black, clinging, stinking mud of a bog.

What did men see then, before they slipped into oblivion? Some evilly beautiful woman who danced towards them, naked, bathed in a cold blue light? Or did horror come swiftly, a black, clammy shape, perhaps—*like that shape before him . . .!*

Good God! That shape, which he had taken for a rock . . . something seemed to move, to writhe!

He stopped. His heart seemed to be pumping icy blood through his veins. His hair stood erect like a terrified dog's. Then . . . he heard a low moan! The fog was shoulder high, just his head above it, and there, somewhere below him . . . yes, something *was* moving, slithering snake-like, and . . . there was another low moan!

Was it *human?* He lived alone with his wife on the top of the hill. No one came up its barren side except visitors to the graveyard . . . or . . . visitors *from* the graveyard!

A WAVE of fog lapped over his head and he was submerged in a dead, grey world. Again came a rustling, dragging sound from below him, and another low moan. He clenched his teeth and, summoning up all his will power, moved forward.

Through the grey mist he saw a figure crawling painfully on the road, crawling, sinking in exhaustion, crawling again. It was an old man.

Colton knelt swiftly at his side. The old man was hatless, coatless. His cheap dark clothes were damp with the fog.

"What . . . what's the matter? Are . . . are you ill?" Colton asked. His voice was unsteady.

The old man's eyes focused on his face. He half nodded, his eyes searching, questioning. He tried to say something, then his head fell forward on his breast.

With an exclamation of pity, Colton seized him by the arm, to pick him up. He started. There were thongs bound around the old man's arm! Thongs and a small box! Was this why . . . ?

Some ingenious, horrible torture . . . ? Some barbaric, unholy rite . . . ? Thongs bound tightly around an old man's arm . . . ?

Then he remembered. After all, he had spent some years under Von Scharr studying Oriental Civilization. He should remember. This was the *tefilah shel yad*, the tefilah of the hand. The old man was a Jew, an Orthodox Jew, and for the evening prayer he had to bind this thong around his arm.

Colton started again to pick up the old man. But there was a convulsive movement in the aged body. The eyes opened again.

"Wait . . ." The old Jew's voice was weak, cracked but urgent. "Only . . . a few minutes more . . . promise me . . . one thing. I come . . . of a long, noble line . . . dying . . . see that I get . . . honorable burial . . . promise! . . . promise!" The weak eyes blazed with his intensity.

"I . . . I promise," Colton said.

Where he was to get the money for a funeral he did not know, but he had promised. The old man half nodded, then his eyes narrowed. He searched Charles' face. "I . . . I have no money," he said. "But perhaps . . . here at my breast . . . worth more than gold . . ." His hand fluttered up weakly.

Charles opened the man's torn coat and saw that there was a bulky pouch tied around his neck. The old man nodded, and he opened the pouch, took out an old parchment scroll. He held it up before the old man's eyes.

And then fear welled up in those eyes as blood wells up in a sudden wound— fear filled that old body with a last surge of strength, so that he staggered to his feet and snatched the parchment from Colton's hand.

"No, no!" he shouted. "I dare not! You do not know . . . it will bring . . . even I . . . destroy . . ." He started to reel off into the fog, toward the graveyard wall. He had taken but a few steps when he groaned, stumbled, and fell flat on his face.

Charles ran forward. He could see in an instant that the man was dead. He picked up the parchment, thrust it into his pocket, then bent and picked up the old man, who, thin and emaciated, weighed no more than a child.

Colton turned with his burden, hurried back to the house. He opened the door, carried the corpse into the one big room. A fire still burned in the fireplace. He laid the old man on the couch. That look of terror was still on the dead face and it found an answer in Charles. He shuddered. He tried to close the old man's eyes. They would not close. He must forget . . . somehow. He must forget the fog creeping up to surround the house and the body of the mysterious old Jew that had come out of the fog to die!

Well, he had wanted company, now he

had it. He tried to laugh but no sound came from between his lips. He tore his eyes away from the cold, waxen face and looked at the parchment on the desk. The old man had offered it to him first, then had died trying to get it away from him, to destroy it. What was it?

HE WENT over to the desk and unrolled it carefully. The parchment was yellow, cracking. It was very old. He spread it out and examined it. It was covered with queer black, faded characters, Hebrew characters. He . . . yes, he could read it! He had to go slowly, laboriously, but he could read it.

They had laughed at him at college. "Study Hebrew? I though you wanted to be a writer. Are you going to write in Hebrew? Wasting your time studying with that old crackpot Von Scharr . . ." He was glad now. He had always been glad that he had gotten to know Von Scharr well, that erratic old genius. He knew more about Orientology, more about Occultism . . . Colton shook his head to pull himself back to the task before him.

Then he sat up in amazement. This was the Kabbala, but a form of the Kabbala he had never seen nor heard of before.

It had always intrigued him, that old mystical science of numbers, letters and their powers. All Occultism made use of it as in the Key of Solomon and the Black Grimoire. But this parchment was more than a study on the Kabbala. It was *the* Key, the Key to the Future, the Key to Knowledge. It told how a question could be written, how the letters which made up the words could be changed into numbers, how the numbers could be manipulated and then changed back into letters . . . and the letters would spell out the answer to the question!

His heart clenched like an icy fist!

Alone in this deserted house on top of the hill, the fog surrounding him, menacing his sanity, a strange dead man behind him and . . . a parchment that purported to draw back the Forbidden Veil!

If only someone, anyone, would come! Someone he could talk to, tell of his fears. Someone who would laugh at the parchment as a piece of medieval nonsense, would explain why the old Jew should have come here to him, certainly the only man for miles around who knew anything about the Kabbala—and tonight of all nights when he was alone and the fog he feared was about him! If only someone . . . !

He laughed suddenly, a sharp, bitter laugh. Then, taking a pen and paper, he wrote, "Will anyone come here tonight?" Referring constantly to the parchment he changed the letters of the question to numbers, manipulated the numbers in the way specified in the parchment, changed the numbers back into letters. And then . . . his hands gripped the table in mortal terror! He had written "Tessa, Von Scharr and Someone Else will come!"

Yes, he had written that, even to the capital letters of the 'Someone Else'! The letters, out of billions of possible combinations, had actually formed a coherent sentence. And such a sentence! It . . . it was impossible, of course. Absolutely impossible! Tessa was in New York. She couldn't possibly be back tonight! And Von Scharr! He hadn't seen Von Scharr in seven years. He hadn't corresponded with him. He didn't even know if he was still at the University. Then, too, that 'Someone Else' . . . what could that mean? . . .

At that moment he heard the door of the house, the door behind him, being slowly opened!

He could not scream. His throat was dry, choked. He sat there and a cold wind whistled through the open door, rustling the parchment on the desk. The door had opened . . . Someone . . . Something . . . was standing there. But he dared not even turn around!

The door closed with a crash. The noise seemed to release him. He whirled around and there, smiling at him, stood his wife!

"Tessa!" he shouted. "Tessa! You! You're back! You're home! I didn't expect you until tomorrow night. But thank God!"

He rushed to her, folded her in his arms. Suddenly he felt her stiffen. She pushed him away.

"Charles!" she gasped, her face white with terror. "Who . . . what is that?"

He whirled around. She was staring at the old Jew on the couch.

"He . . . he died on the road," he answered. "I brought him in here."

QUICKLY he told her all that had happened. The fear did not leave her eyes. In fact it deepened.

"Charles," she said. "I'm frightened! That body there . . . I couldn't spend the night here . . . with—with that! And the parchment. There's something evil about it! There's something evil about the whole house tonight. Didn't . . . didn't you once tell me that the Kabbala was used in Black Magic?"

"Why, yes, Tessa, it is used for that."

In a voice he knew to be strange, she said to him: "All day something has been bothering me, Charles, paining me like a steel chain around my heart, dragging me back here as if I were being drawn back to some unholy ceremony. I couldn't get any money in New York. Your publishers won't advance any more until they see the rest of the book. I was going to sleep overnight at Charlotte's and try again tomorrow when . . . suddenly I found myself on the train coming back here! Oh, Charles, Charles, let's leave

here now, this minute, and go back to New York. I couldn't . . . couldn't stand staying here!"

Colton looked at her, and his heart sank like a lead weight. He had hoped, prayed that someone would come and keep him company tonight, and she, his wife, had come. But instead of comfort, her presence now only gave him additional fears. "Tessa, Von Scharr and Someone Else," had said the writing. Who——

Three slow knocks sounded on the door!

Colton saw his wife staring at him, and their unspoken fear together was like some foul vampire draining the blood and strength from their bodies. What did Tessa fear? Colton was beginning to understand what. That parchment . . . unholy, forbidden knowledge . . . Faustus and his pact with the Devil . . . a phrase of Von Scharr's used in connection with the Jewish religion blazed across his mind. "They did not need a Heaven nor a Hell. They knew that payment for everything was exacted here, on earth!"

Payment! He had asked a question! He had wished!

The door opened. Neither Tessa nor Colton could move. They were facing the door but they were powerless to move.

A tall, dark figure stepped into the room. Above the somber, muffling overcoat was a lean, saturnine face.

"Von Scharr!" Colton gasped. "My God, Professor Von Scharr!"

"Charles Colton!" said Von Scharr, his eyes dilating.

"But, Professor, how did you find us? Why did you come here to see us?"

"I didn't," Von Scharr said slowly, in clipped, foreign accents, "come here to see you. I had no idea you lived near here. I had been working very hard, then

I became tired, could no longer think. My assistant, he is always bothering me. 'Professor, stop this line of research.' 'Professor, forget your work and rest a while, you'll have a nervous breakdown.' Bah, the foolish puppy! I cannot go to sleep yet, I cannot listen to his foolish gabble any longer. I jump in my car and I drive, back roads, any roads that appear, then suddenly, *pfft*, my car stops on a hill. No more gasoline. I see lights. I go towards them and behold, it is your house!"

"Then you didn't start out to come here?"

"Did I not just tell you? I went for a drive to clear my brain . . . Ah, Charles, I am close now, very close. You know my theories of the Occult, its sources, its functions, its influences on man. I have been discovering things, Charles, in the seven years since I've seen you. Strange, wonderful things! But . . . something is still missing, something I cannot find out. It is the one thing I must know to complete my work and it is driving me mad! If I could . . . yes, I would give my soul to know it!" As he paused, his eyes gleaming wildly.

Then he pulled himself together and laughed a deep, booming laugh. "But you two, you look so pale. Look! It is me, Von Scharr, not a ghost!" He took off his hat and coat and was putting them down when he caught sight of the body on the couch.

"My God!" he said. "What is that?"

Colton looked at Tessa. Then he said. "Sit down, Professor, and I'll tell you."

FOR the second time that night he told the story of the old Jew and the Kabbala. When he had finished Von Scharr got to his feet, walked over to the parchment and examined it.

"It is very, very old," he said. "And it it authentic. I have never seen one like it before. It is priceless, Charles, priceless! Almost any library in the world would give a small fortune for it. I myself . . ." He stopped, breathing heavily.

"You, what, Professor?" Colton asked.

"I am mad, of course," said Von Scharr slowly. "I said before I would give my soul to know one thing for my 'Studies in the Occult.' Well, why not go to the Occult for what I want to know? In the darkness you will find darkness, and in the second darkness, perhaps, light! So, Charles, I would give all the money I have in the world just to use this parchment once, to ask it one question!"

"But, Professor, you don't really believe . . ."

"My boy, I have lived too long to believe or disbelieve anything!"

"Then, Professor, if you want to, use the parchment! Not only that, but if you want to buy it for the college library . . ."

Von Scharr's face lit up. He ignored the latter part of the sentence. "I can try it?" he asked. "Oh, thank you, Charles, thank you!"

He sat down eagerly at the desk, the parchment and a pen and paper before him, wild hope in his eyes. Colton took Tessa to the window and watched the fog. A grey tentacle climbed slowly up the window pane as if to grasp at them. Tessa shuddered and Colton did not have to ask why. He tried to comfort her.

"Aren't you glad we stayed, dear?" he asked. "Von Scharr says that the parchment is worth a great deal. We'll sell it and the money will keep us going until my book is finished and then . . ."

Then the most piercing shriek he had ever heard rang out in that room!

They whirled together. Von Scharr was sitting at the desk staring at the piece of paper in front of him. His face was white, bone white, skeleton white. His eyes, black rimmed, were sunk in his head. Saliva dripped from his mouth and he was stiff as stone with a horror that was more than human reason could bear!

"Professor!" shouted Charles. "My God! What is it?"

The professor did not answer. He did not turn around. Slowly, slowly, he pushed back his chair, picked up the paper he had been writing on, and with the mechanical steps of an automaton, walked to the fire. Charles and Tessa watched, fascinated, hypnotized. He sank to his knees and thrust the paper *and both hands into the heart of the fire!*

Horror-struck, neither of the watchers could move. The paper vanished in a puff of smoke. The flames licked Von Scharr's hands like eager dogs. The hair disappeared, the skin cracked, peeled, burned like a hundred small torches. The sickening stench of burning flesh filled the room. Von Scharr bent lower and taking up handfuls of glowing coals, washed his hands with them as though they were water! The flesh was hanging in shreds from his hands, the white bones showing through!

COLTON, with a shrill scream, broke the chain of horror which held him rooted to the spot. Leaping forward, he seized the professor by the shoulder, pulled him away from the fire. The action left Von Scharr on his back, and on his back he lay, smiling, with the smile of a madman.

Slowly, delicately, he raised those blackened stumps, those scorched bones which had been hands. The blood still boiled and steamed as it dripped from the charred flesh. And slowly, carefully, he raised those stumps to his face and started to rub them over his cheeks and eyes!

Colton wrenched the madman by the shoulder, his own stomach retching from the odor which arose straight to his nostrils.

"My God, Professor, what is it?"

Von Scharr twisted out of Charles' hands, leaped to his feet. His mouth was open, his tongue lolled out crazily. He pointed a disgusting semblance of a forefinger at the scroll on the desk. Then, with a hoarse scream, he rushed to the door, opened it and, still screaming, ran out into the night!

Colton leaped for the door. "Quick, Tessa! We must catch him!" He flung open the door and dashed out, Tessa only a few paces behind him.

Fifty feet ahead they saw Von Scharr. He was a darker wraith against the dark curtain of the fog, and he was standing on what seemed to be a rise.

"Tessa! The cliff! He's on the edge of the cliff!" Colton gasped the words frightenedly. And then: "Professor! Wait! Wait! Don't move!"

He rushed forward again. Von Scharr, his hands raised imploringly, seemed to be mumbling a prayer. They heard the words ". . . forgive . . . pay. . ."
They were not ten feet from him when he jumped.

Where the professor had been not a moment before, Colton and his wife stopped. The cliff dropped sheer at their feet. And some two hundred feet below lay Von Scharr's body, broken and shapeless. They could not see it but they knew what it must be like . . .

Shaken, sick, they looked at one another.

"There's nothing that we can do," Colton said. "Simply nothing!" As if they were being sucked into the heart of some vast maelstrom, as if they had to seek out the very heart of the horror which now filled them both, they went back to the house.

The body of the old Jew was still on the couch. The fire was lower, the light dim. Tessa spoke the first words she had uttered since Von Scharr's scream.

"Charles," she said. "In God's name, what was on that paper?"

He turned his white face towards her. "I don't know. But it was something so awful, so terrible, that it drove the most intelligent man I've ever known to madness . . . to madness and death!"

"Charles . . . Before he jumped he said something about paying. Paying for using the parchment! Charles, you used the parchment too!"

The wind whispered outside the house like a soft voice from Hell. It whispered things no man had ever dared to dream of before.

"What does it mean? Who must be paid . . . and how?"

"I don't know," said Colton. He spoke quietly, but in his eyes too, at last, lay a gleam of madness. "I don't know but I shall find out," he went on. "As Von Scharr found out!"

He walked toward the desk.

"No, Charles, no!" She screamed it. "Not that way! Please, please, don't touch it! It's evil, it's horrible! That's what dragged me back here from New York . . . and . . . and Von Scharr, too. How do you know what else it will drag here from . . ."

She stopped, too frightened to go on. But her eyes glared wildly and she was facing in the direction of the graveyard.

"Who else will it drag here? The first answer I got this evening said 'and Someone Else'." Colton paused. For, oddly, queerly and as if far, far away, he seemed to hear a voice crying, "Von Scharr! Von Scharr!"

He looked at Tessa. "But, come what may, I must know! I must know!" Gritting his teeth, his lips white, he sat down at the desk and started to write.

TESSA stood at his shoulder. Once she turned and looked behind her.

The long room was dark. Shadows leaped and twisted in the corners like witches dancing the Sabbath. The door at the end of the room rattled and then was still as if Something were trying to get in. Shuddering, she looked down at the paper. Charles had written, "Who must be paid . . . and how?"

The wind died down. A deadly silence held the house in a weird grip. Tessa Colton could hear her heart beating even as she heard the wind whistling in her husband's nostrils. His face was white, his hands trembled while he worked, changing the letters to numbers. . . "Who must be paid . . . and how?" The words were running through her brain . . . and again, seemingly a little closer, there seemed to be a voice crying "Von Scharr! Von Scharr!" . . . Colton manipulated the numbers and she watched, fascinated.

Then he started to change the numbers back into letters. He was panting like a runner after a hard race, cold sweat dripped unheeded from his brow. . . "Who must be paid . . . and how?" "Who must be paid. . ." His stiff fingers spelled out the answer.

"Turn around and you will see!"

Silence! Dead, empty silence! While they stared at the paper and knew! Knew why Von Scharr had gone mad, knew what the wind had been whispering, knew that . . . Something . . . was standing there behind them in the darkness and silence of that room!

For a moment, rigid, frozen, they stared at that awful sentence. Then, slowly, slowly, they started to turn their heads.

Every muscle, every nerve, every fibre of their bodies was protesting, fighting to keep them looking straight ahead. But Something was stronger than they were, Something was pulling them around, around, further, further. . .

Tessa whimpered deep in her throat and Colton, cursing softly, knew his curses were really prayers... Now they could see the wall to their right, and, on the wall, their shadows. They turned farther, farther.... Then they saw ....

It was not a shadow. A shadow is the absence of light. This was the opposite of Light. The shadows looked pale and grey in comparison with it. If the fog had become inky, the quintessence of night but magnified ten million times, then it would have been—perhaps—something like this!

And alive! Fog was inanimate; this moved with a will and a life of its own. Slowly, like a stain of black, clotted blood, it crept over the wall, closer to their shadows, closer, closer ... It threw out tentacles, then advanced until it had re-absorbed those tentacles, then threw out other tentacles... Now it was just above the couch. Five feet more and it would reach their shadows. Four and a half, four feet ...

Nothing!... Nothing could save them!

Then Charles Colton did the bravest thing any man has ever done! Wrenching his eyes from the wall, he turned them back to the desk.

"No one," he gritted through clenched teeth, "shall ever again . . ." and seizing the parchment he threw it to his right, into the fire. It crackled for a moment with the heat, then burst into white leaping flame.

Colton heard Tessa gasp, and his eyes swung back to where hers were still riveted on the wall.

The burning parchment threw a shadow on the wall, the shadow of the andirons. The shadow fell between their shadows and that ... stain ... which was still creeping toward them, slowly, inexorably. The shadow of the andiron fell on the wall ... and it fell in the form of the Cross!

The Cross grew sharper, more distinct. The advancing, engulfing shadow seemed to have stopped its forward movement. It no longer spread. . . It was retreating! More and more quickly, it shrank back, back farther and farther until it was out of sight, until the wall was white and clean again!

They were both panting now, panting as if they had been holding their breaths for moments on end. Then, together, they swung around and looked behind them ... and there in the semi-darkness was a figure, the figure of a man!

"Von Scharr!" the figure gasped. "An elderly man . . . I'm looking for him . . . I'm his assistant . . . found his car down the road . . . he's gone . . . must find him . . . shouldn't be out . . . his mind . . . too much work. . ." He paused.

Colton looked at him steadily.

"Go down the road about a half a mile," he said. "You will be at the base of a cliff then, and you will find Von Scharr's body there."

He took Tessa's hand in his. "And it is by God's Will alone that there is only one body there!"

BLOSSOMS
OF DOOM

TERROR gripped me after my father had been buried. I had promised him never to leave the Eden in Bermuda he had created for my mother, the first Mary Lynn.

And, now that I was alone, the place was ghastly. While Jon Lynn lived, I, his daughter, had loved it as he did. But had I foreseen the ghastly loneliness, I would never have promised, even on his death-

bed. Yet I had promised, and I knew that he would, if living, hold me to that promise.

Could he still do so, after death?

How could I know? He had been a strange, fierce man, with hidden reserves of weird power. Something inside him had made him internationally famous as a painter, though he had never been satisfied with his work. After mother's death, he

Had Jon Lynn really come back, or did some deeper evil lurk there, investing all that creeping, crawling vegetation with a strange and horrible animation which—for Mary and her lover—meant a ghastly, terror-haunted death . . . ?

By Arthur J. Burks

(Author of "Eater of Souls," etc.)

had been strange, terrifying to everyone but me.

Great God, what had I promised? To live here, never to marry, never to have a sweetheart or children, merely because my father had willed it? Already, five days after his death, I felt his fierce will reaching back to me from the grave.

I feared it the more because already, in a way, I had broken my promise. Clel Urban, whom I had met—and secretly loved—in school in the States, had cabled condolences. I had never hoped that he would love me. He was destined, I knew, for the same fame my father had fought for all his life. Clel would be a great man. And I wanted him! Wanted, while from beyond the grave my father was already warning me, somehow, that to break my promise would mean bringing unnamable horror down about my head.

I had answered Clel. And he had mailed me his picture, suggested visiting me immediately. Now I had to make a decision, and my body seemed bathed in the ice of fear as I foresaw what it would be.

On this morning of which I write, I left the picture of Clel Urban there on my dresser where he could laugh in silence in the room which was mine, and went out of that vast house which echoed only to the footfalls of servants. I went out through the break in the high hibiscus hedge, away from the road where the carriages passed to and fro, down the twisting path to the murmuring stream my father had turned into a thing of beauty. There, I began walking through the scattered forest of red cedars.

How mighty those cedars! So strong were they, that I had not even bidden Salvatore, my gardener, to cut away the strangler vines which encircled two of them. I knew these cedars to be too strong to be bothered by mere vines.

As I walked, peace came upon me.

How to find words to express that peace? There were the nodding morning-glories, light blue, like my eyes. In little clearings among the cedars the sun came through with its golden caress, to nestle like brilliant invisible birds in my hair. I felt the lips of the warm soil kissing my feet. I kicked off my shoes to receive the kisses, and they tingled upward to my heart.

The morning-glories whispered: "You are one with us, Mary Lynn!"

The words were so easy to understand that I answered: "Yes, I am one with you."

The oleanders said: "We are your cheeks, Mary Lynn!"

I nodded, looking upon all the oleanders as they stretched away, and it seemed to me that all of them were part of me, each part flying away to some part of my father's Eden, so that I might, while standing very still, be everywhere at once in this Elysium.

THERE are no words to describe love like that. It was love that fairly welled up within me. From within and without it came. The flowers bent to kiss my ankles. I felt their love as part of mine. Even the strangler vine would not have strangled, and I allowed its many arms to encircle my waist which hungered for caresses.

This was the abode of love, and all of it was mine.

And it went back in Time, beyond all time, to the countless eons of Yesterday, when the first polypi, deep under ancient oceans, had begun to build this Eden. They had gathered together as by some great urge, to die on an ocean floor, to make that floor rise a little. Years had passed, millions upon millions of years; and the polypi had lived and died—and Bermuda had thrust its head out of the sea as, somewhere back in time, my ancestors also must have thrust their forms up out of the sea.

The dead polypi were the foundation of the soil which was my father's Eden.

And the spirits of the little mites, in all the myriads of quintillions, whispered to me as I stepped down and sat beside the stream:

"Our love has built this place out of the ancient walls of time—for *you*, Mary Lynn! *See that naught defiles the sanctuary!*"

I started, sensed a vague new note of fear. There had been a command in that many-lipped whisper, even a hint of threat.

Was it imagination, or as I looked again through all my place of beauty, did I sense a sudden drawing back of the oleanders, the morning-glories, a disapproving whisper of the hibiscus? It startled, amazed me. I was a little afraid.

I thought I heard the last whisper of Jon Lynn.

"Remember, Mary, it must not be defiled!"

But what could the vague unease mean?

I went back to the house. I ran. I had never run before since I was twenty, preferring always to dawdle, enjoying the love I felt for the flowers and knew they felt for me. But with this hint of vague terror I ran, and was more afraid *because* I ran!

"Martha," I gasped to my housekeeper, "what in the world has happened to me? I'm afraid of something!"

Martha had nursed me as a baby. Had taken the place of the mother who had died. She was part of this garden of love. And with my head against her ample bosom, she listened, as I told her everything I had felt during this strange and mystifying morning. When I had finished I detected a vague hint of trouble in her voice too, as she said:

"It is spring, Mary."

"But there have been other springs," I said.

"Ah! But in other springs there were no pictures of handsome young men on Mary's dresser!"

I felt my face flaming, though I never hid anything from Martha.

"You think it's that?" I whispered. "That I'm in love with Clel Urban?"

"It is spring," she repeated. The note of trouble in her voice was more pronounced than ever.

"You know what my father made me promise, Martha?"

She nodded, a little frown between her eyes.

"If, then, I were to fill this place of love with love which is greater still——?"

She shook her head.

"Your father, Mary," her voice rose to no more than a whisper, "was a very strange man. There were rumors—still are, for that matter—among the people hereabouts, of things he did at night, after your mother died . . . ."

"Rumors? But only, Martha, because he shut himself away from his neighbors!"

"More than that," said Martha. She looked at me intently, and carefully began to talk "During his last days he painted things no one ever saw. They are locked, I think, in the attic. I often heard him speak to them, as though he bargained with someone. The day the stroke hit him I heard him say: *"Give me this genius just for an hour and I give you Mary forever!"*

"I heard him say that. And I watched. Nobody came out of the studio after him. And there was no one inside but your father. So with whom, dear, did he make a pact, giving you to someone, or *something*, forever? Do you think that may have been the reason he exacted a promise from you, that you must never leave the place he called his Eden?"

A COLD chill raced all through me. I had known my father to be strange. But I had scarcely given it thought—I had adored him. During his last days, I had seen a strange hunger in his eyes when he had looked at me. His eyes had burned with fires, deeply lit as though from the wells of his very soul. Yet he had not been a frustrated man; the world had called him great and filled his coffers with money.

There was just one thing in which he had been bitterly disappointed: he had never reproduced on canvas, to his satisfaction, this estate which love had built on the road to the beach of golden sands. He had failed even though he had ceased to paint for money, had spent the last five years of his life trying to preserve for mankind the beauty of this Eden in Bermuda. Why? Who knows what inspires painters to delve into their very souls for glories only Nature ever builds but which Nature never seems to save?

Every season Nature destroyed its work. Leaves fell, flowers withered and blew away on the wind, birds vanished into the southern skies.

The painter who could capture Nature's glory on canvas, could keep that glory forever.

But how, and with whom, could Jon Lynn have made a bargain as Old Martha hinted at: to give me forever—to What?—if he but be granted genius for an hour?

I was suddenly very much afraid. I sent for Salvatore, my father's old servant.

"I want to send a radio to Clel Urban in New York City," I told him. "Immediately!"

My rebellious soul had decided.

I think it was the first time Salvatore ever frowned at me, and I wondered why. But he took the message to Hamilton for transmission, reported back that he had sent it, and said: *Death rides a carriage tonight!*"

CHAPTER TWO

The Carriage Comes

I SHUDDERED. I couldn't help it. I felt all at once that Salvatore, whom my father had always trusted, had become my enemy. He knew of course, all about the promise exacted from me by Jon Lynn. And—though he loved me—he would be on his old master's side.

But rebellion was rising in me.

I spoke to Salvatore sharply.

"What do you mean, 'death rides a carriage'?"

"What should I mean, Mary Lynn?" he asked. "Does an old man always need to mean something? But this I do say: no good can come of it!"

"Of what?"

"This message to a young man."

"Did you make the arrangements I directed you to?" I asked sharply.

"Of course. While I may not always approve, I am always, I trust, a proper servant. Yes, when and if the young man answers, the message will be brought to you by the hand of Garten, who drives a carriage. I paid him in advance, though he insisted that the joy of serving Mary Lynn was payment enough."

"Then go about your business, Salvatore," I told him, "and do not presume to criticize your betters."

He grinned, a little, sheepishly, at that. Just so had I talked to him when I had been five years old, imperiously stamping my small foot. He had always loved it. He had looked, when I was five, about as he looked now, fifteen years later. Salvatore would never change.

Yet he was uneasy. And I was growing more so.

The sun was by now vanishing into the west, dropping behind a sullen bank of clouds. Its waning rays reflected little lancets of burnished silver from the white houses on Bermuda's hills, so that they looked like so many piles of snow among the woods.

That sunset seemed to be a goodbye to something. The going of all that warm brightness brought a sort of chill down upon the world. From my high window I could see the ocean, touched in vast patches with the black of the cloud shadow, dappled in between with pools of silver and gold where the sun's last rays reached.

Night was falling.

And with its falling a chill, too, came in a wind off the sea. A wind which whispered about the eaves, murmured through my flowers. The whispering and murmuring made me think of the soft time-talk of the spirits of the polyps which were the soul of Bermuda. Had it been to these that my father had bound me? But that was so ethereal, so unreal, so fanciful. Yet what else? I tried to think of so many things.

I looked down. Now I could see Salvatore puttering in the estate back of the house, along the trail which led down to the stream that was like a silver thread through the trees. Salvatore, big and bulky, moved with the soft grace of a great cat, the silence of a whisper in a storm. Up to now he, with Martha, had been part and parcel of the love which enwrapped the estate of Jon Lynn.

AS darkness possessed the place, vague uneasiness gripped me. I didn't turn on the lights. I kept my eyes glued to the black woods behind the house, where I was usually as much at home at night as at any other time—since night, too, is the time of love. Fireflies darted here and there, until all at once they vanished and I heard the swift pattering of the rain's feet on the runlets of the roof.

I shivered, wondering at my mounting fear. What *was* it that frightened me?

Night? I had never feared it before. The wind? Wind was the song of my heart. The beauty of the estate. That was part of me. What, then?

Salvatore had said: *"Death rides a carriage tonight!"* What had he meant? What had caused the abysmal gloom in his voice when he had made that strange prophecy? Had it anything to do . . . ? Merciful Heaven! Garten was coming to me tonight, bringing an answer from Clel Urban. Was *that* the carriage? But how? Why?

I was rapidly whipping myself up to a kind of silent, torturing hysteria, in which I found myself listening for the clop-clop of a horse's hoofs, the creak of Garten's

carriage—all the while being deathly afraid of hearing exactly that.

But Death wasn't a man, a woman, anything that rode in a carriage! And yet, I knew strange things were often whispered among the natives of this place. Talk of spectral shapes in the deep cuts the road made through the corral of the islands; of dancing witch fires. . . .

I shook myself.

And then I heard, in the road outside, the clop-clop of hoofs.

I knew at once it was not Garten's horse. Garten always hauled me when I shopped or traveled about Hamilton and the roads surrounding the place. I knew the sound of his horse's hoofs as I knew the beating of my own heart.

The wind was rising. The murmuring under the eaves had become a faint wail of sound, like a harp softly played, a harp which sang in words a human being could almost understand—which a human being *could* understand if that human were Mary Lynn, accustomed to talking with the flowers, the streams, the trees and birds.

The wind said: "Death *does* ride a carriage tonight!"

I put a hand to my mouth quickly, barely choking my scream. For the words were plain, unmistakable. I had actually heard them. I heard them again in the rising cries of the wind. A flurry of rain swept the roof, passed over, and the flurry spoke with a pattering of feet. Then the pattering became words:

"Thus Death races to catch His carriage!"

I jumped to my feet. My mouth was open to cry out for Martha and Salvatore, for I was suddenly afraid with a fear such as I had never dreamed to be possible.

But I didn't cry out. I couldn't. I couldn't because, even as I rose to dash for the stairs—at the bottom of which, in the warm cozy kitchen, I knew I would find Martha and Salvatore—I heard the clop-clop of hoofs all over again.

The first clop-clopping had passed. There had been two people in the carriage, their heads close together. A man and a woman, affectionately intertwined, enroute to the beach for solitary love beneath the moon. The woman had been singing softly to the man, her face white in the moonlight. They hadn't even minded the warm rain, falling on them both in those scurrying flurries.

I stared down the road, toward the mouth of the cut through the coral. Out of that cut this second carriage had to come—and I dreaded to see it appear. The cut had become the mouth of a monster preparing to spew forth something ghastly for my sight.

It was Wingfoot, Garten's horse, which emerged from the cut. Moonlight glistened on his harness. The carriage followed, at its front Garten himself, in his black suit, with the derby hat pulled low over his black ears. I could even see the red badge of his calling on his left arm, near the elbow.

Clop-*clop!* went the feet of Wingfoot. There was a halting impediment in his trot. Death *rides* . . . . death *rides* . . . . death *rides a carriage* . . . .

I stared at Garten. He looked like a crow, like a black hobgoblin. . . .

Nonsense! He was merely a negro hackman, bringing me a message. A message from Clel Urban—who wouldn't have answered if he hadn't loved me. And yet—I had to hold myself back to keep from racing out to the road and holding up my arms to Garten and calling to him to stay where he was because "Death rode the curving highway tonight."

I DIDN'T do that. I convinced myself that I was being foolish. That Jon Lynn, if he but knew how I ached for Clel Urban, would have released me from my promise—would have done that because he loved me so.

So I didn't run down—though Garten was a monster, squatting there on the seat of his carriage, a black forbidding monster with the devil's own scepter in his hand. Scepter? But it was only the carriage whip! He never even used it on Wingfoot, because he was a man whose heart was kind. Why, Garten had taken me riding in his carriage when I had been no more than a tot, and he had driven—just as kindly—another Wingfoot. Garten a monster? Absurd!

He stopped before the gate, put his whip in the socket, wrapped the lines about it, stepped down. I heard his feet against the gravel of the walk. I went down to meet him.

In the kitchen I saw Martha, nodding over a newspaper. I didn't see Salvatore anywhere. And I smiled my relief. Everything looked so very much the same that I was reassured.

I opened the door to Garten, who held out the envelope. I took it from him eagerly. I gave him money, which he accepted with a courtly bow such as he had given me when I was five, or even four.

I read the message in the light from the porch.

It was from Clel. It said:

COMING TO YOU ABOARD THE MORNINGSTAR STOP WILL ARRIVE DAY AFTER TOMORROW STOP SHALL SEND ANOTHER MESSAGE IN MORNING OR LATER TONIGHT STOP LOVE CLEL

I had all but forgotten the strange undercurrents of the day when I had finished. Clel Urban would share Elysium with me! That was all—but that would make Elysium perfect.

"Stay awake, Garten," I said. "Here's more money. There will be more messages.

Bring them to me when they come. I'll pay whatever you lose in fares."

He touched his derby hat, turned away, and I went back into the house. I climbed to my room upstairs under the eaves, switched on the lights, and studied Clel's smiling, pictured face.

"Oh," I said to his picture. "I'm sure we shall be happy. Why didn't I decide before father died? Now every hour between us seems ages long and filled with fear. I shall not sleep until you reach me!"

How true that was I could not—by the wildest stretch of imagination—have foreseen.

I sat for a long time with my eyes closed, seeing Clel and myself among the flowers and bees, lazing on the bank of our stream, floating over the water in a cozy boat just large enough for two. My fancy drove the night away and we were in the sun, bathed in it, caressed by it, and Clel had become as much a part of the love about this place as I had always been.

It seemed very simple. In fact it——

At that precise point I heard a scream such as I had never heard before, nor even dreamed about. A scream which came from deep in the estate's woods, down the curving path where night held sway over the red cedars. A scream of agony and terror, in a man's voice. I thought it was Salvatore, but I had never heard him scream. Then I knew it wasn't Salvatore, either.

It was a scream of death. A scream which broke off finally, dying away to nothingness as if snatched into eternity by the wind and rain.

I raced for the stairs once more. Flying down them, I looked out the window, toward the road. Maybe I was thinking subconsciously about "Death riding a carriage," I don't know. But I looked, anyhow.

And the blood fairly clogged in my veins.

Garten's carriage still stood where he had left it, empty. Wingfoot was pawing at the coral dust of the road. His ears had shot forward. He lifted his head, looking toward the house, and past it.

Then he neighed, and his neigh as well was filled with terror—terror all the more awful because it came from the dumb heart of a beast who could neither talk nor weep.

I knew by Wingfoot's whinnying that it had been Garten who had screamed from the black woods—and that Garten was dead.

CHAPTER THREE

Under the Red Cedars

I SCREAMED the names of Martha and Salvatore, who were as much to me as my own parents could have been, had those parents been living.

Nobody answered. But I saw Martha still nodding over the newspaper, and I ran to her, wondering where Salvatore was that he, too, failed to reply.

I shook Martha. The newspaper fell to the floor. I stared into Martha's face. It was set and still. The eyes were glassy, unblinking. Martha was dead.

Death had been gentle to her. Her face told me nothing, even though I did think she must have died of some terrific shock. That was the impression I had.

Nothing could be done for her. My duty was to the living, or to the dying if they could yet be saved.

I hurried outside, not thinking of possible danger to myself, certainly not in this place which had held nothing but love— love enough to fill the hearts of the world. The darkness flowed over me like a well-flung blanket, wet and clammy. Imagination, of course, but the dark blanket seemed to whisper as it fell, whisper in triumph.

I found the path through the red cedars.

I knew every turn and curve, could have found them all in my sleep, as I now found them in the deep blackness of night under their arching tops. I ran down the slope. The odor of the flowers was in my nostrils, rich, cloying—the odor I had always loved and drank in as a tippler drinks his wine.

But at the bottom I paused—quickly, as though hands had fastened themselves about my ankles. Through the shadows of the red cedars I saw a moving bulk. It was shaped like a man. Its arms fought at something which clutched at its throat. I didn't know what it was, but it was too small for Salvatore, and Garten was missing from his carriage.

"Garten!" I called hoarsely. "What are you doing in here? Answer me at once!" But he didn't answer. His arms continued to flail out as though he fought at strangling hands.

I gathered my courage and dashed on. What I wished most to do was turn and run and never stop until I reached the lighted places in the road to Hamilton. I wanted to run because, in the space of a single scream, this place I had loved for so many years had become a place of abysmal terror.

I didn't run. I went on—fearfully. And I came to Garten, to where I could peer at his face.

It was as dead as the face of Old Martha. The eyes glowed in the dull gloom. Rain dribbled down the cheeks like pearls. Garten had been spread-eagled against a boll of red cedar.

Yet—what caused his arms to dance and fling about, since he was so obviously dead?

I stepped closer—and a scream rose unbidden to my throat.

Something I had never dreamed possible had happened to Garten. A "strangler vine" had looped its folds about his throat and about his stomach, and had slain him. It must have happened as he came along the trail quickly, unnoticingly. And now it still held him, strangled to death against the tree.

But it couldn't be. The strangler vine had no such voracious, murderous life. It choked trees to death, yes, but it required years in the doing. It couldn't recognize an enemy, and attack it as it passed, like a python or a boa constrictor.

And yet, Garten had died. I had heard his scream—which must have exploded from his throat when the loop fell home. Moreover, the constricting folds of the vine still held him.

Sobbing, I grasped the loop of vine about hist hroat, tried to pull it away. There was just a chance, perhaps, that he still lived. By releasing the pressure on his throat. . . . .

I MANAGED to slip the fingers of my right hand under the loop about his neck. Then I pulled. I panted with my exertions, for the vine was tough and hard. I felt it give away from Garten's throat. I thought I heard the escaping sigh of his breath. Maybe he lived, after all.

But just as I would have placed my left hand beside my right, to lend the full power of my young body to the task of rescue, the loop tightened—*tightened as though it had been a live and deadly python!*

That tree was suddenly a weapon of murder. It was alive, with a mind of its own, a mind bent on killing?

"God, Oh God!" I moaned. And even as my lips mouthed His name—I realized my own predicament. The tree held me prisoner, too.

My right hand was inside that fatal loop, the knuckles against the black throat of Garten. And even the touch of his cooling flesh set me to shuddering. I heard my own screams go keening through the night, across the stream, out to the road, out through the woods, to flutter about the white roofs of my sleeping neighbors.

"Martha! Martha!" Then I remembered—Martha would never answer me again, not this side of Paradise.

"Salvatore! Salvatore!"

But Salvatore did not answer either. He did not come to free me as I struggled and pulled, my hand pinioned against the black throat of a dead man, a man whom the strangler vine had murdered—*when nothing of the sort had ever happened before, would ever happen again.*

What had inspired the strangler vine?

What had caused Garten to go into this place anyhow, when I had last seen him turning away to carry out my mission in Hamilton? Why had he changed his mind? What dread summons had sent him here to his death? No black man ever went voluntarily into a black abyss such as this under my red cedars—certainly not on the estate of a man who was known, or reputed, to be as queer as Jon Lynn.

I screamed again and again. The corpse shook and did a kind of dervish dance to accompany my writhing and twisting. The loop of strangler vine tightened again. And then, sick with horror at what I was compelled to do—yet seeing no other way out—I put my foot against Garten's dead body and thrust backward with all my might.

Moistured bathed my body. I bit my lips through in my agony of effort. But I managed to get free.

I ran blindly. I did not realize where, until the stream blocked my progress. At that point I was out in vague moonlight.

Across the stream were vines my father had planted, a carpet of them. To my fevered eyes it seemed that they were all in motion, like a nest of snakes. Beyond the patch of creeping vine were several banyans, with their many snaky roots. They, too, seemed alive.

All my Elysium, in which I had been

so happy, had become a kind of Purgatory. The morning-glories had become reptiles to bite and sting me even as they soothed with their odor. The banyan in which I had played as a child had become Laocoön, fighting with many snakes.

The stream was the largest snake of all . . . .

The coral soil under my feet was alive, squirming, all the polyps come to life, eating upward into my feet, reaching for my heart to destroy me.

Why? Because I had broken a promise? But who was to know I had broken it? My father could not avenge such disloyalty, for he was dead . . . .

But suppose. . . .

I REFUSED to think of that as I turned back. I had to reach the house, lock myself in before the terror should slay me. I had to pass the gruesome body of Garten, but that could not be avoided, and I could avert my head. I screamed as I ran.

"Salvatore! Salvatore!"

I passed the body. Its arms still flailed about as though the loops of strangler vine were living things which thus made mock of their victim.

"Salvatore! Salvatore!"

And then I heard him coming.

"What is it, Mary Lynn?" His voice was heavy with anxiety. It came from somewhere near the house. I heard his feet strike on a rock somewhere.

I raced faster, feeling invisible cold fingers against the back of my neck. I ran into his arms. His harsh old body was firm against mine as his great arms held me.

"What happened, Mary Lynn?" he repeated. "What . . . why is Garten's horse in front of the house? Where is Garten?"

I told Salvatore and felt him stiffen as he held me.

"It's working out," he said. "Old Jon

knew what he was doing, knew how to keep his faith with the spirits of the woods!"

"What are you talking about?" I demanded.

"The sanctuary of beauty may not be defiled without punishment," said Salvatore. "Garten is. the first to die. When your lover comes he will surely die."

"But why Garten?" I asked desperately. "I wasn't in love with him! Why should he, in all his innocence, be destroyed because . . . because of . . ."

"He brought the message!" said Salvatore ponderously. "And there will be others, mark my words—and your Clel Urban will be the last, after which the evil will pass out of Jon Lynn's paradise!"

"No, no!" I moaned. "I'll leave this place. I'll run away. I'll go into Hamilton, fetch the police."

He stiffened further.

"There must be no police," he said. "There is no way of knowing what would happen, and British justice is inexorable. They might fasten a noose about the white neck of little Mary Lynn. Come, show me Garten."

I watched as one numbed with horror while Salvatore, as easily as though it had been nothing at all, pulled the loops free of the neck of Garten. As he did so, the corpse fell into the trail and was erased by the deep shadows.

Salvatore gathered Garten up in his arms.

"What do you intend doing?" I asked.

"Hush, Mary Lynn," said Salvatore. "I am always the proper servant. I do the best I may for my little mistress."

He put the corpse of Garten over his shoulder, carried it to the gate. He stayed behind the hibiscus hedge while he studied the road, broad and vague under the moonlight. Nobody was coming, whereupon he set the body in the carriage seat.

Wingfoot turned his head. His ears shot forward, he snorted. His eyes blazed with fear. Salvatore spoke to the animal with the soft reassuring voice of the man who understood horses.

But Wingfoot struck at him when he walked to the creature's head—struck, and started to turn the carriage about, toward Hamilton.

Salvatore spoke again, grasping the bit.

He turned the carriage. Garten sat as stiffly erect in his seat as he ever had alive. His derby hat was low over his ears, his legs braced. Salvatore put the lines in his dead hands, arranged the body so that it would not fall. Then he spoke to Wingfoot. The horse broke into a trot, and loped down the road.

I stared after Garten as the carriage of death rode toward the black mouth of the cut—and Salvatore's words came back to me with numbing force: *"Death rides a carriage tonight!"* Just as the carriage entered the cut, Garten leaned over to the left, as though to balance himself.

"Now, Mary Lynn," Salvatore said, "we wait to see what happens, and keep silent."

Once in the house, I was too numb with terror to ask what had become of Old Martha. I saw that the chair in which her body had sat was empty. It rocked gently to and fro as though she had just risen and gone away somewhere. Still wondering what had sent Garten into the grove of red cedars, I swayed and fell— into black oblivion.

CHAPTER FOUR

Whispering Flowers

I AWAKENED in my own room. Clel Urban stared at me from my dressertop. But as I looked, through bleared eyes, at his likeness, there seemed a subtle difference about him, somehow.

His eyes had changed. There was fear in them, I thought, and dread of meeting mine. And this in a mere photograph!

The room spun. My brain was dizzy, my soul sick with a nameless dread. What had happened, *was* happening here in the place which was my father's masterpiece of architecture and landscape gardening, which he had tried to transmute into a masterpiece of painting?

The house seemed weighted with strange silence.

The whole land was all at once silent, as though it waited for *what?*

I rose from my chair—which I did not remember reaching—and crept down to the first floor. While the floor rose and fell under me like the deck of a ship in a storm, I staggered to the door.

What had caused Garten . . . But I had asked that question times without number, hadn't I?

What had killed Old Martha? Where was she now?

Was Clel Urban doomed when he came to me?

I wouldn't have it! When morning came I would flee this place as from a spot accursed, meet Clel in Hamilton, go away with him. Lightly, even gladly, for the hope of love to come, I would cast aside all the love which had been mine.

"You can't come here to your death, Clel!" I heard myself saying. "You can't. you can't!"

I would leave right away, now, and radio Clel to meet me in Hamilton.

I ran to my door. To my unbounded amazement, it was locked. I tugged. But it was of stout oak and would not budge. It was fastened from the outside.

"Salvatore!" I called. "Salvatore!"

No answer.

I whirled to the window. It wasn't a far drop to the ground. I could open the window and go out that way. But even as I started in that direction, I staggered back, and a cry of sheer terror numbed my throat.

Strange, sinuous tentacles lay across the window!

I stared. And as I did so, the slender creeping things came up over the sill outside—green things, with purple flowers at their ends. They touched the glass of the window-pane, and swayed from right to left like a mess of wriggling little serpents trying to enter my bedchamber.

They were nothing else but purple morning-glories. *Nothing* else, did I say? But if not—how did they grow so swiftly? How did they come inching over the sill in this insidiously horrible fashion—pausing for a brief moment, a half dozen of them, unevenly spaced along the window's width, as though they paused for breath. Six purple flowers. The flowers I loved so well—which my father had said were the eyes of his Mary. Six purple flowers which now put their petals against the glass, as though to administer a caress.

Alive, almost human, were these purple morning-glories! *What did this strange growth portend?*

I STARED at the flowers. The eyes which they were, had suddenly become malignant, threatening. The lips of them had ceased offering kisses, and instead whispered threats. I listened not with my ears, but with my soul, for whatever it was they would tell me.

"No man shall ever have you, Mary Lynn, for you belong to us as we belong to you! Who tries to take you shall die!"

Scarcely understanding the passing of time, I watched the mat of morning-glories rise to cover the lower half of the window, then the upper half—and knew, with a conviction that could not be gainsaid, that I might never escape by way of the window!

Why not?

Because the morning-glories were like the bars of a cage in which I was imprisoned. Somehow I knew that if I tried to force my way through the purple flowers, they would wrap themselves about me, as the strangler vine had wrapped itself about Garten, and I would die.

Then I heard another sound beyond the window. And something happened to the mat of flowers there. They fell apart over the window-pane, showing an opening.

I dashed toward it. The window glass was wet, as though it perspired from some strange, unearthly struggle. I looked out.

Along the road before my home were many people. They were all dressed in black, and wore derbies.

Merely seeing them, my senses almost left me and I grew rigid with terror. For these men who stared so queerly at my house were the black cabbies of Hamilton. And I knew why they were here.

They were a clannish crowd. They had received the dead Garten into their midst. The police had not been notified, else they would have been here long since. But the black cabbies had come out, seeking the answer to the puzzle of dead Garten's ghastly return.

Somehow those silent black men, all standing along the road like soldiers standing shoulder to shoulder at attention, filled me with the deepest, most terrorizing fear I had ever known.

If they had suddenly, like black robots, started marching on the house, directly through my hibiscus hedge, I would have died of terror—knowing that they came for a vengeance which would not be gainsaid.

What they did was worse. They merely stood in the moonlight and waited.

AND something happened. I couldn't tell what it was for I couldn't see it myself. But suddenly one of the cabbies flung his arms high and yelled, his voice pitched to a quivering, unnatural howl: *"Old Jon Lynn!"*

And with that their black ranks broke. All of them were in flight at once, fleeing toward the cut which shut off the view toward Hamilton. They ran swiftly, looking back over their shoulders, their eyes rolling like mad. Yet no sound came from anywhere on the estate that I could hear.

I watched them clamber into their carriages, turn about, lash their horses into a gallop for the return to Hamilton. Then the flowers fell into place again over the window, while on the roof the slithery sound of their miraculous growing increased in volume.

The flowers personified it all. I was chained to this place. Could never leave it. Salvatore forbade. The flowers forbade. The land forbade. Everything here forbade. I was chained to the estate of Jon Lynn.

And what had the cabbies seen? Why had one of them shouted "Old Jon Lynn"?

Had he actually seen "Old Jon Lynn"?

But that couldn't be. There wasn't a man, woman or child in all Bermuda who hadn't known my father by sight. . . But my father was dead!

The country was silent again.

Finally, when I had driven myself to the verge of madness in a fight to get out through the door—desisting only when I thought I heard outside the slithery whisper of the morning-glories, growing up the stairs!—I stopped again. I had heard another sound. It was the clop-clop of Wingfoot's hoofs!

The sound came from Hamilton way. I dashed to the window, forgetting caution in my terror. I knocked out the window-pane with a chair—which I hurled through the vines, leaving a hole which gave me a view of the moonlit road.

But what numbed me further was the fact that the dead Garten still drove his carriage—and he was still bent far over to one side, as he had been when I had last seen him, vanishing into the cut.

As though bathed in a glacier's icy temperature I stood there in that room of madness, waiting for the dead Garten to bring me the latest message from Clel Urban.

The horse stopped outside. But I didn't hear anyone alight. I heard no hail—nothing.

Until—though I heard no step upon the porch—there came the muffled beating of knuckles on the door below.

Hours seemed to pass, while I feared to answer the summons. It did not come again. But then came a new whispering sound. And I stared at the door.

Tentacles of the flowers were thrusting themselves under the door. In their midst was a white envelope. I picked it up, all at once afraid to touch the flowers themselves—which seemed like leeches created to drink away my soul.

I read the message. And fear—this time for the safety of a loved one—reached its pinnacle.

HAVE CHARTERED A FLYING BOAT FROM NASSAU STOP WILL BE WITH YOU BEFORE MORNING STOP CLEL

CHAPTER FIVE

The Secret Masterpiece

HAD the black cabbies, fleeing, given me an inkling of why Garten had gone into the red cedars to his death? Had they seen what they believed to be the ghost of my father? Had Garten, turning away from me to go back to Hamilton, also seen it, between himself and the road? If so, had it driven him, fear-ridden, the other way, there to enmesh him in the coils of the strangler vine?

God, Oh, God, could that be the answer?

If it were, then the possibilities of the whole situation were thrice terrible. For then I knew that I faced, what Clel faced when he reached me.

The spirit of my father possessed this place, of course—for it *was* his spirit. But could that spirit enter into every growing thing, into every morning-glory, every oleander, every bit of hibiscus, even the red cedars—to endow them with superhuman attributes so that they could strangle a Garten, make a prisoner of Mary Lynn, and drive those cabbies shrieking down the road to Hamilton?

How strong had been my father's desire? Would he have slain to keep me as part of the virgin purity of all this loveliness? Would he even destroy me to keep his ideal alive?

What bargain had he made that day Martha heard him talking behind the locked doors of his studio? What, and with whom?

Between periods of fighting at the door until exhausted, and calling for Salvatore until I was hoarse, I listened to the whispering of the morning-glories which thickened all about the house and over it. I listened to the sighing of the wind in the red cedars.

And all the whispers said: *"You are a prisoner. Even death will not release you and whoso tries to set you free shall die!"*

And then, overhead, like a song of defiance, I heard the roaring of a motor. I knew without going out to look—as I could not do—that it was Clel Urban, flying low over the house, setting a course for the nearest possible anchorage for the hydroplane. That would be at Hamilton, less than two miles distant.

Finally, far down the road, muted by distance, muffled by the cut through the coral, I heard a rollicking voice lifted in song:

*"Through the night,
Swift in flight,
I'm coming back to you!"*

IT WAS a rich baritone. It was the voice of Clel Urban. I knew somehow that he wouldn't wish for even a cabbie—not even if one could have been prevailed upon to come back here—to witness our meeting. I knew that he would be coming to me either on foot or on a bicycle—automobiles being unknown in Bermuda. And I wanted to rush out, flee to the cut, and head him off. For I knew that he rode to his death.

The spirit of the place had become a malignant, horrible spirit, lying in wait to destroy my beloved. We'd scarcely exchanged half a dozen words, yet we both knew that a lifetime spent together would not have brought us closer to each other. Time mattered not at all when two people were in love.

I heard Clel outside the gate. He cried: "Hello, the house!"

And someone answered from behind the house!

"This way, Clel Urban."

Unmistakably it was the voice of Jon Lynn!

"Righto!" I heard Clel answer. Then I heard his steps on the gravel path which circled the house.

I flung myself at the window, into the thick of the tentacles. They clung to me. My fingers ripped and tore at the tentacles, through the soft embrace of which I felt myself falling.

My feet touched the ground, outside. I struggled free, to lie panting for a moment on the lawn, behind the hibiscus hedge. My brain whirled as I stared at the house, its side a mass of morning-glories. Oleanders were in my nostrils, the smell of soil.

And then, to the left, striding purposely toward the path which led down to the stream, past the tree where the strangler vine had taken Garten, I saw a black figure: *Jon Lynn!* In his hand he carried something which looked like a strangler's noose!

"Clel! Clel!" I screamed.

His voice replied instantly. "This way, darling! What the devil's going on here, anyhow? I'd like to know. . . ."

Right there his voice broke in a scream of pain. I heard another voice chime in, as though it came through gritted teeth. I heard a body threshing about. I knew it was Clel's.

Again I saw a shadow, and the flailing arms, and found Clel Urban, his feet lifted from the ground and kicking out, held fast in the grip of the strangler vine.

I hurled myself forward.

In the act of grasping the constricting folds I looked up into the shadows of the red cedar—and it was then I discovered that I carried a weapon: the heavy leg of the chair I had broken to fight my way through the morning-glories at the window.

It struck Salvatore, there in the tree, directly on the head. He came tumbling down, while the folds of the strangler vine released the body of my beloved. The next instant, regaining the club, I stood over Salvatore, who was garbed so that at a distance he might have been taken for Jon Lynn. Behind me Clel Urban gasped for breath.

"Don't brain him just yet, dearest," said Clel. "He's got some explaining to do."

YES, Salvatore had to, and did, explain. He had been the loyal servant through everything, but his loyalty had been for my father only.

"I knew he had bound you to this place he loved," whispered Salvatore. "I meant that his will should be obeyed. I killed Garten as a warning to you, but it was not enough. I sent whispers out among the cabbies, who came to stare, and to flee with shouts of 'old Jon Lynn' on their lips. That was not enough, either, so I was ready to slay this man of yours when he came."

"How about Martha?" I demanded.

"I forgot she had a weak heart. She saw me in disguise and thought I was really the Old Master and the shock killed her. You will find her in her bed, where she would have preferred to begin her last sleep."

Old Salvatore's eyes never left my face as he talked. An agony of sweat beaded his forehead. His eyes were filled with something which made me shudder. Clel saw, too, and tightly gripped my arm. Old Salvatore loved me, but with a love which had led to murder, would have led to other murders.

By binding me to Old Jon Lynn's estate he had hoped to have me with him until he died.

"The morning-glories around the windows," panted Salvatore. "Look at them closely and you will see that they are trained on slender trellises, which, when I shoved them up the face of the wall, made it seem, to anyone inside the window, that they grew before that one's eyes. The whispers on the roof were merely dead vines, dragged slowly back and forth. . . ."

So all was explained. The oleanders that had seemed alive, the banyans with their snaky roots, the whispering red cedars, all had been born out of my imagination.

It had all been Old Salvatore, fighting for the thing he most desired: myself. He had failed.

As the horrible old man died, I told Clel the rest of the story. When I was finished, he said:

"You see? There's just as much love here as there ever was. There isn't a curse on the place, save only what old Salvatore placed upon it. We both heard his last words, which will satisfy the police. And so we'll be free to live and love here, until the day we die. . . ."

* * *

The explanation seemed simple, but Clel and I have never been entirely satisfied with it. Old Salvatore—might he not, after all, have been the implement of my father's iron will? The will which had bound me to this Eden because my father had made a bargain?

I hadn't heard the words in which he made his bargain, of course; but in the attic Clel and I, diligently searching, found his last picture. Clel, himself a painter of international fame, gasped when he saw it.

"A masterpiece!" His voice was a soft, reverent whisper.

In the morning we took it out, studied it against the original landscape. And no matter how carefully we studied it, neither of us was able to find anything missing from it. Every oleander was there, each in its exact coloring, so real that it all but waved in the breeze.

Jon Lynn had transmitted his garden, exactly, to canvas.

Had he, in payment for this touch of genius, tried, from beyond the grave, to keep a queer bargain with incomprehensible Nature?

Together, down the years, Clel and I, among the flowers my father started growing, will seek the answer to this question, knowing that father had already forgiven me my broken promise because, loving me with all his soul, he understands this other love which, too, is mine.

THE END

THE BLACK CHAPEL

A FEAR such as he had never known came over Pete Stark. He could feel the
muscles in his jaw aching. He couldn't ask this girl what she had done. He
couldn't! He just stood there, waiting, dreading the words she was going
to say—words which would put the stigma of murder on her!

Her voice came out of the darkness
again, steadier now. "I didn't know it
would kill them. I got it from an old witch-
doctor in the interior. You see, I'm not
any missionary's daughter. I've been lying about everything, but I'm not lying
now. I didn't know it would kill them!"

The girl was tugging at Stark's sleeve
now, but he shook her off. He could feel
anger rising like a hot wave out of his
chest into his throat. This was his first
command. It was his duty to see that the
ship came through—and the whole damn
crew was trying to desert.

And then came the mad laughter, echo-
ing into every part of the doomed vessel.
For one long second, the dark universe
about Pete Stark was utterly still, utterly
empty except for the mirthless, skull-like
laughter that stirred and shook the darkness. He knew he had lost. He knew what
that ghastly sound meant: the laughter
which came invisibly, curdling his blood,

126

was that of a man killed horribly, buried
in the silent depths of the sea!

Thus, in crisp, strong sentences, Wyatt
Blassingame paints the picture of terror
—relentless and vengeful—which stalks a
freighter at night, when the storm gods
leer at the recklessness of mortals, and the
old man of the sea licks his lips greedily,
fingering ivory skulls of those who have
already drowned, and lusting for the helpless humans on that haunted packet.

But that is only a small taste of the
story, and only one story of the many!
From the four corners of the earth, mate-
rial has been gathered to make the next
issue of TERROR TALES the finest ever
published.

Each author, an old favorite—a master
of soul-chilling, eerie fiction—will provide
such a feast of terror as has never before
been included within the covers of a single
magazine. The July issue of TERROR
TALES is a sure-fire winner—eighteen-
karat, blood-speeding fiction!

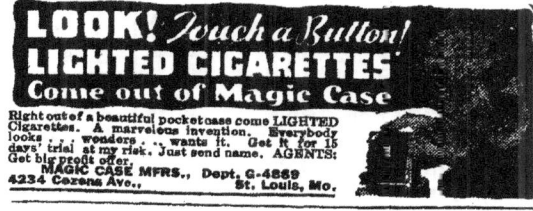